ISBN 978-0-06157-1724-1
Website: janicelanepalko.com
Twitter: @janicelanepalko
Blog: thewritinglane.blogspot.com
Facebook: JaniceLanePalko.writer
Pinterest: Janice Lane Palko

For whatever we lose (like a you or a me) it's always ourselves we find in the sea.

-e.e. cummings

Also by Janice Lane Palko

St. Anne's Day
A Shepherd's Song

CAPE CURSED

By

Janice Lane Palko

Happy Reading,
Jackie!
Janice Lane Palko

Chapter 1

"If you want to know anything about the lighthouse, miss," Parker heard Ernie say as he grasped the screen door's metal handle, "then Parker, there is the fella you should be talking to."

Parker Swain stepped inside The Seafood Shack. The door's spring squeaked before it slammed shut behind him. Hot, greasy air enveloped him. How did Ernie endure working behind those deep fryers on days like this? Parker wondered. If it was ninety-three degrees outside, it surely must be more than one hundred inside.

"Ma'am," Parker said, as the woman leaning against the counter turned and fixed her black eyes on him.

"I was just asking about the lighthouse," she said, tucking a lock of long, lustrous raven-colored hair behind her ear.

What little air there was seemed to have been suddenly sucked out of the place, and Parker felt short of breath. She was

3

heart-stoppingly beautiful in an exotic way that he'd never seen in person but only on the faces of women from faraway lands in the *National Geographic*.

It was nearly sunset; the dinner rush over. She must be a vacationer who had just arrived at Crystal Shoals and was looking for a bite to eat, he thought.

He brushed his sun-bleached hair off his forehead and used the pretense of being responsive to her interest in the lighthouse to take in the sight of her. Her skin lacked a tan, but that was about all she lacked. "I'd be happy to answer any of your questions," he said, feeling desire for her overwhelming him. He'd assumed that he was dead to the wiles of beautiful women, but the quickening of his pulse told him otherwise. Maybe physically he was alive, but emotionally, he knew he was as lifeless as the stagnant air.

Steady, Parker, he chided himself and turned to the man behind the counter. "How you doin' today, Ernie?" he asked, trying to regain his composure. Ernie's face was a leathery cross-hatch of wrinkles, indicating that he'd lived every day of his life, except for those spent in Korea during the war, under the bright North Carolina sun.

"Fine. What can I do you for?" Ernie drawled.

The Seafood Shack was an appropriate name as it was nothing more than a small wooden structure with a few Formica booths. For a fast, delicious meal, however, it couldn't be matched. Taking advantage of the long June days, Parker had worked through dinner. Famished now, he'd planned on picking up a bite to eat and spending the rest of the evening organizing his research material.

Parker scanned the menu above Ernie's head. "How fresh are the crabs?"

"Fresh as them kids you teach."

Parker raised a golden brow. "That fresh, huh? Then, I'll have the platter. And would you be kind enough to slip me a couple extra hushpuppies for Beau?"

"Sure thing. You want somethin' to drink?"

"I'll talk a large."

"What have you been working on?" Ernie asked as he wrote Parker's order on a slip of paper and passed it to Skip Jeffers, the young man behind him who was perspiring over the deep fryer.

Parker pulled his wallet from the back pocket of his well-worn jeans, fished out a ten, and handed it to Ernie. "Porch roof."

4

Ernie rang up the tab, closed the cash drawer, and gave Parker his change. "Bet that was toasty."

Holding out a muscular forearm, Parker assessed his skin, which was the same deep brownish-red shade of a well-worn baseball glove. "I'm about as cooked as your clams."

Ernie set two paper cups down on the counter. "Here, ya'll go. Why don't you talk to this pretty young lady? Tell her about the lighthouse, Parker, and I'll call you when the orders are up."

"Drinks are over here," Parker said, nodding toward the soda fountain. He watched as the young woman in the white Capri pants and lime tank top scooted past him and grabbed some napkins and a straw. She certainly filled out her clothing nicely. The graceful, generous curves of her back and derriere reminded him of the gently sloping dunes hugging the beach.

"Ladies first," he said, motioning to the soda machine.

"Thank you."

Her accent was definitely not southern. Yet Parker couldn't quite place its origin.

The ice rattled into her glass. "I was just asking about the lighthouse."

"Well, what would you like to know?"

"Is it really cursed?" she asked as the Dr. Pepper streamed into the cup.

Parker froze. The bluntness of her question startled him. He felt his defenses rise. Then he forced himself to exhale, telling himself to let it pass. Looking at his work boots, he answered, "There's been some tragedies, and such. But no more than any other place. Just local folklore."

She held her glass to her temple and closed her eyes. "I also heard the markings have some significance."

Who is this woman? Most visitors only wanted to know how tall it was or how old. Why is does she want to know this?

She opened her eyes, and he fell into the depth of them. Canted exotically above her high cheekbones, they were black like the mermaid's purses that washed up on the beach, and seemed to hold fathomless mysteries. *Resist, Parker.* He'd been down the summer romance road before, and it had lead to only one destination—heartbreak. Besides, at thirty-two, he knew better and was too busy for that kind of silliness. He needed to focus on preserving The Keeper's House.

5

"They're so unusual," she said as Parker held in the ice button.

"Not another one in the world like it," he said, filling his glass two-thirds full with cubes. "Originally, it was to be painted like a barber's pole."

He loved talking about the Cape Destiny Lighthouse, but the vacant stares and yawns that often greeted him when he tried to enlighten others about it warned him to temper his enthusiasm. He figured he'd better be polite and not monopolize the conversation. "Where are you from?"

She seemed to stiffen. "What do you mean?"

"Nothing. Just that I've never seen you around before. Take it you're not a local?"

"No," she said appearing to relax. "I'm from Pittsburgh," but then she quickly changed the subject. "What do the markings signify?"

His eyes fastened on hers, and he paused a moment as his throat suddenly went dry. "Eternal love," he rasped.

Quickly, he filled his glass with lemonade, took a long sip that cooled his parched throat, but did nothing for the heat this woman was generating in him.

"Eternal love . . . " she repeated wistfully.

"Legend has it," he continued, "that the first keeper insisted it be painted with the two intertwining stripes to symbolize he and his wife—their love spanning their lifetime and reaching into heaven."

She sighed, her small, firm breasts rising and falling. "Now that's what I call romantic." Then she looked pointedly at him. "How do you know so much? Are you a lighthouse aficionado?"

Aficionado? No, she definitely wasn't from Crystal Shoals.

"Order's up," Ernie called, breaking the spell that had come over Parker. They walked to the counter, and Ernie handed each of them a bag.

"Thanks, buddy. You take it easy now," Parker said.

"You too. Enjoy your stay, ma'am."

The young woman gave a small wave to Ernie. "Bye."

Parker held the screen door for her. They walked outside together into the thick June air and the slanting sherbet-colored rays of the setting sun.

"I like lighthouses," Parker said, "but I'm particularly attached to Cape Destiny." Now that they were out of the greasy air, he could smell her scent. Honeysuckle. His mouth began to water, and he wasn't sure if it was from hunger or desire.

She pointed over her shoulder. "I'm parked around the side."

"Mind if I walk you over?" he asked, not wanting to let someone so interested in the lighthouse get away. She shook her head no.

A dog barked. They both turned. A large Golden Retriever leaped from the bed of a pickup truck parked in front of The Seafood Shack and came bounding over.

"Beau!" Parker said sharply. "You know better than to do that."

The dog reached out with his paw and hit Parker's bag. Shaking his head and holding the bag higher, Parker said, "He knows I have hushpuppies in here." Taking out a golden fried ball of cornmeal, Parker fed it to the dog, which gobbled it in one bite.

The woman crouched and petted Beau's silky coat. "Aren't you a pretty boy?" The dog yammered and stared adoringly at her.

"This is Beau, and my name is Parker Swain. The Swains have always been lighthouse keepers at Cape Destiny."

"How charming," she said, stroking Beau under the chin.

Charming? Definitely not from Crystal Shoals.

Beau responded to her affection by giving her a slurpy lick on the cheek that made her giggle.

She rose and smiled coyly. "Are you as romantic as your ancestors?"

Good lord, she's flirting with me.

Beau nosed around the bag. "Get in the truck now," Parker said. The dog snorted, meandered back to the pickup, and jumped into the bed.

Parker grinned at her. "I can be. When I'm properly motivated." *What am I doing flirting with her? This is no good. This can only bring trouble.*

She laughed and began walking. Parker followed along. "Well, Parker Swain," she said, looking coyly over her shoulder, "if you're ever feeling motivated to talk about the lighthouse, I'd love to hear more. I'm staying up the road. The Destiny Cove." She stopped and turned toward him, offering her slim hand. "In case you're wondering, I'm Bliss—"

He shifted his dinner to his left hand and shook hers. "Did you say Bliss?"

"Yes. It's a long story."

"I'm a history teacher. I love long stories." He was still holding on to her slim hand.

She smiled and slid it out of his grasp. "Well, I have five older brothers. When I was born, they put me in my father's arms, and my mother asked him what he thought of a daughter. He replied, 'This is bliss.'" She shrugged. "That's how I got my name."

It sure would be bliss to hold her in my arms, Parker thought. They walked around the back of her black Ford Explorer.

"My last name is—

"*Sherman?*" he cried, reading the lettering on the side door: *B. C. Sherman Engineering. Moving Heaven and Earth for You.*

He looked at her, his face burning scarlet with anger. "You're Sherman Engineering? You're the destroyer of my lighthouse?"

Chapter 2

"Destroyer of your lighthouse?" Bliss cried, shocked that Parker had shifted from Southern gentleman to bully so quickly. "What are you talking about?"

"I'm talking about your jeopardizing a national treasure."

Bliss was well aware that some of the residents were opposed to the move, but she didn't expect to be blamed. "Look, I came down here to save it," Bliss said, trying not to further raise his ire. She wanted this move to go smoothly. Her career was riding on it, and she didn't need any more enemies. Jonathan Lavere was enough.

"What do you know about my lighthouse?" Parker asked, puffing out his chest.

"I know that if it's not moved, it'll soon be swallowed up by the sea."

"I don't believe that."

She tossed her hair back. "Have you checked the beach? There's only fifteen feet separating it from the Atlantic."

He sniffed. "Checked the beach? I don't need to check the beach. I've lived here all my life, and I don't believe it's worth risking my lighthouse just because some pinhead in the capitol thinks it should be moved."

"Well, I've seen the studies, and I'm telling you, Mr. Swain, one more hurricane and *your beloved lighthouse* could be washed out to sea."

Parker swept his hand toward the direction of the beach. "I know this place. No one can predict that ocean. With the next storm, it could very well add ten feet of new sand to the shoreline."

Bliss sighed impatiently. "That's highly unlikely."

Parker's soft brown eyes hardened as he glared at Bliss. "I believe in the unlikely. I know the impossible happens."

"And I know that your mind is closed," Bliss replied. "I'm no longer going to argue with you." She turned on her heels, her black hair spinning behind her.

"Oh no, you don't," Parker called, following after her. He touched her arm. She flinched and jerked it away. "Don't come down here thinking you can turn this place upside down and then walk away on me without me saying my piece."

Bliss looked at Parker, and in his cold, dark eyes she detected more than anger but a flicker of desperation, and she inexplicably felt a twinge of sadness for him. She sensed that he was raging against something more than the move of the lighthouse.

"You don't know what the lighthouse means to the people down here," he said. "It's the axis that life on these shores revolves around. No matter where you are, you can always look up and see it reaching to the sky, and you know where you belong. It's like a guardian angel watching over you."

Bliss inhaled deeply, trying to draw some patience. She had enough to worry about without alienating the natives. "Mr. Swain, I'm sorry, but I don't agree with you. The lighthouse needs to be moved. Besides it doesn't matter what I think, does it? Moving the lighthouse was not my decision. I'm only here to carry out the government's wishes. Like they say, don't shoot me. I'm only the messenger."

"So that salves your conscience? You don't feel any remorse for coming down here and disrupting all our lives?"

Any sympathy Bliss felt for him dissolved in her rising anger. "Look, I'm trying to be understanding, but I've got a job to do. One that can make or break my career, and I'm not going to stand here in this heat and argue with someone who obviously cannot discuss this rationally." She stomped away, the heels of her sandals clicking on the asphalt.

"Go ahead," Parker shouted. Two sandpipers squawked and took flight. "Walk away, General Sherman. What do you care if you come down here and destroy my lighthouse! The only curse on Cape Destiny is Sherman Engineering!"

*****

"Oh, the nerve!" Bliss said, gripping the Explorer's wheel so tightly her arms shook. "General Sherman? I'm a curse on Cape Destiny? It's not my fault his stupid old lighthouse is falling into the Atlantic."

As she drove up Beachfront Road, she pulled a French fry out of the bag and bit into it with such force, it was as if she were tearing off Parker's head.

"Oh, what a fool I am! Suckered by Hayseed Hank's muscles and manners. When are you going to learn, Bliss? After Jonathan, you'd think you'd know that men can never be trusted."

She stepped on the gas. "Well, there's no way I'm going to let some Gomer Pyle on steroids get in the way of this project. I don't care how handsome he is. I've worked too long and too hard to get here."

Behind her, she heard a siren. Her eyes went to the rearview mirror. A patrol car with lights flashing pulled in behind her. She slapped the steering wheel. "Oh great!"

Bliss hauled the Explorer onto the sandy shoulder in front of the Taffy Factory. In the mirror she watched an officer step out of his cruiser and saunter to her window. She lowered the glass, the scent of cooking candy sweetened the warm sea air, and she looked up meekly at the baby-faced officer.

"Evenin', ma'am," he said. "I see from your Pennsylvania plates that you're a visitor. Ever been to the Outer Banks before?"

She tried to control her annoyance. "Briefly."

"I don't know about where you come from, but down here, we obey the traffic laws."

"Yes, sir."

Cars slowed down and peopled gawked at her. She wanted to slide under the dashboard and hide.

"They teach you to read numbers and letters up there in Pennsylvania?"

11

Anger flared in her—an automatic reaction whenever anyone questioned her ability to read—but she knew this was not the time to unleash her wrath. It was bad enough that Parker had it out for her. She didn't need the police gunning for her too.

She smiled demurely. "Yes, sir."

"Then why were you barreling down Beachfront Road doin' 40 when the signs say 25?"

"Um . . . um, because I was so overwhelmed by the beauty here, I didn't see the speed limit sign?" She batted her long dark lashes at him.

Redness gathered above his collar and spread over his pudgy cheeks. He chuckled and shook his head. "That's understandable, ma'am, but you might see more if you slowed down."

"Yes, sir."

"So as you don't say that we're an unfriendly lot here on the Outer Banks, I'm going to let you go. For now. But, miss," he tapped the car door, "I'd pay more attention to the speed limit or the next beauty you're going to be admiring is a dilly of a citation."

She flashed him one of her million dollar smiles. "Oh, thank you, officer—" She tried to get a look at his badge. Never hurts to have the police on your side.

He touched the brim of his hat. "Officer Bevans. Wayne Bevans. And you're welcome, ma'am."

"Talked yourself out of that one," Bliss muttered as she watched the young officer walk back to his patrol car. In her rearview mirror, she noticed an aqua Chevy truck slow down and pull along side her. She looked out her side window and caught Parker Swain and his dog staring back at her.

Quickly, she turned her head.

"Kiss my grits, Parker Swain," she snapped and shifted into drive.

*****

Parker glanced in the rearview mirror. "Well, General Sherman is certainly off to a fine start." Bliss's tires threw a plume of sand as she pulled back onto the road.

He'd heard that the person heading up the lighthouse move was a woman—an Amerasian woman. Some magazine had run a profile on her a while back, setting all the local tongues wagging. But he'd paid no mind. He wasn't interested in reading anything about the people invading the Cape to ruin his lighthouse. He'd pictured an older, brainy type—a cross between Yoko Ono and

Hillary Clinton—not some beauty. Mother Nature had taken the best of both gene pools and created an exotic goddess.

In his mind, he could hear his granddaddy warning him, "Parker, now you watch out for those pretty gals, they bring nothing but trouble." Then he'd wink at his grandmama. "I should know. Done married the best looking girl in all the Carolinas and look at the trouble she done bring me."

With that angel's face and temptress's body, Parker thought, as he headed home, Bliss Sherman would be off the charts in terms of trouble. And trouble was one thing he didn't need.

The rush of evening air streaming in the truck's windows cooled his skin and rippled Beau's coat and ears. Instinctively, his eyes sought out the Cape Destiny Lighthouse above the tree line. Then he remembered with melancholy that the beacon's 1,000-watt beam had been extinguished in preparation for the move. Ever since he could remember, its light had been cutting a swath in the darkness. The sun ruled his days and the lighthouse his nights.

Parker propped his elbow on the truck's door and glanced over at Beau, whose head was sticking out the window, his lips fluttering in the wind. She probably thinks I'm a lunatic for getting so upset, Parker thought. He'd heard the others in town whispering that he seemed obsessed with the Cape Destiny Lighthouse, that he'd fallen under its curse. How could he make them understand what it and the keeper's house meant to him?

Lost in thought, he steered the truck off Beachfront Road, leaving behind the traffic and stores and entering the Cape Destiny National Seashore. A national park, it closed at dusk; and his was the only vehicle heading north. At the gate, Mary Jane Mullins, the Park Ranger, sat in the booth and waved him through.

The lighthouse lay directly ahead and seemed to grow taller as he drove nearer. "Hmph, move a lighthouse?" he said to Beau. The dog looked at him with more understanding than he usually got from people. "Why risk destroying something that's been standing since 1875? It's bad enough what they let happen to the house."

Through the low-growing bayberries and sea oats, he caught glimpses of the Atlantic to his right and the Sound to his left. Then the land flattened and the vegetation became so sparse that he had an unimpeded view of water on both sides. Blazing ribbons of clouds hung above the expansive Sound, receiving their crimson color from the setting sun.

Parker reached over and ruffled the dog's golden coat. "Bliss Sherman was gorgeous though, wasn't she, Beau?" The dog yammered. "She was even more beautiful when she was angry. You see how her eyes turned that turbulent black and how she swung that cute little behind when she stomped away."

Beau opened his mouth wide and yawned loudly.

"If you weren't neutered, buddy, you wouldn't be so complacent."

The small road leading directly to the lighthouse had been barricaded when the state had passed legislation to move the lighthouse nearly two years ago. He made a sharp left, turning onto a crushed limestone road. The vegetation picked up once again then became a tall wood that surrounded the lighthouse and its grounds.

"Sad thing is, Beau. I think she liked me."

And I liked her too.

He pulled into the lot and shut off the engine. A shorebird sang a lonely tune and the wind rustled the leathery leaves of the old Magnolia. Leaning over the steering wheel, he took a good look at the Victorian Keeper's House.

He'd made considerable progress since beginning to renovate it over Easter vacation. Last fall the Keeper's House had been moved back so that it now overlooked the Sound. He hoped to have it completed by next summer, so that he could then approach the government about having them accede it to him.

With loving hands, he'd restored the place, pouring his cash and free time into it. As he sat there admiring his handiwork, he could almost feel his ancestors with him approving of the job he'd done. They were all gone now; most of them buried in the plot not far from the house. Knowing that his family had lived there until the lighthouse was automated in 1939, and remained there in death, and that he was now occupying it, gave him roots and a sense of his place in the universe.

Beau lifted his nose and sniffed.

Across the lawn in the fading light a fat old mama raccoon and two babies waddled toward the Sound, disappearing into the brush.

Beau danced on the seat. Parker grabbed the dog's collar and stared into the animal's big, soulful eyes. "Listen here, Beau, when I open that door, don't you dare take off after those raccoons. You hear me?"

Parker stepped out of the truck with his dinner. Beau followed at his heels, along the path carpeted with rust-colored needles that had fallen from the towering pines.

The breeze blew again, carrying a whisper of honeysuckle. Thoughts of Bliss invaded his mind, sending a chill up his sun-baked back. Her dark, exotic eyes flashed at him again. Her soft, pink lips curled into a seductive smile. He remembered her hand, cool and slim, when he'd shaken it. How wonderful those delicate fingers would feel massaging his knotted muscles.

Something stirred in the bushes. Beau froze, barked, and then bolted.

"Beau!" Parker shouted. "Come back here!"

The dog was a gilded flash in the twilight as it ignored his command and pursued the raccoons.

"Aw, Beau." Exasperated, Parker raked his hands through his blond hair. "You know chasing after things you shouldn't only leads to trouble."

Chapter 3

Bliss tucked the bag of food under her chin and riffled through her purse for the key. She stuck the plastic card into the slot and before the green light could flash, the door opened.

"Here, let me help you, Bliss," Nancy Klempner said as she reached out and plucked the bag from under her chin.

"Thanks," Bliss said, amazed that Nancy, once again, had anticipated her every need. As she stepped into the hotel room, Bliss congratulated herself once more for hiring Nancy away from Jonathan's firm nearly two years ago.

Nancy took the bag over to the small oak table, extracted the plastic utensils and napkins, and began to set a place for Bliss.

"You don't have to do that," Bliss said as she slung her purse on the bed and walked over. "You're not my maid."

Nancy stepped back. "I'm sorry. I just thought you could eat while I go over some things with you."

Bliss looked around the room. Since arriving earlier in the evening, Nancy had managed to sort all Bliss's paperwork into neat piles on the desk and unpack the many handheld microrecorders that Bliss used.

Bliss also noticed that her luggage was no where to be seen and guessed that Nancy had unpacked her too, even though Bliss had warned her not to before heading out to get some dinner. Nancy was her girl Friday, Saturday—all seven days of the week.

"Oh, I'm too hungry to work," Bliss said, shoving the utensils back into the bag. "Take a break. Come out on the balcony. I brought you some key lime pie."

Bliss opened the sliding door; the caress of the ocean breeze feeling refreshing on her skin. It was nearly dark now. She could hear the ocean's roar, but could no longer see the waves crashing on the shore. A light from a boat bobbed on the black sea and four floors below, shadowy figures strolled the beach. Bliss, exhausted from the long drive, plopped into a plastic chair and kicked off her sandals. Setting the bag on her lap, she fished out a Styrofoam box and handed it to Nancy, who sat stiffly in the other chair.

Nancy's thick fingers held the box as if it were a bomb. "Thank you, but I think I'll save it for later, back at the cottage." She set the box on the small white table between them.

The twilight had softened Nancy's chiseled features. Bliss knew from pictures she'd seen of her when Nancy had first joined Lavere Engineering in the early eighties, that Nancy had once been striking. Tall and blond in her younger days, she looked like a model, an athlete, or one of those Swedish bikini team girls. Now, twenties years later in her early fifties, Nancy's hair had dulled, her shoulders and waist had broadened, and her high cheekbones and firm jaw were less cover girl material and more the reflection of the harsh ravages of time. All work and no play had left her looking haggard, Bliss thought.

Although Nancy was everything an employer could ask for, Bliss sometimes worried about her assistant. She wished Nancy would lighten up a bit or learn to enjoy life a little more.

"Are you sure you want to stay all the way out on Wellington Island?" Bliss asked, taking the box containing her dinner out of the bag.

Bliss watched Nancy run her index finger under her watchband. She always did that when nervous. "I know renting a private cottage is more expensive, Bliss, but I've taken care of it. I've figured out the difference between staying here and the cottage, and I'm going to deduct that sum from my paycheck and reimburse the company the added expense."

"I don't care about the expense," Bliss said.

"But I do. This company has to succeed, and keeping a tight control on the finances will ensure that."

"The only reason I mentioned it," said Bliss, "is because don't you think staying here would be more convenient, and you could enjoy the ocean view?" Bliss set the box on her lap.

Nancy sniffed. "I'm not a beach person."

Bliss pulled out the plastic utensils from the bag. "Really?"

In the soft light emanating from the room, Bliss saw Nancy frowning. "All that sand getting everywhere. Salty water," she shuddered. "Went once in my younger days to St. Thomas. Haven't been back to the beach since."

Bliss closed her eyes, feeling the cool ocean breeze lift her hair and tickle her skin. *How could she not enjoy this?*

"No," Nancy said, straightening up in the chair, "the cottage will suit me fine."

Perhaps, Bliss thought, disliking the beach was just an excuse to cover Nancy's desire for her privacy. From the time they had met, they had always enjoyed a great rapport, but with the other workers, Nancy had kept mostly to herself, and Bliss had heard the guys in her crew speculate about the mysterious Nancy behind her back, cracking jokes that she probably led a kinky sex life and wore a black leather G-string under her Pendleton suit. Bliss thought her mysteriousness more a result of her innate bashfulness. She'd confided once in Bliss that she'd been painfully shy as teen and had been bullied. It wasn't until she'd gone to work at Lavere that Nancy had felt competent and confident.

Bliss had been to the cottage she'd rented when they were down here a few weeks ago making arrangements for the move. It was located on a small, wooded island off the mainland about fifteen miles from here. The cottage was charming, but it was located in a desolate, marshy place with few inhabitants, and Bliss thought it a bit creepy, the kind of area where a sci-fi movie about swamp monsters would be filmed.

Bliss opened the Styrofoam box set to devour her meal. "Darn!" she snapped. "Now I've got his crabs."

"Pardon me," Nancy said.

"Crabs. I've got Parker Swain's crabs!"

"What?"

"Not those kind of crabs," Bliss said. She showed the box's contents to Nancy. "I ordered clams. Oh, Parker Swain, you owe me."

19

"Who's Parker Swain? And why does he owe you?" Nancy asked.

"Some local yokel who jumped down my throat for moving," she rolled her eyes, "*his lighthouse*. I wanted clams. If there is a curse down here, I hope it's on him."

"His lighthouse? A curse?"

"Yes, some legend about the place being cursed."

"I never heard that before. Sounds ominous."

Bliss shrugged. "Just some nonsense. Apparently, they call this place Cape Cursed instead of Cape Destiny. He's related to the people who used to be the lighthouse keepers." Bliss shut the lid and tossed her unwanted dinner onto the small table. "He's obsessed with the lighthouse. Probably something psychosexual—a phallic symbol to make up for his own poor excuse for manhood."

Nancy looked alarmed. "Do you think he'll pose a problem for the project?"

"You mean like chaining himself to the lighthouse?"

Nancy nodded.

Bliss riffled through the brown bag until she found a small container of coleslaw. "No, he's just annoying, that's all."

Nancy exhaled audibly. "Probably just one of those old history buffs who can't let go of the past."

Bliss removed the lid of the coleslaw. "Oh, he's not old. He's young. And gorgeous."

Nancy rose and eyed Bliss. "Gorgeous?" she asked, her voice sounding concerned.

Bliss stuck her fork into the cabbage. "Oh yeah. He's blond and tanned and muscular. And has brown eyes as deep and yummy as dark chocolate."

"And you were attracted to him?"

Bliss could feel her watching her as she ate. "Well, any woman with a pulse would be," she said then swallowed. "That was until he hopped all over me."

Nancy sat back down. "Good."

Bliss looked over at her assistant. "Good that he hopped all over me?"

"No, that you're no longer attracted to him."

I didn't say that, Bliss thought.

Nancy pursed her lips and shook her head. "We don't need another man interfering with the business."

20

Bliss saw Jonathan's cold blue eyes in her mind. How murderous they had become when she'd told him that she was leaving him, leaving the firm, and taking his best employees to launch her own company.

A company that would compete head-to-head with his.

She recalled how red his face had become, like someone had tightened his silk tie and was choking him when she reminded him that he'd never had her sign a no-compete clause. She heard, once again, his threats that she'd be sorry, that he'd ruin her as she left his office. No she didn't need any more trouble from handsome men.

"Don't worry, Nancy," Bliss said. "I've learned my lesson with Jonathan. This company and this project are too important for me to allow anything to mess it up."

Bliss gazed out at the dark ocean and silently vowed: *I'll never let another man come between me and my career.*"

Chapter 4

Bliss pulled into the lighthouse's empty parking lot. She'd been down to Cape Destiny several times before. Once, to scope out the site when they were preparing to bid for the contract, and most recently when she'd come down to oversee the preliminary stages of the project—the clearing, grading, and compacting of the move corridor; installation of the sensors to monitor the stress on the structure during the move; and the separation of the lighthouse from it's base. But that had been in the winter. Then it had been a gray, unfriendly place whipped by biting winds.

On this June morning, however, it was different. Like magic, the shafts of golden light filtering in through the canopy of pines transformed the barren landscape she'd known in the winter into an idyllic dreamland.

From her car, The Victorian Keeper's House with all its charms—wide front porch, peaked roof and gingerbread—was visible through the trees. What a shame that it was in such disrepair. Sitting on the western side of the thin tongue of land, the house had been boarded up when she'd last been here, but it now looked as if someone had been refurbishing it. With the lush grounds of azaleas and yuccas and wisteria framing it, she envisioned the house, upon completion, gracing post cards.

A sandy path from the parking lot meandered to the middle of a wide flat lawn in front of the house. From there it forked with one part leading to the house and the other disappearing into heavy brush that wound its way to the lighthouse and the ever-encroaching sea.

She stepped out of the coolness of the air-conditioned Explorer into the humid air, heavy with salt and the spice of a pine forest. Before seven a.m., the heat was not yet in the air, but the steaminess was. Birds chattered and twittered overhead and the distant sound of waves crashing on the beach came to her in a hush.

Bliss's stomach fluttered from fear and excitement. The next few weeks would make or break her career. Since founding the firm, she and her crew had successfully moved several smaller structures, but moving the lighthouse was such a high-profile, technically challenging undertaking that if all went well, her business would be catapulted to the forefront of the industry.

If it failed? Well, Bliss didn't want to think about that. She'd risked everything to land this contract—putting her small company in financial jeopardy and burning bridges behind her. She didn't care about the bridges; she had no intention of ever crossing them again. But her financial solvency worried her.

Reaching into the Explorer, she grabbed her briefcase from the front seat and set it on the ground. Then she slid over two bags each filled with three boxes of doughnuts. Bliss had wanted to kick off this critical phase of the project on a positive note, and doughnuts, she thought, would do the trick. On the way out to the site, she'd stopped right before the bridge that linked the Cape with Crystal Shoals, at Decadent Doughnuts and picked up six dozen. She slipped her hand through one of the plastic handles and the other bag she carried in her arm.

With a shift of her hip, she nudged the door closed, and carefully balancing the boxes, she then grabbed the briefcase and began walking. Half way up the path, a branch caught the stack of boxes and knocked the top one askew. She lurched to balance the stack, and the boxes shifted. One hit the ground and opened. Jelly-filled, chocolate-frosted, and maple-glazed doughnuts rolled away like hubcaps from a speeding car.

"Oh no," she groaned, setting the briefcase on the soft earth and bending over to try to salvage her goodies.

*****

Parker pulled the keys out of the truck's ignition and shoved them into the front pocket of his jeans. He was now accustomed to seeing Sherman Engineering vehicles in the parking lot. Through the winter, he'd come over on the weekends and worked inside the house, and when the weather had broken in the spring, he moved from his small clapboard bungalow in Wingina, the nearest town on the mainland to the cape, to begin the renovations in earnest.

Usually the only thing that welcomed him during the winter was downed limbs littering the lawn, cobwebs suspended from the corners, invading field mice, and leaky roofs. This spring, however, a construction crew brought in to prepare for moving the lighthouse greeted him. By now, he was used to them. But being used to something didn't mean the same as liking it.

With coffee cup in hand from his breakfast at the Belle Island Fishing Pier, Parker lowered the tailgate, and Beau jumped out. He slid a bundle of shingles to the edge of the bed, then with a low grunt, hoisted it to his shoulder. His yellow Wingina High Warriors T-shirt was already sticking to his skin the air was so sultry. Picking up his cup for a sip, he then decided he didn't need anything hot to drink and left it sitting in the bed.

"Gonna be another scorcher," he said to Beau, who was nosing around the edge of the wood. He spied a few burrs tangled in the underside of his coat left from his foray into the forest the previous night, and Parker made a mental note to brush the dog first chance he got.

He started up the path, and although he may have been used to the Sherman Engineering vehicles on the property, something he was not used to seeing when he rounded a curve in the path, made him nearly drop the shingles. Before him, highlighted by a shaft of morning light was a shapely, firm female behind.

Savoring the view, he watched as Bliss, in khaki shorts, blue cotton short-sleeved shirt, and work boots, bent over and scrambled to gather falling boxes and rolling doughnuts.

Quietly, he moved closer. "I hope you're better with lighthouses," he said.

Startled, she gasped and quickly straightened up. "I can assure you I am," she snapped, shock evident on her face.

25

Bliss felt a blush rise from her chest to her cheeks. What a way to start the day, she thought, dropping my doughnuts and then having to endure Parker Swain's gloating.

Beau loped over. He sniffed a chocolate doughnut and wolfed it down in two gulps then headed for another.

"Now, cut that out, Beau!"

"I don't mind," Bliss said. She liked the dog, but his owner she could do without. "But won't he get sick?"

Beau's tail wagged happily, beating against her thigh. She crouched and petted him, catching her hand on a burr. While gently removing it, she whispered in Beau's ear loudly enough for Parker to hear, "Your owner should brush you more often."

Parker nudged Beau away with his leg. "Now get on the porch, you old glutton." Beau reluctantly scampered away.

Parker flipped the bundle of shingles onto the ground and bent to help Bliss. "He chased a raccoon last night. I thought I got all the burrs," he said, feeling guilty for not properly grooming his dog. "And he won't get sick; he has a cast iron stomach. I think he's part goat."

"I can clean this up by myself," Bliss said, rebuffing his attempt to start a conversation. "Lord, knows I wouldn't want to be accused of ruining *your* property along with *your* lighthouse."

Parker looked into her black eyes; they were as cold as a grave.

"Did I really say it was *my* lighthouse?"

"Yes, you did," she said, avoiding his gaze, keeping her focus on the ground, gathering boxes and dirty, pine needle-covered doughnuts.

When they both reached for a jelly one, their fingers brushed. Quickly, she snatched back her hand as if touching a live wire.

It was clear to him now how much he'd offended her, and he felt guilty.

"Bliss," he said.

She kept her head down. "That's Ms. Sherman to you."

He crouched next to her, angling his face so that she had no choice but to look at him. "Ms. Sherman, I'm sorry. It was way out of line for me to rip into you like that yesterday. I know you didn't make the bullets, you're just firing them."

She stared him down. "So I'm not General Sherman?"

He collapsed onto the ground, sitting on one hip, one of his long legs stretched out, the other drawn up. Resting his elbow on his knee, Parker covered his face with his powerful hands. "Oh, man, did I really call you that?" He looked between his fingers sheepishly.

She stood and tossed her dark hair back and turned her eyes to the sky. "Yes, you did. And you said I was a curse on Cape Destiny."

He gazed up at her——a pillar of feminine flesh. "Hope you're better at giving up grudges than we Southerners."

He rose and spread his arms plaintively. "Ms. Sherman, I'm terribly sorry. Most people round here know me to be an agreeable fellow. It's just that when it comes to the lighthouse, I have a blind spot." He shook his head and frowned. "Lighthouse or not, I'd have to be a blind fool to want to offend a lovely lady like you. Someone as beautiful as you could never be a curse. Please accept my apologies."

How could she refuse his honey-dipped, Southern-fried apology? Parker waited while she thought for a moment. Then Bliss smiled devilishly, and he felt like a lost vessel sighting the beacon of the lighthouse.

"I'll forgive you on one condition," she said, tapping her foot.

He stepped closer; a rush ran through her.

"And that is?" he said all gooey with charm and sex appeal.

Tilting her head, she looked up at him. "That you'll help me finish cleaning up this mess and then find me a place where I can wash my sticky hands."

"Bliss, if you'll forgive me for being such a lout, why I'd gladly lick your fingers clean."

Chapter 5

"Mind the mess," Parker said as he led Bliss up the steps, where lumber, sheetrock, and various tools were stacked.

It was cool under the shady porch, and she shivered as Parker set the doughnuts on a plank lying across sawhorses and unlocked the door. Expecting him to proceed on inside, Bliss stepped forward to follow.

"Ladies first," he said sweeping his hand back and hitting Bliss hard in the abdomen. A strangled wheeze escaped her lips as she doubled over.

"Gracious!" Parker exclaimed, gently laying a warm palm on her back as he crouched and peered querulously into her face. "Are you OK, Bliss? Oh, I'm so sorry."

Her face twisted with discomfort, as she struggled to recover her air. He pushed her long black hair out of her face and asked again. She nodded that she was fine although she felt as if her lungs had been deflated. Some long seconds later when she nearly gave up hope of ever breathing normally again, she got her breath back and straightened up.

"You sure you're OK?" Parker said, the worry on his tan face making the furrows on his forehead bleed white in the creases.

"Sure," she said her chest sounding tight. "Just got the air knocked out of me." She wasn't used to men being mannerly around her.

"I'm sorry," he said.

As president of a nearly all-male company, she made it a point to be treated as their equal. She'd have to remember that she was in the South now where social courtesies like letting ladies go first still mattered.

Parker raked a hand through his blond locks and shook his head. "Oh, lord this hasn't gone very well, has it? First, I argue with you and insult you, now I darn near kill you. How about if we start over? I'll just step inside and close the door, and you can knock and we'll pretend we've never met before."

Bliss, not thinking he was serious, only laughed. But when he went inside and shut the door, she was flattered that he was so concerned for her feelings. Playing along, she inhaled deeply, smoothed her hair, and straightened her clothes.

Holding herself erect and with a serious, professional look on her face, she knocked on the screen door. Parker opened it wearing a genial smile.

"Pardon me for bothering you so early in the morning," she said, "but I wanted to introduce myself. I'm Bliss Sherman of Sherman Engineering." She pointed in the direction of the beach. "My company is in charge of moving the lighthouse."

Parker smiled and nodded respectfully. A lock of his yellow hair fell across his forehead and made Bliss's breath catch, this time in a good way.

"Please to meet you, Miz Sherman. I'm Parker Swain," he said as he smoothed the hair away. "Would you like to come in?"

"Yes, please."

He held open the door for her, and she gracefully walked inside.

He extended his hand to her, but she held up her sticky fingers. "Oh, right," he said. "Forgot."

He touched her arm. His fingertips were callused, his grip firm and powerful. An odd sense of comfort filled Bliss. She trusted the hands of working men. There were strength and honesty in them. Their roughness revealed the nature of a man, how he spent his time, how he made his living. Her late father had been a mechanic in the Air Force, working on fighter jets. His large, strong fingers with their grease-stained knuckles flashed in her mind. Sadly, she recalled the way, after suffering a stroke in his early fifties and lingering for several years, how his hands had slowly lost their roughness and griminess and eventually became as pink and smooth as a boy's just before he died.

As Parker kicked some tools out of the way, she thought of Jonathan's hands with revulsion. They were soft, unblemished, and feminine. Why, he even got manicures. They told no tale, revealed nothing about his character, only covered his deceitfulness.

"Now let's see about those sticky fingers," Parker said. "Just watch your step. Might be a stray nail. I try to be careful, but I wouldn't want you tramping on one."

Bliss made her way from the small foyer down a dark, stuffy hallway. The plank floor was dull and scarred and the walls were gutted, exposing new two-by-fours. The place smelled old and new at the same time—the air of an ancient house and the smell of fresh lumber and adhesives.

Holding a degree in civil engineering, Bliss was drawn to his work. She wanted to stop and examine the materials he was using, observe his craftsmanship, but as if she were a child, he took her gently by the wrist and led her to the kitchen in the back of the house. The cabinets, partially stripped to bare wood, were off the wall and scattered about the floor.

He rushed ahead of her to the sink, grabbed a pair of pliers and latched them onto the copper stems, turning the water on. "Sorry about the state of this place. I was working in here until the roof decided to leak. I had to drop everything."

"This is quite a project," she said as she put her hands under the cool stream of water.

"Let's get some air in here," he said as he opened a door that led to a porch. The back of the house faced the wide blue expanse of the Carovista Sound. A breeze rushed in off the water that lay fifty yards from the back porch.

Bliss washed her hands and felt the breeze cool the dampness at her hairline. When she was finished, Parker moved beside her, and using the pliers, once again, he turned off the water.

31

Tearing a paper towel from the roll on the counter, he handed it to her with an apology. "Wish I had guest towels, but that's not for a while."

"You're expecting guests?"

"Not anymore. Originally, I had dreamed of turning this place into a bed and breakfast."

"And you're not going through with the idea?" Bliss asked as she dried her hands."

"No. Not now."

She looked around. The place was big enough, had enough charm and history, and was situated in such a beautiful setting as to make it a great place for a bed and breakfast.

"Why not?"

He tossed the pliers into a toolbox sitting on an old Formica kitchen table then gazed out toward the Sound. "I guess you could say I lost my partner to the dream." He looked back at Bliss and for a moment his warm brown eyes grew cold like a cloud passing in front of the sun. Then he smiled weakly. "So it's just me now. I finished renovating the upstairs during the winter. Hope to finish the first floor before school starts again."

"School?" Bliss asked.

"Yes, remember, I'm a teacher. History at Wingina High."

"Oh, I thought you were a contractor. You're work is very professional."

"Coming from a pro like you, I appreciate the compliment. But no, I'm a teacher. During college, I worked summers on construction crews building beach houses around here. You pick up a lot."

"So you own this place?" Bliss asked leaning against the counter.

"Would you like some coffee? I always put a pot on when I get here. Probably not the thing for a steamy day like this, but the aroma adds a homey quality to this disarray."

Bliss glanced at her wristwatch. She really wanted to get an early start. When she looked back at Parker, he was smiling expectantly at her. "I guess one cup wouldn't hurt." She thought it smart to keep him as a friend, and she was interested in hearing about his renovations.

He cleared the tools from the table and moved a chrome and vinyl chair over for Bliss. "Have a seat."

She sat and watched as he navigated the kitchen. "So you own this place?" she asked again.

He held the coffee carafe under the faucet. "Well, sort of. My ancestors lived here and kept the lighthouse for decades. Then in 1936 it was automatically lighted and the Coast Guard took over. The house fell into disrepair and by the time they turned it over to the state in the 1980s, it was a shambles. Broke my heart to see it just falling apart." He put the pot under the coffeemaker and turned it on. Then Parker leaned against the sink, the morning sun streaming in the uncovered windows behind him, firing the blond streaks in his hair and turning the stubble on his cheeks and the tips of his long eyelashes to gold. She told herself to be tough. She had a construction crew to oversee and a project to run. If she allowed every man with soft brown eyes and hard, tanned muscles, to make her melt like a stick of butter in the heat, she'd be ruined. She tried to focus on his words.

"About four years ago, I began to petition the state as a descendant of the keepers, about buying the place. After the house was moved last fall, they worked out a deal with me. I formed the CDLC, The Cape Destiny Lighthouse Conservation group, and pledged to open and operate a lighthouse museum out in the old oil house. That little building right out there." He pointed out the kitchen window to a small out building. "That's where the oil was kept for the lighthouse when it was illuminated by a mineral oil lamp with five concentric wicks."

Bliss looked out the window. "They hauled oil from there all the way to the lighthouse?"

"Yes, they did," Parker said proudly. "Anyway, the arrangement provides for the proceeds to go to the state. I'm required to renovate and restore the place, and when it's complete, in exchange, they'll deed the place to me. If I fail to do any of that, the state can take the house back."

"Works out well for everyone," Bliss said.

Parker crossed his arms in front of his chest. "It does. The state gets a museum and revenue from it, and I get to keep my ancestral home."

Parker poured two mugs of coffee. "How do you take yours, Bliss?"

"A little sugar, please."

He opened up the metal spout on the box of sugar sitting on the counter and poured some in. "Here you go," he said, setting the mug in front of her, "sweet and strong." He took a seat across from her. "Like the President of Sherman Engineering."

She laughed. "Where'd you study at the Rhett Butler School of Southern Charm?"

He took a sip and then deadpanned. "Graduated Magna Cum Lordy." They both laughed at his awful joke.

"Seriously," he said, "how'd a sweet thing like you wind up moving lighthouses?"

Bliss sighed and looked into the mug. "Oh, that's a long story."

"Bliss, this is the South. Down here we take the time for long stories."

"Well, you asked for it. Let's see. My father was in the Air Force stationed in Korea when he met and married my mother. She was Korean."

"That explains your lovely black hair."

She felt herself blush. "Thanks. Do you believe when I was a rebellious teen, I used to dye it blond?"

"Be like painting a mustache on the Mona Lisa."

She shook her head and waved a hand at him dismissing his compliment.

"Anyway, I was a military brat, and we moved all over the place. I think that's how I got into moving things. Never stayed put for very long. Guess I can't stand to see buildings and lighthouses in one place either. I studied civil engineering in college and joined Lavere Enterprises after graduation."

"Forgive my chauvinistic inclinations," he said, "but if you liked moving things so much, wouldn't it have been easier to study interior design and just move sofas and tables around instead?"

"Maybe for some, it would have, but my strong suit is numbers and equations. So I majored in engineering."

"The universities love women who major in traditionally male fields. They're always coming to my school trying to encourage the girls to major in those careers."

An involuntary laugh came from Bliss.

"What's so funny?"

"They certainly didn't encourage me."

Puzzled, he stared at her, waiting for the rest of the story. She hesitated. Only her closest friends knew of her greatest shame,

34

but since he seemed so kind and he was a teacher, she thought it safe to share her secret.

"I'm dyslexic. But strangely only when it comes to letters and words, not numbers. That's why I stuck with the sciences."

Parker looked shocked. "I've taught dyslexic students. They struggle so. What an accomplishment to come so far. It must have been very difficult for you."

"I have lots of assistance."

"You'd be a real source of inspiration for my students with learning challenges."

Learning challenges? Bliss snickered to herself. They never labeled her so gently when she was in school. She remembered how her classmates taunted her by calling her the half-Jap dummy. She didn't know which angered her more being called dummy or that they didn't know there was a difference between being Japanese and Korean. "I'd be happy to."

Parker wrapped his hands around the mug and leaned toward her. "So how did you become president of your own company?"

"With a lot of help." She thought of Jonathan and her days with Lavere. *And a lot of heartache*, but she couldn't tell Parker that. "I learned the business at one of the best civil engineering firms in the nation. I had a great mentor, Nancy Klempner. She's my assistant now and a minority owner in my company. She does everything for me that I can't do—composing letters, typing, computer work—she's fills in for the part of my brain that doesn't work properly. At Lavere, she took me under her wing and the usual story. I was promoted and given more responsibility, until it was time for me to strike out on my own."

"Well, you should be quite proud of yourself," Parker said. "I know how stiff the competition was to land this lighthouse project."

Bliss looked at her watch. "Speaking of lighthouses. As much as I'd like to sit here and continue to let you praise me, I have one to move."

Parker rose and accompanied her to the porch.

"Well, thanks for letting me wash my hands," Bliss said. Then she covered her mouth as she remembered something. "Oh, no. I've forgotten the soap!"

Parker screwed up his face. "Soap?"

She pulled a microrecorder out of her pocket and spoke into it. "Buy a case of soap." She released the button. "We use it to grease the skids so to speak when moving things. Works better than grease."

"That's a pretty high-tech little gizmo there," Parker said.

Bliss held out the recorder. It wasn't much bigger than the palm of her hand. Told you—can't type, have trouble reading and writing, and obviously remembering things——thank God for technology. Makes up for what I lack."

She bent and picked up her briefcase, and when she rose, Parker was leaning against the porch pillar, arms crossed, grinning at her. "Bliss Sherman, I don't think there's anything you lack."

She blushed deeply, feeling as if someone had taken a blowtorch to her cheeks. "Thanks," she said softly and turned to pick up the doughnuts to avoid his gaze.

He came to her side. "Let me help you carry those."

She looked up into his eyes, and felt her breath catch in her throat. "I'm fine."

She hurried down the wooden steps, knowing she wasn't fine at all.

As she walked across the lawn in the bright morning light, she scolded herself for allowing herself to be so easily seduced by his smooth, easy charms.

No, Parker, she thought I do lack something——sense.

Chapter 6

As Bliss rounded the path, the work site came into view. Squinting into the morning sun, she peered up to the top of the 196-foot lighthouse. She still had trouble believing that she was in charge of moving such a massive structure. She felt like Atlas, trying to lift the world.

Everything was ready to go. The tower had been cut from its base between the first and third plinth and raised by hydraulic jacks. Steel beams, acting as a support frame, had been slid underneath. The monolith had then been lowered onto steel travel beams that were fitted with rollers. The push jacks were now in place, and beginning tomorrow, they would slowly nudge the 130-year-old tower more than 1,700 feet to the northwest.

Swarms of workers were busy reading sensors, monitoring hydraulic jacks, and welding steel beams. It reminded Bliss of that scene in the *Ten Commandments* where the Israelite slaves were laboring to build the pyramids.

As she walked down the packed sand and gravel of the move corridor, the path cleared for the lighthouse to travel to its new destination, many of the workers greeted her respectfully with a, "Morning, Ms. Sherman."

"Morning," she replied confidently to all of them, but she was shaking in her steel-toed boots. She had every confidence in her expertise and crew, but she knew that there were many variables—everything from equipment failure to foul weather—that could prevent the success of this project and meeting the deadline of having the lighthouse installed in its new site by September 1. She'd gambled and spread their resources thin to acquire this project. She didn't even want to contemplate the monetary penalties she'd accrue if she failed to meet the deadline.

Bliss walked up the wooden ramp to the trailer that would serve as Sherman Engineering's offices for the duration of the project and opened the door.

Inside, it was cramped. Three desks and file cabinets filled the space and the air conditioner strained to keep the temperature slightly cooler than the outside.

It was nothing like her corporate office back in Pittsburgh, where she'd left only a small administrative staff behind.

Nancy's back was to her as she clicked away at the computer's keyboard. Turning her head, she peered over her bifocals. "Oh good, you're here now, Bliss. I'm working on some purchase orders that need to be signed as soon as I print them."

Randy Barstow, her chief foreman, was pacing behind his desk as he hung on the phone. A burly, quiet man, his massive biceps gave the impression that he was strong enough to pick up the lighthouse and move it by himself. He covered the mouthpiece. "Trying to get some two-by-fours delivered so we can finish off the platform for the press conference."

Press conference. Bliss had completely forgotten. No, that wasn't accurate. She hadn't forgotten it. She'd dismissed it from her mind. Of all the tasks associated with the move, the press conference was the one she dreaded most. With the difficulties she had reading, speeches were not her strong suit.

Several times she'd sat down and made a valiant attempt to compose her remarks, but each time she flashed back to her sixth grade book report on Vasco da Gama. She saw herself standing before the class, the letters and words on her note cards making as much sense to her as bowl of alphabet soup.

She moved aside some papers resting on top of a metal credenza and set the remaining boxes of doughnuts there. "I tried to get an early start. Even bought treats," she said as she opened the boxes, "but I had a minor disaster."

Nancy, with a look of alarm, swiveled her chair to face Bliss. "What happened?"

Bliss selected a coconut topped one. "Oh, nothing serious. When I was walking through the parking lot, the boxes shifted, and I lost about a dozen cream-filleds and glazeds." She took a bite and picking up a napkin, walked to her desk. "But I guess it wasn't a total disaster. I met that Parker Swain again, and he apologized for last night."

"Well, he should," Nancy said, shuffling some papers. "The nerve of some people."

Bliss finished her doughnut and licked her fingers. "Oh, don't be so hard on him. He's really quite nice."

"Nice?" Nancy snorted.

"No, he really is. He helped me clean up the mess of doughnuts and had me into the keeper's house for coffee."

Nancy looked sharply at Bliss and began to fiddle with her watchband. "You went into his house?"

Randy hung up the phone. "Mornin', Bliss. They're going to send the lumber by noon. Other than building the stairs up to the platform, we're all set for tomorrow."

"Good," Bliss said. "I brought doughnuts."

Randy came over and selected a chocolate one with crushed peanut sprinkles.

"Have you tested the equipment to see if it works?" Bliss asked.

"Yep, a little bit ago," he said. In three bites, he consumed the doughnut. "Everything worked perfectly."

"Great," Bliss said. "Wouldn't that be embarrassing to turn the switches on only to have the thing not move?"

"No chance of that," Randy said. "This is the best crew we've ever assembled, and I've made sure everything is ready to go when you give the green light."

"I must be the smartest woman in the world to have hired you two away from Jonathan."

"Not to discredit your intelligence," Nancy said, "but it didn't take much to persuade any of us to leave him."

Randy selected another doughnut, this time a maple glazed. "His father would be ashamed of him."

Bliss didn't want to think of Jonathan anymore. She'd spent too many minutes and too many tears on him the last few years. She changed the subject. "Any idea of how big a crowd we're expecting tomorrow?"

Nancy moved to the printer and waited for the machine to regurgitate her file in hard copy form. "I talked to the Governor's office when I got in. They're telling me to expect a thousand or so. Seems there's a lot of lighthouse groupies, people who are fond of them."

Bliss felt sick. She wasn't expecting to have to speak before that many people.

Randy went to the coffee maker and filled his insulated mug. "There's that many fools willing to stand in the heat to hear a bunch of blow hard politicians? It's not like the lighthouse is going to do the hundred-yard dash up the move corridor. The thing will be traveling so slowly, it'll be barely noticeable. It'll be like watching paint dry."

"Well," Bliss said, settling in at her desk, "this lighthouse is a National Landmark and from my conversation last night, I've learned just how much it means to the people around here."

"Well, in that case," Randy said as he snapped the lid on his mug, "I better get to work. Don't want to disappoint the masses."

"Nancy, have a doughnut," Bliss said.

Nancy rubbed her jaw. "No thanks. One of my molars is giving me trouble. I think I've chipped a tooth or lost a filling."

"Randy says everything is under control. Why, don't you find a dentist and get it taken care of today?"

"Are you kidding? What if the dentist is one of those locals who is against the lighthouse move? Don't want someone with a vendetta and a drill anywhere near my mouth. No, I'll wait until we get back to Pittsburgh."

"Randy," Bliss said, "why don't you take the rest of them to the crew."

"OK."

"I'll be down later. I have to run out and get soap."

"Better get a case or two," he said as he went out the door with the doughnuts.

Nancy came and placed the purchase requisitions in front of Bliss. She waited until Randy had closed the door then she looked down disapprovingly at her and slid her finger under her watch's strap. "Do you think that was wise, Bliss, to go into his home?"

Bliss picked up a pen. "Who? Parker?" Bliss chuckled. "I'm a big girl, Nancy. I can take care of myself."

"I know you are, but—"

Bliss looked up at her. "But what?"

"Well, a lot of the people down here are against this move and it's just that sometimes you're too . . . "

"Too what?" Bliss said impatiently.

Nancy pushed her glasses back. "Oh . . .well. You're too kind and naïve."

"What?" Bliss exclaimed and backed her chair away. "I am not naïve. Gullible people don't come this far."

"OK, so maybe you're shrewd in business, but sometimes you're too kind. And trusting. Look how you were taken in by Jonathan."

Bliss stood and tossed her hair back. "May I remind you? We were all taken in by him."

"Yes, we all were—professionally. But you married him."

Bliss felt her anger rising. "OK, so I was blind to his faults. Aren't we all entitled to one youthful indiscretion?"

Nancy's shoulders seemed to sag. "Yes, I'm sorry. I guess we're all entitled to that. But what I'm saying is, Bliss, you think the best of everyone. That's admirable but not always wise. Take this Swain character. He could have taken advantage of you or worse."

Bliss could see that Nancy was truly concerned for her. "OK, maybe I should have been more cautious." She made her black eyes huge and hunched her shoulders like she was cowering from an evil entity. Then Bliss thought about the curse and dropped the act. "Next time I'll be more careful. But Parker was very nice and he did apologize. With him right next door, I thought it best to befriend him."

"As long as it's just friends."

Bliss's cheeks flushed crimson. "Oh, be serious, Nancy. I'm not going to get involved with him."

Nancy looked dubiously at her.

"Why would I? There's no future. We'll be gone in a few months. I'm from Pittsburgh. He's Southern. He's more rooted to this place than the lighthouse, and I . . . I move things."

Bliss looked out the window toward the Keeper's House. Parker was up on the porch roof working. His shirt was off and the sun was glistening on the muscles of his back as he hammered. Sadly, she turned away. And besides, she thought, he'd never want me if he learned the true reason why Jonathan left me. No man, not even someone as kind as Parker, would ever want her.

She faced Nancy. "Rest assured. There's no way I'd ever get tangled up with Parker Swain."

Chapter 7

After Bliss returned a few calls, signed the purchase requisitions, and took a walkthrough of the site to make sure everything was progressing as planned, she returned to the trailer. It was nearing lunchtime, and she wrestled with the urge to put off working on the speech and drive down Beachfront Road to find something for Nancy and her to eat.

She forced herself to work for another half hour, dictating thoughts into the microrecorder then finally deciding she'd work much better on a full stomach. When she suggested lunch, Nancy said she wasn't hungry. Bliss interpreted her reply as a suggestion that she continue with the speech.

Taking a seat at her desk, she looked at the program for the press conference. She was to speak right before the governor.

As she was about to dictate some more notes, she heard a knock at the door.

Nancy rose. "I hope it's the lumber. They said they'd be right out with the delivery, but these people down here don't know the meaning of hurry." She opened the door.

"Excuse me, but is Miz Sherman in?"

Bliss looked up when she heard Parker's voice. He was standing in the bright sunshine, holding a brown bag. Beau was sitting at his heels.

"Parker," Bliss exclaimed as she quickly came around the desk. "Come in."

"I don't want to disturb y'all when you're busy."

Bliss was surprised at how glad her heart felt to see him. "No, no. I'm not that busy."

Out of the corner of her eye, she saw Nancy's lips become tight.

"Come in," Bliss said again. Nancy may be the engine that drives this office, but I'm the one controlling the gas pedal, thought Bliss. She would not allow Nancy to dictate who her friends would be.

Parker stepped into the trailer and turned to Beau, "You lie there quiet now."

"Oh, it's so hot, Parker," Bliss said, "let him come inside. He'll be good." Bliss turned her gaze to the dog. "Won't you, handsome?"

When Bliss's eyes fell on Beau, he leaped to his paws, bounded into the trailer, and jumped on Bliss slathering her with kisses. She giggled.

"Beau!" Parker commanded. "Get down!"

"I'm sorry," Parker said, grabbing his collar. "Now you sit."

Bliss kneeled beside Beau and petted him. She looked up at Nancy. "Nancy Klempner, my right arm and right brain, or whichever hemisphere it is of mine that doesn't work properly, this is Parker Swain, our neighbor for the next few months."

Parker transferred the bag to his other hand and extended his free one to Nancy. "Pleased to meet you, ma'am."

She slowly extended her hand to him.

"And this," Bliss said, her neck being washed by the dog's large tongue, "is Beau." She whispered into the dog's ear. "Say hello to Nancy."

The dog stood and went to Nancy and licked her hand. Nancy withdrew it and shoved it into her pocket. "Is there something we can help you with, Mr. Swain?" Nancy said curtly.

"Parker," he said as warmly as Nancy's remark had been cold. "Please call me Parker."

Beau must have smelled the scent of doughnuts because he began sniffing around the credenza, his brush of a tail generating enough wind to stir the papers lying on Randy's desk.

Nancy set her jaw and slapped her hands on top of them.

"I'm sorry," Parker said. "Beau, get on over here."

"Is there something we can help you with?" Nancy asked with more insistence this time.

Parker looked at Bliss and smiled. He held out the bag to her. "What's this?"

"Clams," he said. "I owed you a meal."

She laughed. "You didn't have to do this." Her cheeks colored because she was flattered that he'd gone to all this trouble.

He turned and looked at Nancy. "I'm terribly sorry. Had I known you were here, I'd have brought you lunch too."

"That's OK. I'm not fond of seafood, Mr. Swain."

"Well, if you judge seafood by what you get in Pittsburgh," Parker said, crossing his arms in front of his chest, "I'd probably not like it either, but down here the seafood is so fresh, a lovely woman like you has to slap its face for impertinence. I guarantee you'd like it. Next time, I'll bring y'all some crabs."

"Save your money, Mr. Swain. I can assure you I won't like your seafood."

Her frosty attitude, Bliss thought, made the trailer cooler than if they'd turned up the air conditioner.

Bliss came and stood next to Parker. "Well, I love seafood, and I can't wait to finally eat my clams."

"Well, then," Parker said, "we'll clear on out of here and let you get to them. Come on, Beau." He headed toward the door.

Bliss followed him outside and pulled the door closed behind her. "Thank you again, Parker, and I apologize for Nancy. She's really a good soul; I'd be lost without her. But she's a little overprotective and a whole lot anal retentive."

"No need to apologize," he squinted in the sun. "I'll just need to ratchet up the charm."

"I'm afraid it'd be lost on her. She's really out of her element here. She's not a beach person," Bliss said as she stared at his handsome face and wondered how Nancy or any other woman could resist him.

"What about you, Bliss?" he grinned. "What kind of person are you?"

Bliss was taken aback by the bluntness of his questions. *Who was she?* She wasn't sure. Was she the confident businesswoman or the dyslexic masquerading as the President of Sherman Engineering? The woman attracted to Parker Swain or the wounded divorcée terrified to trust her heart again with any man?

"I don't know," she said. Then she looked out over the ocean. The sun glinted on the surface of the blue water, and she hugged herself as a feeling came to her that her time at Cape Destiny would define exactly who she really was.

Chapter 8

When Bliss went back into the trailer, she was annoyed with Nancy for being so rude, but she knew from experience that if she confronted her, Nancy would only sulk, making life more difficult. Bliss didn't need any added stress so she made no comment and went to her desk to eat her lunch.

While she enjoyed the golden fried clams, she dictated some more notes for her speech. After finishing her meal, she crumpled the wrappings and stuffed them back into the brown bag.

As she was about to throw them away, Nancy looked up from her desk. "You're not going put that foul-smelling stuff in the trash, are you?"

Bliss dug her nails into her thighs to keep from saying, Listen, I'm the boss here, and if I feel like cutting paper dolls from the wrappers, I'll do it.

"No," Bliss said with quiet control, "I've done all I can on the speech." She picked up the bag and her recorder, walked to Nancy's desk, and set the recorder on it. "Please type it up for me.

I'm going to take this to the trash and pick up the soap. When I get back, I'll make revisions."

"Let me pick up the soap, Bliss. That's my job. You've got enough to do."

"That's OK," Bliss said. "I need a few other things." What she felt like saying was that she needed some space, to clear her head. "I won't be gone long."

When Bliss stepped outside, the sun was high over head and the heat was intense. She strode to the garbage barrel and the odor of refuse cooking in the sun overwhelmed her. She pulled out a second microrecorder that she always kept in her pocket and pressed the button. "Have someone empty the trash before the conference."

Instead of cutting across Parker's lawn, which was baking in the afternoon sun, she took a more circuitous, shady route, walking behind the trailer, through the pines and bayberries on a path made soft with sand and fallen needles.

When she got into the Explorer, the heat inside was oppressive. She turned on the engine, and hit the button opening all the windows. As she backed out, she set the air conditioner to high. Pulling out of the lot, Bliss headed away from the Cape Destiny Seashore. At the guard shack, she waved to the ranger on duty, who looked to be suffering in the heat.

By the time she hit Beachfront Road, the breeze whipping into the car had cooled it off inside. Bliss enjoyed the feel of the wind in her face so much that she shut off the air conditioner and left the windows down. The sound of gulls, crashing waves, and roar of motorcycles as they passed invigorated her. She always rode with the windows up, but now as she took all the sounds in, she felt as if she had been living in a display case.

A display case was an accurate description of her life. She felt like she was always being observed and judged. As a child, the eyes were always on her because of how she looked. As a biracial child, people were constantly scrutinizing her face, trying to figure out just what she was. Even in college, she felt as if she were being judged. "How could she be Asian and have learning disabilities?" asked one blunt girl in her dorm. "That's an oxymoron."

Then she had gone to work at Lavere. And the feeling of being watched had only intensified. The more she distinguished herself, the more attention she drew. And marrying Jonathan Lavere had brought even more scrutiny to her life.

Now she had really reached the pinnacle of attention with the lighthouse move. *People Magazine* had recently interviewed her.

It seemed as if the whole world were watching, waiting for her to fail.

She stopped for a red light. At the crosswalk, two teenaged girls in brightly colored bikinis scurried across in flip-flops. The coconut scent of their suntan lotion came to her on the breeze. She sighed.

She was so tired of feeling she had to perform for an audience. She wanted to come out from the behind the display case, to join in life.

When the Beach Mart and Pharmacy came into view, Bliss slowed down in front of the pink stucco building and pulled into the lot along side. The blacktop was gooey under her work boots from the heat as she walked across the parking lot. When she opened the door, a bell jingled. The blast of cold air from the air conditioner made goose bumps rise on her arms.

A woman, who appeared to be in her seventies, greeted her from behind the counter in the front. She had short, gray frizzy hair and wore large pink button earrings that matched her smock. The woman smiled at Bliss as she headed down an aisle filled with inflatable whales, inner tubes, and sand chairs. "If you need any help, give a holler."

Bliss headed toward the pantyhose. She'd only packed one pair, and she wanted a spare for the press conference in case she got a runner. The selection was limited. Bliss guessed that not many women wore hose at the beach. She then went to the soap aisle. There were about fifteen bars on the shelf. She needed much more than that.

She walked to the counter and waited until the clerk rang up a boy who was buying post cards. Bliss turned the rack of cards. There was one of the Cape Destiny Lighthouse taken at dusk, its beam scanning out to sea. The title on the card said "The Faithful Sentinel."

The boy walked out; the bell jingled again. Then the woman turned her attention to Bliss. "Can I help you, honey?"

"I need some soap," Bliss said.

"Aisle five, past the toothpaste."

"Oh, I found the soap. What I mean is I need more than what is on the shelf."

The woman looked puzzled. "Honey, don't they give you soap at your hotel?"

"It's not for me. It's for the lighthouse."

The woman looked at Bliss like she was waiting for her to spring a punch line.

"Let me explain," Bliss said. I'm in charge of moving it, and I need soap to lubricate the beams it's going to slide along. Soap works better than grease and is safer for the environment."

The woman's shoulders quaked as she snickered. "Oh, I thought maybe you was going to give it a bath."

Bliss laughed and tossed her hair back. "Moving yes, bathing no. I draw the line somewhere."

"Now I recognize you," the clerk said. "You're that Bliss Sherman. Read about you in the new *People Magazine* that just came in, but you're just a little bitty thing. I guess being part Chinese and all you'd be petite."

"Korean," Bliss said. "I'm half Korean not Chinese."

"Whatever. That picture made you look older. Maybe it was that fancy suit you was wearing and posing in that big old office. I'm June Maynard. It's a pleasure to meet you."

Bliss shook her hand. Coming from as large a city as Pittsburgh, it felt strange to get so personal with a clerk.

"Now, how much soap do you need, honey?"

"How much do you have?"

June put a ring bell for service sign on the counter and came from behind it. She wore opaque hose and thick, white rubber-soled shoes, that made little squishy noises on the tile floor.

"Come on back to the stockroom with me, and we'll see."

In the back of the Beach Mart, the raised counter of the Pharmacy ran the width of the store. Behind it a jowly man whose glasses had slid down his nose was bent over pecking at a computer. If he got any closer, he could type with his nose.

"Hey, Boyd," June called. He raised his head, holding an amber pill bottle and pushed his glasses back up the bridge of his nose. "This here is Bliss Sherman, the lady in charge of moving the lighthouse."

He nodded. "Pleased to meet you."

"Boyd here is our pharmacist," June said. Then she whispered to Bliss. "Just got us a computer. He's having a dickens of a time catching on." June opened a door and took Bliss into a dimly lit area in the very back of the store. "He's a Stafford. My second cousin on my mother's side. Boyd's a might shy, but a real good druggist. My maiden name is Swain. You probably heard of the Swains bein' all involved out there at the lighthouse."

"Then you must be related to Parker Swain?"

June beamed. "Why, I sure am. He's my nephew. His daddy and I was born out at the lighthouse." She slyly eyed Bliss from head to toe. "I'd heard you met Parker."

"You did?"

"Oh, word travels round here faster than a case of the grippe. Handsome fella, ain't he?"

Bliss laughed. "Why, yes I'd say he's nice looking."

"Nicest darn fella too. Deserves better," June tsked to herself. "Here we go," she said touching a cardboard box. "Got a case of Ivory and case of Oil of Olay."

"Can I have the Ivory, if that won't run your stock down?"

"Sure thing, honey. And I'll be sure to order more in case you need it."

June lifted the box off the shelf.

"Let me get that for you," Bliss said.

"Nonsense, my late husband and I had a farm outside Elizabeth City. I've slung bushels of peaches all my life. Box of soap ain't nothin'."

June hauled the carton to the counter where Bliss paid for it and the pantyhose.

"So," June said, "paper says the big move starts tomorrow."

"Yes, right after the press conference."

"So much fuss over a silly old lighthouse."

"You mean you're not attached to it like the rest of the people around here?"

"You mean like Parker?"

Bliss looked at her surprised. "Honey, everybody in these parts knows each other, and I know how obsessed Parker Swain is with that lighthouse." She paused and looked intently at Bliss. "And I also know that he's taken a fancy to you."

Bliss's mouth fell open.

"Ernie over The Seafood Shack told me. Heard tell Parker bought you lunch today."

51

"Oh, we accidentally got our dinners mixed up last night, and he replaced my order. We're just friends. Actually, acquaintances would be more accurate."

"Just friends is how me and Skeeter Maynard started out 48 years, five kids, and nine grandbabies ago."

Bliss opened her mouth to set her straight on her relationship with Parker, but June Maynard kept on talking.

"Well, I'm glad Parker's got something else to occupy his mind and heart instead of that old lighthouse. With all the trouble it's attracted, you'd think he'd be glad to let it get swallowed by the sea. I swear that lighthouse ain't nothing but a big old lightning rod for trouble."

Bliss felt a chill go up her spine. "Trouble? You believe it's cursed then."

"If I wasn't a Christian woman who didn't believe in that nonsense, I'd think it was. All know is that place has seen its share of tragedy. Shipwrecks. Pirates. My granddaddy getting washed out of it." She shook her head sorrowfully. Then what happened a few years ago."

"What? What happened?"

"You mean you ain't heard about it? Oh my, so terrible."

"June," Boyd called from the pharmacy counter.

She raised an arthritic finger. "Wait a second, Bliss. Yes, Boyd?"

"Got Mrs. Fletcher on the phone. Said Tucker forgot to deliver her Metamucil when he brought her Ben Gay. You want to check on that."

June turned to Bliss. "Sorry, honey. That Tucker is dumber than dirt. I know I packed that up for him before he left." She picked up the phone and began dialing. "Maybe I can catch him before he gets too far."

Half of Bliss was curious about what had happened out at the lighthouse and the other half told her to leave well enough alone. She was already stressed about the move. She didn't need any beach superstition adding to her anxiety.

She waved goodbye to June, who waved back as she argued over the phone with Tucker.

As Bliss drove toward the office, she noticed the lighthouse towering on the horizon and a sense of uneasiness settled over her. What happened out there? Was the lighthouse cursed?

Bliss, don't be ridiculous. There's no such thing as a cursed lighthouse.

Chapter 9

Bliss was glad she bought the extra pair of pantyhose yesterday, because in her haste to get dressed for the press conference, she put her nail right through the first pair.

She checked herself in the vanity mirror. Bliss had selected a navy linen sheath with a matching short sleeve blazer. She wanted to look beautiful and intelligent. "Well, what woman doesn't?" she said to her reflection.

After pinning her hair up in a French twist, she inserted gold loops into her ears and fastened an understated gold chain around her neck. Bliss wedged her feet into a pair of navy strappy sandals.

Did she look as tired as she felt? She patted her upper eyelid. Being part Asian, her lids normally looked more fleshy, but today she thought they looked puffy. No wonder. After returning from the Beach Mart, she had spent the night rehearsing her speech. She wanted to know it by heart, in case she became nervous and had trouble reading. She'd hardly slept because she'd had dreams of not remembering her speech or that the note cards went blank.

Bliss checked her watch. It was eight-thirty. She'd intended to leave fifteen minutes ago. Grabbing her purse, she stuffed her microrecorder inside, picked up her briefcase, and headed out the door.

As much as she wanted to roll the Explorer's windows down and enjoy the ocean breeze, she refrained because she didn't want to show up on the stage with wind-whipped hair.

As she came to entrance of the Cape Destiny National Seashore, two state police cars were parked there. At the guard shack, three park rangers were on duty today, and they were stopping cars. When Bliss pulled up, the ranger recognized her and waved her through.

When she arrived at the lot, she found another ranger directing the cars where to park. She knew there would be a lot of visitors to see the press conference, but she hadn't expected such a crowd. They were parking cars on the lawn in front of Parker's house. She looked for him, but he wasn't up on the roof working.

Before the ranger approached, Bliss dug her Sherman ID badge out of her purse. When he saw it, he directed her to the VIP Parking area. On the perimeter were satellite news trucks. Her fingers began to tremble as she gripped the steering wheel. If she flubbed the speech, it would be broadcast everywhere.

When Bliss stepped out of the car, the heat slammed into her. Just what she needed. Another reason to sweat. It was difficult walking in heels. When the work site came into view, she was pleased to see that the stage had been completed. Last night when she had left for the hotel, Randy and his crew were putting the finishing touches on it.

She stepped into the trailer, and immediately could tell from Nancy's ramrod posture that she was tense. Dressed in her best black suit, she was rushing between the desk and the credenza.

"Morning," Bliss said.

"Oh, my God," Nancy said. "Where's your speech? We need to change it. Just got a call from Governor Shay's office and he's bringing his wife. We need to add her to the greeting."

Wonderful, Bliss thought. I have it all memorized and now I have to change it. *Don't panic.*

Bliss went to her desk and snapped open her briefcase. She fished out the cards and handed them to Nancy.

Can I just write it in on the cards," Nancy asked concerned, "or do I need to print you out new one?"

"You can just write it. By the way, what's her name?"

"Savannah."

"Oh, great," Bliss groaned. As she repeated the name, it came out like 'Shavannah Says' instead of "Savannah Shays." "It's like a tongue twister." Her knees begin to knock. "I know I'll mess it up."

Nancy put her arm around her and gave her a squeeze. "You'll be fine. I'll just have you address them as 'Governor and Mrs. Shays.' How's that?"

"I'll be glad when this day is over," Bliss said, taking a seat at her desk. Nancy had printed out her schedule. It was packed with appointments with the media right until lunch at noon, which would be held at the Destiny Dunes Restaurant.

By the time eleven-thirty arrived, Bliss had already given four interviews, even one to the BBC. She drove Nancy and Randy to the luncheon. After meeting all the dignitaries, she sat down to her meal. With her speech looming, she had no appetite. She ate only the crab bisque soup and nibbled on a roll. Bliss wished she could box up the shrimp scampi and the devil's food cake with the miniature replicas of the lighthouse done in white and dark chocolate for decoration and take them home to eat later.

After lunch, a police escort led them all back to the lighthouse where the crowd had swelled. Bliss estimated three thousand people.

She checked herself in the rearview mirror, hurried back to the trailer, picked up the note cards, and headed toward the stage.

Taking her seat next to the Secretary of the North Carolina Department of the Interior, she sweltered in the insufferable afternoon heat, listening to one politician after another add to the hot air as they boasted about how they had come to be involved with the lighthouse project. She felt as if she had her own personal sun, beating on her head, broiling her. Clammy now, she cursed herself for wearing a dark colored dress. It seemed to trap the heat. Why hadn't she had the foresight to bring a bottle of water with her?

After Earl Walker, The Mayor of Wingina spoke, it was her turn. She walked to the podium on shaky legs. When she looked out at the crowd, the faces seemed to shimmer in the scorching sun like a mirage.

She licked her dry lips. *Take it easy, Bliss.* She began by thanking Governor and Mrs. Shays and all the other dignitaries for attending. *You practiced this. You can do it. Nice and slow.*

"It is my honor to be here today." Her voice boomed out of the speakers, but she could barely hear it for the thunder of the blood rushing through her ears.

Her hands were sweaty on the note cards, and she forced herself to take a deep breath, to consciously relax, so she could concentrate on the words.

"As President of Sherman Engineering," she continued, "the firm entrusted with moving the Cape Destiny Lighthouse, I am well aware that I am relocating not only a structure, but also a National Treasure, an axis around which this community revolves."

More comfortable now that she had gotten past the introduction, she reminded herself to make eye contact with her audience. She looked out over the sweating mass of humanity gathered at the base of the lighthouse and spied Parker off to left, the sun glinting off his blond hair. "As one resident told me, this lighthouse is like a guardian angel watching over the residents of Cape Destiny."

She caught his eye, and he smiled knowingly back at her.

"I assure you my firm will exercise the utmost care in moving this beloved structure to its new home, where future generations of Americans and residents of this fine area can look to the darkened sky and once again see the Cape Destiny Lighthouse beaming safely in the night.

"Now, I have the privilege of asking that Governor Shays, Mayor Walker, join me at the lever to set the Cape Destiny Lighthouse on its journey to its new home."

Bliss stepped away from the podium and walked over to a giant lever. It was only a ceremonial device; it wasn't actually linked to the equipment used for moving the lighthouse. The governor, mayor, and Bliss posed briefly before the oversized switch to allow the print media time to take a few photos.

Then as the three of them together pulled the lever, Bliss glanced to the left of the stage and her heart stopped. It was Jonathan. He was there glaring at her in the sun.

Fireworks exploded, diesel horns tooted, and the equipment rumble to life. Governor Shays and the mayor shook her hand. Perspiring and feeling weak in the knees, she looked back to where she saw her ex-husband in the crowd and no one was there. *Must have been my imagination.* It's the heat, and stress, she told herself.

Lightheaded, she needed to get out of the sun and into the cool trailer.

Before she could leave the platform, a covey of reporters cornered her, including a correspondent from *American Horizons* who was doing a feature on the move. Ninety minutes elapsed before she could drag herself away.

Her stomach rumbled with hunger, and she was so thirsty from speaking. The crowd had mostly dispersed except for a few stragglers. She was heading up the move corridor, when she heard a small voice call, "Ms. Sherman?"

She turned around to see a young girl, a camera around her neck, holding a notepad approaching her.

"Yes?" Bliss replied pleasantly, while groaning inside.

"My name is Julie Marshall. I'm a reporter for the *Wingina Wind*, the high school newspaper. "May I ask you a few questions?"

Bliss wanted to say no, but as she gazed at the youthful face, the black slanted eyes, and black straight hair, she saw herself. This girl was a mixed-race child too. She couldn't refuse.

"Certainly. What would you like to know?"

Bliss led Julie back up to the platform where the young girl flipped open her steno pad. Bliss could see the pen quivering in her hand from nervousness.

Although Bliss was beyond hot now, almost cold and clammy, she didn't have the heart to rush the interview. When she asked for Bliss's educational background, Bliss promised to get her a bio.

The budding reporter asked the same questions Bliss had answered at least ten times today. Then Julie looked shyly at Bliss and asked, "How was it for you?"

Bliss knew exactly what she meant. She was referring to growing up being mixed race. "At times it was difficult," Bliss said recalling the years of isolation in high school and then how she became a novelty in college to the people who prided themselves on being diverse and collecting minorities. She thought of all the ugly names Jonathan had called her when she was awarded the lighthouse contract over him.

But she knew her life had been much easier than her mother's. When her father had brought her mother, Mee Na, to the United States it was during the Vietnam War, and many people assumed she was Vietnamese. She clung to Bliss's father, and they had made their own little world. Looking back, it didn't seem at all surprising to her now that her mother had passed away five months after her father had died. Walter Sherman was her lifeline to the world. When that was severed, her mother withered and died.

"How about you, Julie?"

"Oh, OK. I guess. We moved here from Washington two years ago. I wasn't so much of an oddity in a cosmopolitan place like that, but here," she shrugged. "They mean no harm, they're just clueless. They call me 'Sue She' to be funny. Every one assumes I know karate and only watch Jackie Chan movies."

Bliss laughed. "I was referred to as 'Kim Chee' and everyone thought I knew Bruce Lee. When you get older, it won't seem to matter as much." Bliss wished that were true, but she knew it wasn't. When you're an adult, people disguise their prejudice with politeness.

The girl's dark eyes brightened. "Thank you, Ms. Sherman for all your time."

She rose to leave and when Bliss stood too, her head swooned. Taking a deep breath Bliss then said, "I'll walk you up to the trailer and my assistant can get you my bio sheet."

Bliss felt as if she had been freeze-dried. Her throat was parched and she had stopped perspiring. She just wanted to go back to the hotel, take off her pantyhose and hot dress, get something to eat, and cool off by the pool.

As they neared the trailer, she saw Nancy giving some instructions to the crew who was in charge of dismantling the platform.

"Nancy," Bliss said, "this is Julie Marshall. She's a reporter for the Wingina High School newspaper. I promised her my bio sheet. Could you please get that for her? I'm going to head on back to the hotel. I'm exhausted, and we can't do much today anyway. See you bright and early tomorrow."

"It was a pleasure meeting you, Sue." Bliss said with a wink.

A smile brightened the girl's round face. "Bye, Kim," she said, going along with the joke.

Bliss retrieved her purse, and then slowly walked to her car, her legs feeling new-colt shaky.

A piece of paper was lying on the lawn, spoiling the natural beauty. "Darn litterbugs," Bliss murmured and bent to pick it up. It was the size of a business card. She turned it over and gasped. It said Jonathan Lavere, President, Lavere and Son.

"Oh, my God. He was here."

As she straightened up, her vision faded to black and her ears began to ring. Then she collapsed.

Chapter 10

In the parking lot, Parker waved goodbye to Louisa Barnhart, the state official who had overseen the lighthouse deal. He'd spent the last hour or so since the press conference had concluded giving her a tour and updating her on the progress of the restoration of the Keeper's House. She seemed quite pleased. And that pleased him.

As he made his way through the pines back to the house, the top of the lighthouse came into view above the treetops to the right. By the end of summer it would be directly in his line of sight. Would he ever get used to looking there for his beloved lighthouse?

Parker knew he'd eventually grow accustomed to it just as he had grown accustomed to living with far worse changes.

When he cleared the grove of pines, he glanced toward the beach to see if the crowd had dissipated. It appeared that everyone had left. Except, of course, Bliss. Near the edge of the lawn where it rose to sandy dunes, he saw her. Just as Parker waved, she stooped to pick something up and didn't see him. He headed her way because he wanted to congratulate her on her lovely speech and thank her for quoting him.

As he strolled toward her, he saw her straighten up, then crumple to the ground.

"Bliss!" he shouted and sprinted toward her. "Bliss," he yelled as he came to her and touched her. She was still breathing, but her skin was cold and clammy, and her coloring was as pale as the sand. He'd served as a lifeguard in his teens and had been trained to recognize the signs. Bliss appeared to have collapsed from heat sickness.

Slinging her purse over his shoulder, he scooped her up into his arms, and quickly carried her across the wide expanse of grass and into the house. Beau, who had been locked inside the house so as not to get in trouble with the crowd, barked when Parker opened the door.

He placed Bliss on the sofa, dropped the purse, and started for the phone to call an ambulance, but he knew that by the time they made it through all the traffic and reached the cape from the mainland, Bliss could be in serious trouble. He wished he had a thermometer to check her body temperature.

Running to the kitchen, he wet a towel and dashed back to lay it across her forehead. He needed to reduce her body temperature. Sprinting upstairs to the bath, he opened the cold water faucet all the way, and stuck the rubber stopper into the drain of the white claw-footed tub.

When he went downstairs, Beau was licking Bliss's limp hand. "Bliss!" Parker shouted, trying to jolt her back to consciousness. Her eyes fluttered, which he interpreted as a hopeful sign. He went to her feet, and unbuckled her navy sandals and slipped them off.

Then he picked her up and carried her upstairs to the bathroom. By now the tub was halfway full. "Forgive me, Bliss," he whispered, "if your suit is not washable."

He plunged her, clothes and all, into the cool water. "Aah," she gasped as she came to. Her eyes flew open as she thrashed in the water. "Where? . . ." she sputtered. What? . . ."

Parker took her hand. "It's OK, Bliss. Relax. You collapsed out on the lawn."

Even had she wanted to get out of the tub, she couldn't. "I'm so weak," she whispered.

"You're dehydrated. It's the heat." He cupped his hand under the faucet then gently poured the water over her head. She shuddered as it ran down her neck. Her hair washed out of the French twist.

"How do you feel?" he asked as he shut off the faucet.

She pushed the hair out of her eyes. "Nauseated. And wilted."

"Do you feel like you're going to pass out anymore?"

She tried to get up, but he put a hand on her shoulder. "Oh, no you don't. I want you to soak for a while, but we need to start getting some fluids into you. Can I leave you alone for a moment?"

She nodded, feeling like a wrung out dishrag.

Beau, who had followed them into the bathroom, sat near the tub. Parker touched the dog's head. "You watch Bliss now." He dashed out.

Parker returned a few minutes later with a large glass of water and pitcher of lemonade. He set the pitcher on the sink. "We'll start you out slowly with sips of water to see how you tolerate it before we try the lemonade.

Kneeling beside the tub, he put the glass to Bliss's parched lips. "Just sip."

She closed her eyes, and when the water hit her tongue, she fought the urge to gulp the rest of it, but she knew if she guzzled it, she'd vomit.

Between sips, Parker gently poured water over her neck, baptizing her in kindness. If she weren't feeling so horrible, she'd have found it wildly exciting to being bathed by such a handsome man, even if it was with her clothes on.

"My clothes," she gasped, looking down at the blue linen suit as it clung to every curve of her body. She felt vulnerable and exposed.

"Sorry 'bout that, Bliss, but you were in such a bad way, I couldn't worry about them."

He felt her forehead. You seem to be cooling off nicely. "Want to try some lemonade. The sugar will revive you."

With each sip of the tart, sweet, cool drink, she felt as if she were a sponge sopping it up.

She looked at him. "How did this happen?"

"It's easy in this weather. You were up on that platform so long while that blowhard Shays went on and on, you perspired all the fluid out of your body."

Her long black eyelashes were clumped in wet spikes and her hair was black and glossy, the ends waving in the water around her shoulders. She was so beautiful, he thought, she could have been a mermaid.

"And I was so nervous, I couldn't eat my lunch."

"You were nervous?" Parker said, sitting now on the tile floor facing her as she became pruney in the cool water. "You looked relaxed up there."

"Didn't anybody tell you, Parker Swain, that looks are deceiving?"

He didn't need anyone to tell him. He could look at himself. On the surface, he knew everyone thought him to be a pleasant, confident man. If they only knew the demons plaguing him. That's why he couldn't allow himself to fall for the beautiful woman soaking in his tub.

"Glad you reminded me." He patted her arm. She seemed to be perking up and her coloring had come back. "Think you want to get out now?"

She held up her fingers. They were puckered. "Yes, think I've taken on more water than the Titanic."

He grasped her hand and helped her up. The wet dress was as heavy as a suit of mail.

"How do you feel?" he asked.

"Like reconstituted orange juice."

"Are you OK to stay here while I rustle you up some clothes?" He pulled the rubber stopper and the water began to swirl down the drain.

Still a little shaky, she placed a hand on the wall to steady herself. "I think I can manage."

Parker disappeared. She stretched so she could look at herself in the mirror over the sink. She was pale and her black hair was a wet mess. "Gee, Beau," she said. "If there are demons out at this lighthouse, one look at me should frighten them away."

Beau barked at her.

"Hey, you don't have to agree."

Parker returned. "I'm sorry this is all I could find that might fit." He held up a pair of gray cotton gym shorts and red T-shirt that said, "The Seafood Shack. Home of the Seafood Diet. When I see food I eat it." He put them on top of the toilet.

"Here are towels," he said. "Beau and I will leave you to get changed, but I'll sit right outside the door, just in case."

Bliss stripped off the soggy jacket, dress, pantyhose and navy lace underwear. She rung them out and tossed them into the sink. After toweling off, she grabbed Parker's clothes.

No underwear. Well, he's a single man, Bliss. *Did you expect him to have a selection of Victoria's Secret's finest?*

As she pulled the clothes over her bare damp skin, she was glad she was going directly home, she felt wicked for not wearing panties and a bra around a man she barely knew. Nancy would have a hemorrhage. Thank God the clothes were baggy.

She found a comb and ran it through her hair. After hanging up the towels, she retrieved her wet clothes and opened the door.

Parker and Beau were sitting at the top of the stairs just outside the bathroom. Both heads turned, and she suddenly felt naked. "You certainly fill those out better than I ever did," Parker said.

She held the wet clothes in front of her like a shield. "If you have a plastic bag or something to put these in, I'll just get out of your way."

He stood and took the clothes. "That's what you think."

"Pardon me," Bliss said, crossing her arms in front of her chest. She could feel her nipples pressing into her arms.

"You're not going anywhere until after you've had dinner, Bliss Sherman."

"Oh, I'll pick something up on my way back to the hotel."

"And pass out at the wheel? No siree, missy." He wagged a finger at her. "You're staying for dinner."

She stared him in the eye, trying to make herself look fierce. "Do you always rescue damsels in distress, and then hold them against their will?"

In an instant Parker's features hardened, and the look that came over him chilled Bliss more than her plunge into the cold bath.

He turned and headed for the stairs. "I learned a long ago, you can't hold onto someone who doesn't want to be held on to."

Chapter 11

Before Bliss could ask what he meant, Parker went down stairs. She sat on the top step not sure what had just happened.

When he started back up the stairs, the softness had returned to his eyes. "Your clothes are in a plastic bag on the picnic table. I'll help you down."

She rose; he put an arm around her waist, and began to slowly walk her down the stairs. She wondered about him as her bare feet padded down the wooden steps. Who had Parker ever tried to hold onto who wouldn't want to remain with him? He was handsome, charming, educated and kind—an irresistible combination. Yet, from his remark, she sensed a sadness about him. The same sadness she'd glimpsed before. Who was Parker Swain? The genial teacher or the mystery man obsessed with the lighthouse?

"Now, I'm going to set you out back, where it's cool," Parker said. "Watch your step. Don't want you tramping on anything in your bare feet." He led her back the center hall and through the kitchen. She noticed the cabinets were now attached to the wall and the handles were on the faucet.

Opening the back door, he guided her to a large screened porch that spanned the width of the house. There was an assortment of plastic lawn chairs and chaise lounges. He walked her to the far end where a large wooden porch swing with a red calico cushion was suspended from the ceiling. He held it steady for her. "You sit right here and enjoy the breeze, Bliss, while I hang up your wet things and then rustle up something for dinner. Beau will keep you company."

"Yes, sir," Bliss snapped as she sat on the swing. "And you accused me of being General Sherman."

Parker stopped and shook his head at her. "You're never going to let me live that one down, are you?"

She pushed off with her barefoot. "Depends on how good your dinner is."

He put his hands on his hips. "Is that the thanks I get for saving you?"

With her foot, she stopped the swing. Reaching out, she touched his hand. "I'm only teasing. Thank you, Parker. If you hadn't found me, I don't know what would have happened."

He squeezed her hand and looked away. "I'm glad this time there was something I could do." His hand slipped out of hers. He picked up the waterlogged pile of clothing.

"Parker," Bliss said softly as she watched him turn and walk toward the door. "Was there another time?"

He halted, his fingers on the latch, turned, and faced her. "I lifeguarded here for years. This place isn't called the Graveyard of the Atlantic for nothing. I'm sure there's not a guard down here who ever patrolled these shores, who hasn't felt the utter frustration of not getting there in time."

He pushed open the weathered door; the boards creaked as he went down the wooden steps. The door slammed behind him as he headed across the backyard in the late afternoon sunshine toward the clothesline.

Beau hopped up into the swing beside her and laid his head across her thigh. She stroked him and watched as Parker hung her clothes. What was haunting him? Did it have to do with what June had alluded to when she said Cape Destiny was a lightning rod for trouble?

She felt hot again, but this time from embarrassment as she watched him drape her panties and bra over the line. Then she wondered another thing. Why, when she had no plans of becoming involved with him, did she care so much to know what was troubling him?

******

After hanging up her clothes, Parker went into the kitchen. She heard pots clanging and water running. Then he brought her another glass of lemonade before heading off toward the bank of the sound. There she saw him step onto a boardwalk that meandered through the tall grass, growing smaller in the distance until the marsh grass swallowed him.

Approaching sunset, the light was taking on a mellow glow, making the water of the sound look like hammered gold and turning Beau's coat the color of new pennies.

She closed her eyes and the breeze caressed her body and carried all her cares away. She was so tired. She could just curl up next to Beau and drift off. When the screen door slammed again, she startled and opened her eyes. Parker was carrying a metal cage filled with squirming crabs.

"Here's dinner," he said holding up the trap proudly.

"You caught those?"

"Sure did." He eyed the crustaceans rattling inside. "Some of the Carolina's finest." He headed into the kitchen.

"You need any help?" Bliss asked.

"No, you just sit and regain your strength."

After ingesting so much fluid, Bliss needed to go to the bathroom. She came into the kitchen and saw a large kettle of water boiling on the stove and Parker chopping some herbs. "I thought I told you to rest," he said.

"Got to go to the bathroom."

"That's a good sign. The kidneys are functioning." He wiped his hands on a towel. "Let me help you."

"No, I can manage. I'm feeling much better."

"Ok, but watch for nails."

By the time Bliss had returned, Parker had spread a tablecloth on the picnic table and was setting out dishes and silverware.

"Look at you," he said as he watched her wearing his clothes take a seat on the porch swing, "walking around in your skivvies in your bare feet. Why you'd think you grew up in the South."

"Next, you'll have me chewing and making moonshine," she said.

71

He laughed as he placed two wine goblets on top of the watermelon-printed cloth. "Dinner's almost ready. Have a seat."

Bliss was famished. She sat at the table and from the delicious smells wafting from the kitchen and the magnificent view of the sound, she couldn't imagine *The Michelin Guide* coming up with any finer dining establishment.

Parker brought out two salad bowls filled with greens, tomatoes, and cucumbers and then two plates heaped with lump crabmeat broiled in garlic butter, a baked potato, and biscuits.

"Oh, this smells heavenly," Bliss said before he disappeared into the kitchen once again.

When he returned, he was carrying a bottle of Pinot Grigio. "I don't think a little glass would hurt you," he said.

Bliss looked at her plate. "With all this food to absorb the alcohol, I think I'll be fine."

They chatted amicably through dinner talking about the press conference and his visit with Louisa Barnhart. After dinner, Bliss poured herself another glass of wine. She felt much stronger now, and she helped Parker to clear the dishes and wash up.

"Now it's time for the show," he said.

"What are you talking about?"

He topped off his glass and then took Bliss's hand. "Come on, you'll see." Bliss grabbed her drink, and Parker led her to the backyard with Beau following behind. The grass was soft and cool under her bare feet. The intense heat had gone.

They strolled along the boardwalk, where birds warbled in the tall marsh grass. At the end of the planking was a small gazebo. They walked into it and took a seat on the benches that ringed its perimeter.

They had a spectacular view of the sun setting over the sound. The clouds blushed pink and red and reflected on the still water. As the waves softly slapped against the shore, lulling Bliss, Parker tapped her arm and pointed to the bank toward her left. "Look!"

A large knock-kneed bird was pecking at the water. "What is it?" she whispered?

"A blue heron."

While she watched the sun slowly melting into the water, Bliss felt all stress leaving her, and she shivered.

Parker glanced at her. "You cold?"

"No. Just got a chill."

He looked at her arm. "You're sunburned, Bliss. That's probably why."

She looked at her arm, even in the diminishing light she could tell that her forearms were the color of the crab shells after they'd been boiled and her skin felt tight. "I didn't realize," she looked up into his eyes and felt them lock with hers, "how intense it is down here. I usually don't burn."

"Everything is intense down here," Parker whispered. After a moment, he gently stroked her arm. "Does it hurt?"

She gulped and felt goose bumps rise. "A little."

"Come on," he said, placing a hand on her back. "I have just the thing for sunburn in the house."

In the increasing darkness, they made their way back to the house. Fireflies put on a light spectacular to rival Disney's parade.

He opened the screen door for her and motioned to the swing. "Have a seat," he said. "I'll be right back."

Bliss returned to the swing, and Beau took up his post beside her again. With her foot she sent it gently rocking. She finished her glass of wine and set it on the porch rail. When was the last time she felt this relaxed?

When Parker returned, he lighted several candles about the porch. Then he shooed Beau off the swing and took a seat next to Bliss. "Here," he said, handing her a plastic bottle "this is an aloe vera and peppermint gel."

Bliss squeezed a dollop on her arm and began to rub it in. It smelled like Christmas and felt cool as icicles.

After she had slathered it on her other arm, Parker said, "You're neck's burned too."

"Old clothes, bare feet, and a red neck," Bliss said with a laugh, "you certainly have managed to transform me into a Southern girl."

"I'll have you saying, 'y'all' before the night's over."

She lifted her hair and tried to reach the back of her neck and shoulder with gel.

"Here, let me, Parker said. She shifted so that he was behind her. He moved her black hair aside and massaged the cool cream into her feverish neck and shoulder. She could feel his breath on her skin as he gently worked the soothing cream in. She wanted to turn to him and kiss him, but she restrained herself. She was not going to get involved in another dead end relationship. Especially now when the most important project of her life lay before her.

But if she couldn't kiss him, there was nothing however to stop her from enjoying his strong yet gentle fingers as they worked in the gel and the knots out of her muscles.

Exhausted from the day, she allowed her eyes to close, and sighing, she leaned against him.

"That feel better?" he whispered in her ear.

"Uh-hmm."

When Parker noticed her breathing slowing, he peeked around and saw that she had nodded off. She looked so peaceful he didn't have the heart to wake her. And to be honest, it felt comforting to have someone snuggled up to him.

When comfort made the leap to desire, he gently slid out from under Bliss. She only half opened her black eyes, then sighed again and curled up on the swing.

Parker moved to a lawn chair. After listening to her softly breathing and watching her in the candlelight for an hour, he went into the house, got a quilt, and covered her.

Then he went to sleep on the chaise lounge, but he didn't need a quilt because the mere thought of the beautiful woman sleeping on his porch kept him warm all night.

Chapter 12

Something tickled her hand. She opened her eyes and startled when she saw Beau's nose in her face. *Where am I?* Quickly sitting up, she looked around. Parker, in T-shirt, jeans and his hair damp, sat in the lawn chair sipping coffee. A gentle rain pattered on the porch roof.

"What happened?" Her heart raced as she tried to recall how she gotten into these clothes and onto this porch swing.

Parker smiled at her. "Morning, Bliss. How do you feel today?"

As the sleep clouding her brain lifted, the previous evening came back to her with her last memory of leaning drowsily against Parker.

"What time is it?" It was so overcast, she couldn't tell if it was day or night.

He looked at his watch. "A little after eight."

"In the morning?" She'd been so tired last night, she wouldn't have been surprised at all to have slept until evening.

"Yes, it's morning."

Bliss scrambled off the swing. It was cooler now and the thin clothes provided little warmth. She wrapped the quilt around her. "Oh, my God. I have to get going. Why did you let me fall asleep? I wanted to get an early start."

He smiled as he watched her rushing about. "You're breakfast is ready."

"Where are my shoes?" She looked under the picnic table. Where had she taken them off? "Are my clothes dry?" She glanced out to the clothesline and it was empty.

"They're dry and after you eat, I'll give them and your shoes back to you."

"I need them now."

"You'll get them after you eat. Now be good and sit."

She stood beside his chair looking like a petulant child. "Cut it out, Parker."

He was surprised that she wasn't stomping her foot.

"Last night it didn't matter if I stayed, but I'm needed at work. I told Nancy I'd be there by seven-thirty. She's going to be hysterical."

He held out a portable phone. "Call her and tell her you'll be late."

"I can't be late. I'm the boss, and they're depending on me."

He rose and towered authoritatively over her. "All the more reason for you to stay for breakfast. Listen, Bliss, you have to take care of yourself or you're not going to be any good to anyone."

Parker handed her the phone. "You call her while I get your breakfast."

Parker was right. She did need to take better care of herself. As she punched in Nancy's number, she hoped that she'd get the voice mail. When Nancy picked up, Bliss was tongue tied for a second. "Nancy, it's Bliss. I'm running late."

"I've been so worried. Where have you been? I called your room last night, and when I got up. No one answered. Early this morning I drove to the hotel on my way out here and let myself into your room. Your bed hadn't been slept in. A few more minutes, and I was going to call the police."

"Look, I'm fine. I'll explain when I get in. Is everything a go at the site?" Bliss asked, knowing that if she wanted to check, she could walk right out Parker's front door and see for herself. The thought of Nancy finding her wearing nothing but Parker's shorts and his T-shirt after spending the night in his house was a scene she didn't wasn't to envision. However innocent last night may have been, she knew Nancy would never see it that way.

"The thunder and lightning that went through last night is gone," Nancy said. "Between worrying about you and that storm, I don't think I slept a wink."

It stormed during the night? Bliss thought. I must have been more tired than I thought not to have heard it.

"It's just drizzling now, so the crew can get started."

"Good, I'll be there in a little while."

Bliss went into the kitchen and handed Parker the phone.

"Did your dorm mother buy your story?" he asked as he poured her some orange juice.

"I don't answer to her."

"Then why is she the first one you called?"

"That was just common courtesy."

"I think you're afraid of her."

"Afraid? I am not. It's just . . . that I don't want to disappoint her."

"You're the president, aren't you? Shouldn't she be afraid of disappointing you?"

"You don't understand," Bliss said taking a seat at the table. "Certainly, I'm the boss. But I needed capital to start this business. She quit her job at Lavere, gave up everything, and invested her life savings in it. She believes in me, and I owe it to her to do a good job."

"But you must admit, she's unusually protective of you," Parker said, taking a plate out of the cupboard and moving to the stove. "Hope you like bacon and eggs."

"I do," Bliss said, hoping that his breakfast was as delicious as his dinner. "I know Nancy's very protective of me. She's been an administrative assistant all her life. They're so used to looking out for their employer, they can get a little possessive and territorial. I think it's because she has nothing else in her life but me and Sherman Engineering. I'm kind of like a daughter to her."

Bliss was cold again, and she noticed how Parker's eyes kept straying to her breasts. She pulled the quilt tightly around her. He set a plate before her.

"She has no husband? Or children of her own?" Parker grabbed the coffeepot. "Want a cup?"

"Please," Bliss said. "She never married, and no kids. Although I think she may have been involved with someone when she was young, but from what I've inferred, it ended badly."

He set a mug before Bliss and took a seat across from her. She looked into the mug, and was flattered that he remembered how she took her coffee.

"I know she's your friend," Parker said resting his elbow on the table and holding his mug chin-level, "but she seems as sour as spoiled milk."

Bliss frowned. "I don't know if you'd call our relationship a friendship." Bliss ate some eggs. Why did they taste so good here? Was it because of the setting? As Bliss thought about it, she had to admit that she was confused about her relationship with Nancy. Certainly, she relied on her and Bliss was grateful for all the years she'd spent mentoring her at Lavere. She wouldn't have achieved the success she enjoyed now without her, but friends share thoughts and feelings. Nancy was much too buttoned down for that.

She looked back at Parker, who was watching her intently, and felt the same way about classifying her relationship with him. He rescues her and remembers small things like how she took her coffee. Were they merely friends? If so, then why when he touched her, did her heart surge and looking into his soft brown eyes make her feel weaker than when she'd passed out?

"I think Nancy looks on me like I'm her prodigy," Bliss said. "I don't think she cares so much about my personal life but my professional one. For whatever reason, I believe she thinks she can live out her thwarted career dreams through me."

"Thwarted career dreams?" Parker asked.

"I sense she wanted to do so much more with her life, but she was raised in a different time. Her options were limited."

Parker set his mug on the picnic table and stretched. "I see her as a crabby old maid."

"Oh," Bliss said waving a piece of toast. "That's typical! Why does every male think that a woman can't live without a man?"

He stood and went to the coffeepot and refilled his mug. "Because it's true."

Bliss put her dish in the sink. "Look at me," she said, holding out her hands. "I don't have a man, and I'm OK."

He sized her up, then grinned. "You're shoeless and wearing my old rags all because you forgot to eat and drink and passed out in the heat." He winked. "Yep, you're doing real well for yourself."

"Hmph," Bliss said turning away from him. "And you aren't so hot yourself. At least I'm not stupid enough to bring home girls who so are so dumb they don't know enough to come in out of the sun."

Parker laughed. "Well, then we're made for each other. Dumb and dumber."

Bliss turned around and eyed him playfully. "Which one am I?"

"Dumb," Parker said. "I'm not stupid."

Bliss glanced at the clock on the stove. "Oh my gosh! Look at the time! I better get going. Where are my clothes?"

"They're in the living room," Parker said. Bliss walked carefully down the hall and found the clothes folded on the couch. Her sandals were on the floor next to her purse. Tossing off the quilt, she folded it neatly, then picked up her belongings and headed for the door.

Stepping out onto the porch, she heard the rain gurgling in the downspout. Beau, curled up in the corner, lifted his head and yawned. The air was heavy with the scent of wet earth.

Parker followed behind. When she got to the steps, she stopped and turned around. Hugging her clothes to her chest, she gazed up at him. She felt so small without her heels as she stood next to him. "Parker, I don't know that in all instances a woman can't live without a man, but certainly yesterday, I know I couldn't have lived without you. Thank you. Thank you for everything."

He moved closer and gently touched her sunburned neck. "Make sure you get some sunscreen." His hands lingered on her flesh while his eyes lingered on her face. Then suddenly he tipped her head back, and kissed her.

Bliss dropped her clothes and wrapped her arms around him and enjoyed his warm, coffee flavored lips until the words she'd said to Nancy, *I'd never get involved with Parker Swain* intruded.

She pulled away and breathing heavily, looked up into his eyes. "Parker, what are you doing?"

He kissed her neck and then whispered in her ear, "Trying to make you realize that it's a whole lot more than one night that you can't live without me."

Chapter 13

Bliss scooped up her things and hurried down the steps. The rain pelted her, soaking Parker's thin T-shirt. As she dashed across the wet grass in her bare feet toward the Explorer, the rain was like a bucket of cold water thrown on her passion. Why had she allowed Parker to kiss her? And more importantly, she wondered as she entered the copse of pines, why had she responded when she had no intention of falling for him?

Her pace slowed while she traversed the wet, sharp needles carpeting the ground. The T-shirt clung to her skin, and she knew she would have made a big hit at a wet T-shirt contest. How was she ever going to go into the hotel looking like this?

When she came to the parking lot, she looked up and gasped. Standing next to her Explorer was Jonathan. He was wearing white linen trousers, blue and white striped buttoned-down collar shirt, and deck shoes. He looked like he'd just disembarked from a yacht. A large golf umbrella kept his thick head of dark hair and his expensive clothing dry.

"Jonathan, what are you doing here?"

His blue eyes burned into her like a welder's torch. "I was going to ask you the same thing."

She pulled out her keys. "I'm late," Bliss said as she edged past him.

He blocked the door. "I came down here to propose a business deal. My contacts tell me that you're strapped for cash. I thought perhaps you'd like to partner with me on the proposal for moving The Old Coast Guard Station below Cape Hatteras. With Lavere's reputation and your advantages, we'd be sure to win that contract."

"My advantages?" Bliss asked, tilting her head and eyeing him warily.

"Your status as a minority and female."

She was so angry it was a wonder her wet clothes didn't start to steam from the fury boiling inside her. "You think I was awarded the lighthouse contract because I'm part Asian and female?"

"Well, it certainly wasn't because of Sherman Engineering's illustrious track record. I hardly call moving a few homes and a chimney stack a major accomplishment."

Any affection she'd felt for her ex-husband died. She'd heard the snipes that she'd gotten preferential treatment because of her race and sex, but that was false. If anything, she had to work doubly hard to overcome them to be taken seriously. "We were awarded this contract because I've put together the finest bunch of engineers and staff in the country."

Suddenly, Parker came jogging down the path. "Bliss, you dropped this on the way out." He was holding her navy lace panties. When he saw Jonathan, he came to a halt. Beau, at his side, barked.

Jonathan chuckled sarcastically. "Oh, very professional, Bliss. Screwing a member of the crew."

She snatched the panties from Parker. "I wasn't screwing anyone. And Parker is not a member of my crew. He owns the Lighthouse Keeper's place."

Jonathan took a step back and shook his head. "Now I get the picture. How could I have been so naïve? You got the contract by doing a Lighthouse Commissioner."

"I did no such thing, and Parker had nothing to do with my being awarded the contract," she snapped. "He's been allowed to inhabit the keeper's house because it's his ancestral home and because he agreed to improve the property for the state in exchange."

Jonathan eyes fixed on Bliss's breasts visible beneath the clingy, wet T-shirt. He moved closer to her. "Come on, Bliss. It's me you're talking to." He put an arm around her waist and held her tightly. She tried to wiggle away.

Beau growled, baring his teeth.

"You always knew how to work it," Jonathan sneered. "Why would you change now? That's the oldest strategy in the books. Sleeping your way to the top!"

"Let go of her," Parker said.

Jonathan faced him as he moved his hand higher until his fingers were digging into the side of her breast. "Does she ever call my name when you're plugging her?"

Parker's fist connected with Jonathan's chin, snapping his head back and making a sickening bone-cracking sound as knuckles met jaw. The umbrella sailed into the air, then cartwheeled away. Jonathan slammed against the Explorer, bounced off, then landed with a large splash on his side in a mud puddle. His white pants were splattered and blood gushed from his lip. Beau stood over him barking as if Jonathan were a raccoon.

Parker, his fists clenched, his chest heaving with exertion and rage, stared down at Jonathan. "Men who talk like pigs deserve to wallow in mud."

He turned to Bliss. "He didn't hurt you, did he?"

Tears streamed down her face. She couldn't speak. She shook her head no.

"You're going to be sorry," Jonathan said as he licked his bleeding lip and struggled to stand.

Parker took Bliss's dress jacket and draped it over her shoulders. Then he wrapped an arm around her as she trembled.

Jonathan rose and, wobbly on his feet, he strode toward Parker. Sticking a mud-covered finger in Parker's face, Jonathan glared at him. "No one messes with Jonathan Lavere and gets away with it. You're going to pay for this." Then he poked his finger in Bliss's face. "Both of you."

Beau danced around Jonathan, barking wildly.

"Get out of here now," Parker commanded, "before I set the dog on you."

Jonathan staggered to his Mercedes and climbed in. Gunning the motor, he sped out of the lot.

Bliss's wet hair hung in her eyes. Parker moved it aside and searched her face. "Are you OK?"

She was cold and shivering. "Uh-ha."

"Who was that?"

"My former boss . . . and ex-husband."

"You were married to that animal?"

"Until I came home early from a business trip and found him in bed working out with my personal trainer."

She covered her face with her hands.

Parker hugged her allowing her to cry it out. "Come on back to the house and calm down."

She pulled away. "I can't. I've got to get to work."

"Bliss, be reasonable. Look at you. You're drenched and covered with mud. Come back to the house. Clean yourself off. I'm sure I have another T-shirt." He touched her chin and raised her head so that she had to look him in the eye. "Although this wet one looks pretty spectacular."

She had to smile. "OK. But I swear this is the last time you'll have to rescue me."

"I'm starting to enjoy it."

They headed back to the house. "I'm so sorry to get you involved. I'm afraid Jonathan will have it out for you too now."

"Oh, I'm shaking in my boots."

"I'm serious," Bliss said. "You don't know him."

"That'll be the day when I'm afraid of a pretty boy who's stupid enough to wear white pants on a rainy day."

Bliss laughed. "Those pants will never come clean."

"I hope his Mercedes has cloth seats," Parker sneered.

By the time they got to the house, they were both soaked. As they stood on the porch dripping, Parker said, "Why don't you take a hot shower?" He stripped off his wet shirt and hung it over the porch rail.

Standing there in nothing but his worn jeans and boots, he raked his fingers through his wet hair. "I'll make you a cup of hot tea, or would you rather have coffee?"

He looked hotter than anything he could ever brew, thought Bliss. His tanned muscular chest, covered with soft golden hair, narrowed to a slim waist. It was dangerous being with him. She needed to refocus. Remember why she had come to Cape Destiny-

—to move a lighthouse, not to fall for the grandson of the lighthouse keeper.

"I'll take a shower back at the hotel. I really need to get going."

He gave her a towel and a clean shirt. After going into the bathroom and wiping off the mud, towel-drying her hair, and putting on the new shirt, she walked into the kitchen.

He smiled. He had on a fresh shirt too. "Sure I can't talk you into a cup?"

In truth, he could probably talk her into anything. Before he did, she replied, "Thanks, but I can't."

Parker had put her wet clothes into a bag. He walked her to the porch. Standing in the spot where he had kissed her before, he touched her arm. "If he bothers you again, let me know."

Bliss kept her distance because if he kissed her again, she knew she wouldn't leave.

"You hear me, Bliss?"

"Loud and clear." She dashed down the steps.

Loud and clear, Bliss thought. Just like the voice in her head whispering, *Bliss, you're falling for Parker Swain."*

Chapter 14

Bliss inserted the card in the security lock on the hotel's side entrance door and scurried down the hall, hoping no one would see her. When the elevator doors parted, an elderly couple inside stared wide-eyed at her.

"Went for a run on the beach," Bliss said. "It's really coming down."

Entering her room, she caught a glimpse of herself in the full-length mirror. It's a wonder that elderly couple hadn't summoned security. She checked her messages. They were all from Nancy, and she sounded frantic.

Shivering now, she blamed it on her wet clothing and the air conditioner, but she knew it was from what had happened in the parking lot. Jonathan's threats chilled her to her core. Parker had laughed it off, but he didn't know the depths of Jonathan's malice.

She stripped off the wet clothes and lingered longer under the hot shower than she should have. Bliss toweled off, rejoicing in being dry, and put on navy cotton shorts and a short-sleeve yellow and white striped shirt monogrammed with Sherman Engineering. It felt rough against her sunburned shoulders.

She dried her hair and only put on some lip gloss as her face need no more color with the sun on the bridge of her nose.

After putting on socks and lacing up her work boots, she went to the desk. She found the microrecorder in her purse and depressed the record button. "Pick up sunscreen. Find some way to thank Parker. Oh, and remember to return his clothes."

*****

When she entered the trailer, Nancy was on the phone, the directory open on her desk. "Beach Pharmacy seems to be closest," she said into the receiver. Her index finger brushed against the page as she read a number out of the book. "Thanks so much," Nancy said before hanging up. She looked at Bliss, holding her jaw awkwardly. "That was my dentist."

"Is it still hurting?" Bliss asked, grateful that she didn't have to be grilled about where she spent the night.

Nancy closed her eyes. "Like someone driving a nail into my jaw. He's going to phone me in a prescription for some pain medication until I can get home and have it taken care of." She closed the directory. "Now enough about me. What in the world happened to you? I was so worried."

Bliss sunk into her chair and grabbed her head. "I don't even know where to begin. I collapsed from the heat near Parker's house."

She briefly filled Nancy in on how Parker had found her, and how she'd fallen asleep on his porch swing. Before Nancy could start into her about getting involved with Parker, she told her about Jonathan showing up.

Nancy said she wasn't surprised as he'd stopped by the trailer right after Bliss had first called in. He was looking for Bliss, before he headed south to consult with some subcontractors he'd lined up for the proposal on the Coast Guard Station. When Bliss failed to show up, he accused Nancy of tipping Bliss off to avoid the office and him. Nancy said he'd been very hostile.

Bliss told her about all the awful things he said and how Parker had decked him.

That was the first time that Bliss had ever seen Nancy smile in association with Parker.

88

Then Bliss exhaled wearily. "He threatened Parker. . . . And me."

Nancy's smile faded. "What did he say?"

"Something to the effect that we'd be sorry."

"Be careful, Bliss," she said as she fingered her watchband.

"Oh, don't worry. He's all bluster. He threatened me when I left him and the firm, but nothing ever came of it."

"But I heard his business isn't doing very well. And Laveres can be cruel. It runs in the family."

"He must not be doing well. He'd never swallow his pride and come to me to team up on that new contract unless he felt that he had no choice."

"That's why I'm saying please watch yourself, Bliss. He must be desperate."

"Nancy, you worry too much. Jonathan Lavere is not going to intimidate me."

Bliss spent the remainder of the morning returning calls, catching up on paperwork, and reviewing the bid Randy had drafted for moving The Old Coast Guard Station. A wealthy man from Virginia was willing to pay top dollar to have the dilapidated station moved off the beach so he could turn it into an inn. The station was located near the South Carolina border. Bliss hoped Jonathan would soon be heading down there and forget about her.

Although she'd put on a brave face, she was worried. When she'd left him two years ago, his business had been flush, but recently she'd also heard rumors that things weren't going well at Lavere, that their accountants had cooked their books and inflated Lavere's earnings. If that was so, no wonder he seemed more out of control, more on the ragged edge.

After ordering sandwiches from the nearest deli that delivered, Bliss did an inspection of the project. The foul weather had cleared, leaving a sun-drenched afternoon in its wake. Randy and the crew were busy monitoring the lighthouse, checking the numerous sensors to ensure structural integrity as it slowly slid on the rails toward it's new home.

The afternoon sun shining on Bliss's face intensified the pain of her sunburn and reminded her that she needed to get sunscreen. After returning to the office, she told Nancy that she was going to run to the pharmacy to get some and asked if she needed anything.

"You could check to see if my prescription is filled yet."

As Bliss strode past the site to the parking lot, she noticed how the morning's moisture had evaporated into the air, making it a humid, thick afternoon.

"Miz Sherman," she heard her name being called, as she was about to turn onto the path toward the parking lot. She turned around and saw Stu Hall, one of the local welders they'd subcontracted, hustling toward her.

"There a problem, Stu?"

His hair had been buzzed and Bliss could see beads of perspiration glistening on his scalp. It must be unbearable under a welder's mask in this heat.

"No, ma'am." He smiled. His skin was as brown as beef jerky. "Just wanted to give you this." He held out a silver, shiny metal oval.

"What's this?" Bliss asked, holding it between her thumb and forefinger.

"It's a North Carolina state quarter. Some of us Tarheel boys put it on the rails while the Lighthouse passed over."

She looked more closely and could make out the image of the Wright Brothers' first flight smeared across the silver. It was like when she was a child and made images of the comic papers with silly putty then stretched the putty.

"Thought you would like something to commemorate the move."

Bliss was touched. "Why, thank you, Stu."

"I know you're not from around here," he said, "so I don't know if you appreciate the significance of what we're doing. This," he nodded toward lighthouse, "has been here longer than my granddaddy's daddy." He pointed to the coin. "Even before the Wright brothers."

She'd felt intimidated by the task before, but now she felt even more so. Not only was she moving a beloved structure, she was moving history itself.

"Tell the guys thanks, and I'm honored to be working with them."

"Miz Sherman, we just want you to know, that not all of us locals were against this move. The ones who reasoned with their heads and not their hearts knew she'd be in the sea before long if she hadn't been relocated."

Bliss folded her hand around the quarter. "I'll treasure this always." Then a bubble of an idea rose to the surface of her brain. "Stu, do you think you could make me a few more of these? I'd like to have one for everyone who worked on the project."

"We got nearly 2,000 feet of track to cover. Can make you as many as you want. Just need to get our hands on some more state quarters. I think Burt, on the forklift—his wife works on over at the bank. Maybe she can get a line on 'em."

"Thanks, Stu. I'll reimburse you for them."

His two-way radio squawked. He put it to his ear. "No, I ain't run off and joined the circus. I'm talking with the boss. Be there in a minute." He turned to Bliss, "Best be going."

"Tell everyone I appreciate their thinking of me."

She turned and headed toward the Explorer.

*****

It was nearing dinnertime when she drove down Beachfront Road. Children toting rafts, fathers holding babies, and mothers carrying mesh bags filled with sand toys and chairs, crossed over from the beach, heading back to their vacation homes to make dinner plans.

Before Bliss went to the Beach Mart and Pharmacy, she pulled into Desiree St. Jacques Custom Creations parking lot. The A-frame building looked like a Swiss Chalet right down to the window boxes. She wondered what misguided architect thought an alpine house would look appropriate at the seashore.

However inappropriate the exterior, the interior looked like Blackbeard's Treasure chest.

The lighting was situated to give the gems and metal creations under the glass of the display cases the most brilliance and sparkle.

A tall woman in a lavender tank top and floral printed, ankle-length gauze skirt greeted Bliss when the bell chimed on the door.

"May I help you," she asked with the faintest of Southern accents. She had plain features and mousy brown hair laced with gray strands, but she wore the most exquisite lapis lazuli choker and matching drop earrings. Encircling her wrist was a thick cuff of hammered gold and each finger was graced with a ring, one more stunning than the next. Her nondescript looks made her seem to be nothing more than a device for showing off her creations, much the way a plain black velvet box accentuates the brilliance of a diamond.

Bliss was tempted to look over the counter and peer at the woman's ankles and toes because she felt certain that they must be decked with some jewelry too.

"Are you Desiree St. Jacques?"

"Yes, I am. How can I help you?"

"I saw from your billboard that you design custom jewelry." Bliss pulled out the pressed quarter from pocket. "I was wondering if it would be possible for you to design something so that this might be worn on a chain?"

She examined the metal disk. "I'm certain I could come up with something." She looked up at Bliss. "But I'm not sure it would be worth your spending the money for what it would cost to create something for it."

"Yes, I know it doesn't look that attractive, but it's the sentimental value. You see, I'm working on the lighthouse move, and some members of the crew put this on the move rails while the lighthouse passed over it."

"I thought you looked familiar from the article in *People Magazine*." Bliss was stunned that so many people knew of her. The article had been small, yet it seemed that with the extinguishing of the lighthouse, the spotlight had shifted to her.

"You know," Desiree said, studying the smashed quarter, "you might have something here. If you could supply me with these, we could sell them. There are so many people interested in this lighthouse move."

"Well, I don't think the government would take to my making a profit on the side off the move, but I'll have a few more for you to make. And if you like, I'll make sure that there's an extra coin for you." If Jonathan was out to get her, wouldn't his finding out that she was making money by selling jewelry associated with the move be the ammunition he'd love to use against her.

Desiree took the coin and dropped it into a small manila envelope. "If you ever change your mind, let me know. I should be able to have this to you rather quickly. I'll call you in a day or two."

Bliss thanked her and went to her car.

Chapter 15

Bliss walked into the Beach Mart. June, who was arranging cartons of cigarettes behind the counter, looked up when the bell on the door jangled.

"Hello, June. How are you today?" Bliss said as she walked up to the counter. "As you can see, I need something for this sunburn, and I came to pick up a prescription.

June shoved a carton of Marlboros into a vacant space and turned to Bliss. "Well, if it isn't the celebrity herself. Fancy a star like you gracing the Beach Mart."

Bliss chuckled. "I like keeping in touch with the little people."

June leaned over the counter and exclaimed. "Did you know you were all over the news last night? Why, my sister-in-law out in Phoenix even saw you on the national news!"

Bliss smiled, "Oh, I'm quite the media darling these days."

June smiled knowingly. "I hear tell it you're not only their darling but somebody else's as well."

Bliss stared at her. "What are you talking about?"

She looked up into the air. "Oh, a little birdie told me that somebody didn't come home last night. Spent the night at the Keeper's House with one Parker Swain."

"How do you know that?" Bliss asked, astonished that not only was she the center of attention around here, but she was being spied on.

"Oh, some sissified fellow, with a split lip, came in here looking for some bandages and an ice pack. Told me he got into a scrape this mornin' with Parker Swain over a woman. Josh Mooney, my cousin, is the night desk clerk at the Destiny Cove, and he said there was a frantic woman who called all night trying to get in touch with you. She looked at Bliss with the satisfaction of Miss Marple after solving a case. "Now, I wonder where you were last night?"

Bliss blushed, making her sunburn more vivid. "Nothing happened. It was completely innocent. I passed out from the heat, and Parker found me. He gave me water and dinner. I fell asleep on his porch swing."

"Uh-hmm." June was not buying it.

"Look," Bliss said, her black eyes widening, "I got sick and he helped me. That's all." She started down the aisle toward the sunburn cream, shaking her head and mumbling, "I don't know why I'm even explaining myself. It's nobody's business."

June followed after her. "If you're looking for . . . " she lowered her voice, "condoms, they're in aisle seven."

"Condoms?" Bliss cried, making a woman with small children perusing the various sand toys give her a dirty look.

June sidled up to her. "I didn't fall off the turnip truck. Don't be shy. I know the score. People who work in pharmacies are wise to everything. I know who's taking Viagra. Who has hemorrhoids. What girls are on the pill. Whose kids have cooties. But I'm discreet. Your secret affair with Parker is safe with me."

"I'm not having a secret affair with Parker!"

"Whatever you say, honey," June said, waving her hand, dismissing Bliss's protest. "I'm tickled to death. It's time that boy found a nice girl and settled down." Bliss rolled her eyes, then bent over, and scoured the lower shelf for an ointment that contained the same soothing ingredients that Parker had massaged into her red skin.

"Mind, I'm not passing judgment," June said. "What two consenting adults do is their own business. Although I think a girl is mighty foolish to give it away so freely. But on the other hand, it's about time Parker joined the land of the living again. I know he can be standoffish, but that's just to keep from getting hurt. Some folk believe he was to blame for what happened, but I know Parker Swain, and he'd never meant to hurt no one."

Bliss straightened up. "Blame Parker for what?"

June looked panicked for a moment and avoided Bliss's gaze. "For—for causing a ruckus about moving the lighthouse."

"Well, how would that hurt someone?" Bliss asked certain that June was hiding something.

"Hurt feelings is what I meant. Some people wanted it moved. Others didn't. There was a lot of hurt feelings regarding the move." June lowered her head and moved around Bliss. "You said you needed a prescription. I'll check with Boyd to see if it's filled yet."

"It's not for me. It's for my assistant, Nancy Klempner," Bliss called after her, knowing that if June saw a prescription for pain pills, she'd have it all over town that Bliss was a drug addict.

Why had June shut down like that? What was she hiding? Bliss picked up the nearest sunburn cream and followed her to the pharmacy counter, where June was riffling through bags of prescriptions.

"June, I said it's not for me. It's for my assistant, Nancy Klempner." She riffled in another drawer. "Don't see it." June raised her head and said to Boyd. "You get a prescription for Klempner?"

"Filling it now. Be just a sec."

"You heard that, Bliss? Be just a minute."

June, whose mouth previously had been stuck in overdrive, was now silent. She busied herself with straightening pamphlets entitled, *Detecting Osteoporosis*, and *High Blood Pressure: The Silent Killer*.

Bliss wanted to ask what she meant about Parker not meaning to hurt anyone, but she could tell by June's defensive posture that she would get nothing more out her. And deep inside, Bliss was afraid of what she would reveal.

When the prescription was filled, she brought the bag to the counter. Bliss paid for it. As June took the cash, Bliss caught her hand. "You're hiding something. What is it?"

June looked grim. "I'm not hiding anything. I'm a pharmacy clerk, and I've got to maintain privacy."

"But we're talking about Parker here, not some bottle of pills."

June looked sympathetically at Bliss. "All you need to know is that Parker Swain is a good man, who never hurt nobody."

Somehow as Bliss drove back to the site to deliver the prescription to Nancy, June's defense of Parker did nothing to reassure her.

*****

Bliss pulled into the parking lot the next morning, meeting her goal of arriving earlier than the crew. Finally, she felt on top of things. The press conference was behind her, she'd mended fences with Parker, and she even was armed with sunscreen.

When she stepped out of the Explorer, the exotic scent of Cape Destiny, a spicy mixture of bayberry, hydrangea and salt-air came to her and gave her a sense of being fully alive. Working on location always sparked her senses. From the butterfly that flitted past, she knew this was going to be a good day.

Yesterday, they'd been able to move the lighthouse two extra feet than they had originally projected. At this rate, they'd make the September 1 deadline with no trouble.

Clearing the dense pines, Bliss strode across the short-stubby Bermuda grass lawn then stopped cold when she heard someone scream. Dashing toward the work site from where the sound had come, her heart pounding, she prayed that there hadn't been an accident.

When the site came into view, she saw no one, but looking toward the right, she spied Nancy, who was standing outside the trailer, white with shock, her hands covering her mouth. It was then that Bliss knew all notion of it being a good day had evaporated.

Chapter 16

"Nancy, what is it?"

"Who would do such a thing?" Nancy mumbled, shaking her head.

Bliss turned her eyes to what Nancy's was staring at and gasped. Spray-painted in shameless red on the side of the white trailer were the words: WHORE! BITCH SHERMAN LEAVE CDL! SLUT!

Bliss's blood ran cold as she absorbed the malice of those words.

"Who would do this?" Nancy asked again, turning to Bliss.

Bliss immediately thought of the fortune she'd invested in equipment. Dropping her purse and briefcase in the sand, she ran toward the lighthouse. She did a cursory inspection to see if any of the hydraulic hoses had been cut or any of the instruments been touched. Upon first inspection, nothing seemed to be amiss. She'd need Randy, when he arrived, to do a more thorough inspection.

Bliss hurried back to the trailer and met Nancy, who was returning from the direction of the shoreline. "I found this bobbing around in the surf," Nancy said. She held out an aerosol can of spray paint.

The words on the trailer humiliated Bliss, and she felt vulnerable like someone had written her name and phone number on the bathroom wall. She wanted those words gone. "Let's see if we can scrub this off before the crew arrives," she said heading toward the trailer. Nancy kept some cleaners in the supply cabinet.

She grabbed Bliss's arm. "We need to call the police first."

Bliss was stunned. She didn't want the police involved. It was only the cruel work of some vandals. "Why? There seems to be no other damage."

"I think you should file a report. There may be some that we don't know of, and if there is, our insurance carrier will require one. Besides maybe they can catch whoever is responsible."

As always, Nancy was the voice of reason. She and Bliss went to the trailer. When Nancy unlocked the door and flicked on the light, they were both relieved to see nothing inside the office had been disturbed.

"Do you want me to call?" Nancy asked.

Bliss slumped into her chair and sighed. "No, I'll do it."

*****

When Bliss heard the siren wailing, she regretted having called the police. She stepped outside the trailer intending to meet the squad car and tell the officer to can the theatrics, but she was surrounded by several of the crew who had begun to straggle in. Most of them would have never even noticed that the trailer had been vandalized had it not been for the piercing police siren. They began to ask what was going on.

Randy had arrived half an hour earlier and was, at Bliss's request, inspecting the equipment. She saw him double-timing it back to the trailer. When the men saw him, they gathered around him clamoring for answers.

Randy whistled, getting everyone's attention. "Look, gang, nothing's wrong. Some kids vandalized the trailer last night. I checked around and everything seems fine. You might want to look around and see if you notice anything." Satisfied, the crew dispersed and headed off.

Bliss groaned when she saw Officer Bevans, the baby-faced patrolman who had pulled her over on Beachfront Road, walking toward them in the misty morning sunshine. He was carrying a clipboard, and Parker was at his side.

This was proving to be humiliating. She could understand the how rape victims were reluctant to report the crime. It stripped one of all privacy.

Parker, wearing jeans that were worn in all the right places and a gray T-shirt, looked at her with concern. "Wayne here tells me you had some trouble overnight. You OK?"

"I'm OK," Bliss said. "You know each other?"

"Wayne," Parker said as he gently slapped Officer Bevans on the back, "was in one of the first classes I taught at Wingina. We've been friends ever since. Pays to have friends in the law."

Officer Bevans looked puzzled by that remark. Then with a respectful dip of his head, he said, "Morning, Miz Sherman. What seems to be the problem?"

"Over here," Bliss said leading them to the trailer. When Officer Bevans saw the graffiti, his only reaction was to pull out a pen and make notes on the clipboard.

"Oh, Bliss!" Parker exclaimed taking a stance like he was ready to do battle. "If I get my hands on the lowlifes who did this."

Officer Bevans looked up. "When did you first notice the vandalism?"

"When Nancy and I arrived for work," Bliss said. "She found a spray paint canister on the beach."

"Who's Nancy," Officer Bevans asked.

"My assistant."

"Is she around?" he asked. "I'd like to ask her some questions too."

"She's inside," Bliss said. "Why don't we go into the office. It'll be easier for you to write and cooler."

Bliss introduced Nancy to Officer Bevans. Nancy related how she had found the vandalism and the canister of spray paint. After he asked Nancy if she had noticed anyone unusual hanging about lately, Nancy handed him the can of spray paint.

He pulled a pair of rubber gloves out of his pocket and picked up the can. "We might be able to get some prints, although if it's been in the water I don't know how successful that'll be."

"How would anyone get at the site?" Bliss asked. "The ranger closes the gates at dusk and won't let anyone past unless they have authorization."

"That maybe," Officer Bevans said, "but they can't patrol the shore."

"Any kid who grew up in this area certainly knows how to avoid the rangers if they want to," Parker said. "I don't know how many times I've broken up drinking parties down on the beach after dark."

"I'm not so sure it's kids who are responsible," Wayne Bevans said.

"What do you mean?" Nancy asked, looking concerned.

The policeman took an at-ease stance. "Well, we don't have much trouble with graffiti down here. That's more of an urban problem. And whoever did this singled you out, Miz Sherman. Do you have any enemies?"

Bliss froze, a vise grip of fear clamping her chest. "Enemies? No, I don't have any enemies."

Parker glanced at Bliss then spoke up. "Yesterday morning, Wayne, Bliss was threatened."

Was nothing private here? Bliss wondered. "It was just my ex-husband and former business associate. He's harmless."

"I punched him out for calling Bliss names similar to what is painted on the trailer," Parker said. "He said we'd both be sorry."

"It was probably some teenager who heard his parents complaining about me moving the lighthouse," Bliss said, not wanting to consider the possibility that Jonathan could stoop so low.

Officer Bevans capped his pen. "Well, Miz Sherman, it's a well-known fact that most victims know their attackers. Has your ex done anything like this before? Has he ever gotten violent with you?"

"No," Bliss said emphatically. "Jonathan attacks verbally. He'd never do something like this."

Nancy spoke softly as she looked at Bliss. "This seems more than a verbal attack."

"But I know him," Bliss said, the words ringing hollowly in her mind. She thought she knew what kind of a man Jonathan was when she was married to him too, yet he had been cheating on her. "We've been divorced for nearly two years. Why would he start to harass me now?"

"Has anything changed for him?" Officer Bevans asked, tapping the pen on the clipboard.

"We've heard rumors that his firm isn't doing very well," Nancy said.

"And he believes Bliss and I are involved," Parker said.

Wayne Bevans's doughy cheeks pinked as he raised his brows and looked at Parker expectantly.

Bliss saw Nancy fold her arms across her chest and lower her gaze.

"It was a misunderstanding," Bliss explained. "I spent the night at Parker's, but nothing happened."

Parker winked at Bliss. "Wasn't for lack of trying."

Bliss's eyes became two fireballs as she stared at Parker.

Officer Bevans cleared his throat. "Anyway, Miz. Sherman, you might consider hiring additional security."

Another expense, thought Bliss, to stretch their strained budget.

"And," he continued as he picked up the can with his gloved hand, "you might want to vary your routine a little. Pay extra attention to see if you're being followed. That kind of thing."

"I can assure you," Bliss said. "I'll be fine."

Officer Bevans walked toward the door. "If you need anything, just give a holler."

The policeman stepped out into the morning sunshine. "You coming, Parker?" Officer Bevans started down the ramp to the sand.

"Be along in a minute."

Parker took Bliss by the arm and led her outside and whispered. "I'm sorry I had to tell him about Jonathan, but I think you're blind to the rage that guy had in his eyes when he left here."

"OK, but did you have to tell him that I spent the night at your house?"

"I did that for Nancy's benefit. Give her something to gnaw on."

"The only thing she'll be gnawing on is me."

"Seriously, Bliss. Jealousy is a powerful emotion."

"But he has nothing to be jealous about. I wasn't 'with you,'" she said rolling her eyes at the implication "with you" meant.

He moved his hand up her arm and touched her sunburned cheek. Then he kissed her briefly and grinned. "At least, not yet. I'm working on it though." He trotted down the ramp, leaving Bliss stunned at his audacity and tingling from his lips.

She floated back into the office feeling like she was enclosed in a golden bubble like the kind in which the Good Witch in the Wizard of Oz traveled.

Nancy was standing by the window, her arms crossed and her lips pressed tightly together. "He kissed you," she said disapprovingly.

"Yes, he did," Bliss said dreamily as she drifted toward her desk.

"How could you allow him do that?"

"I didn't allow him. He just did it."

"It's a mistake, Bliss," Nancy said, shaking her head.

"Don't get upset. It's only a harmless flirtation."

"That kiss didn't look harmless," Nancy quipped.

"Oh, Nancy," Bliss said rising and gliding to her assistant and putting a hand on her shoulder. "Don't worry."

"I can't help it. You're not seeing the big picture."

Bliss chuckled. "Explain to me then what I'm not getting."

Nancy looked toward the door as if to make sure no one was coming then she turned to Bliss. She lowered her voice. "I didn't want to raise the possibility when they were here, but it may not be Jonathan or some teenagers who did this."

"Who then?" Bliss asked expecting to hear a theory worthy of the *Weekly World News*.

"Someone who also sees you as a threat. Someone who has reacted explosively to you before. Someone who has acted violently in the past."

Bliss scanned her memory, coming up with no one who fit Nancy's description. "Who are you talking about?"

Nancy spat out the words, "Parker Swain."

Bliss felt the golden bubble of euphoria encasing her pop.

Chapter 17

Bliss dismissed Nancy's hypothesis, but she could barely concentrate on her work after Nancy had accused Parker of spray-painting the graffiti. Maybe Cape Destiny was cursed. Maybe he was part of the curse. Maybe Nancy was right. Bliss hated to admit it, but Nancy had some valid points. Parker was opposed to moving the lighthouse and had reacted explosively when he first met her, and by punching Jonathan, he demonstrated that he was capable of violence.

When Bliss had scoffed at Nancy's accusation, Nancy had come back with a question that unnerved her. "What do you know about him, Bliss?"

Not much, Bliss had to admit. Parker Swain was an enigma, a Mr. Rochester living in his own Thornfield, but she sensed that behind the veil he had a gentle heart.

As Bliss sat at her desk staring at a mish-mash of words that was the bid for the Coast Guard Station move, her normally rebellious mind was even more distracted. Thoughts of Parker kept intruding. Why would he rescue her and then try to frighten her? It made no sense.

By the time Randy brought the OSHA official, who had arrived for an impromptu inspection in the midst of all the turmoil, to her office to give his safety report, she'd convinced herself that she had nothing to fear from Parker.

Bliss's mood elevated considerably when Mr. Sanders, a paunchy man in navy Dockers and short sleeve denim shirt, handed over his report. He'd found only minor violations and recommended moving the orange mesh safety fence farther back from the site to keep the crowds safely at bay.

Shortly after he left, Bliss was surprised to receive a call from Desiree St. Jacques informing her that the quarter pendant was done.

Bliss made arrangements to pick it up on her way back to the Destiny Cove after work. She summoned the discipline that had gotten her through college, despite being dyslexic, to tackle the proposal. After spending an hour making corrections, she pushed herself away from the desk and stretched. Then she walked the revisions to Nancy's desk. They had barely spoken all afternoon.

Their relationship was as delicately balanced as the sensors on the lighthouse. While Bliss welcomed and valued Nancy's opinions and expertise, she wanted to make sure that Nancy observed the line between personal and business. They had worked together so long and Bliss relied on her so, that sometimes the line blurred. It wasn't all Nancy's fault either, Bliss admitted. She often crossed the line by involving her in things that were really none of Nancy's business. But since she had no mother or sister to confide in and her brothers were living all over the globe, Nancy was easy to turn to when Bliss needed emotional support.

They'd both worked so hard Bliss didn't want anything as trivial as the vandalism to jeopardize their relationship. Intending to mend fences, Bliss set the proposal on Nancy's desk. She immediately swiveled away from the computer and replied evenly, "Good, you're done reviewing that. I can make corrections and have the new copy to you by tomorrow morning."

Bliss touched her shoulder. "There's no rush, Nancy. It's been a trying day around here. I'm going to leave now, and I suggest you take it easy too."

Nancy smiled. "It has been a rather unpleasant matter."

Bliss sat on the edge of the desk. "I think you should be careful too, Nancy. If Officer Bevans thinks this is more than a youthful prank, then whoever did this might also be a threat to you as well."

Nancy gathered the papers together and straightened them by tapping them on the desk.

"Oh, Bliss, don't worry about me. Who'd bother with me? You're the face of Sherman Engineering."

*****

"Oh, this is exquisite," Bliss exclaimed, staring at the medallion lying in her palm. Desiree had encased the oval coin in a silver twisted rope and the loop where the chain was threaded resembled a mariner's knot. "It's perfect."

"I'm glad you like it," Desiree said. "I wanted to give it a nautical and masculine touch."

Bliss was so delighted with the piece she couldn't wait to give it to Parker. Tucking the velvet box into her purse, she decided to deliver it right after getting a bite to eat.

As she drove up Beachfront Road, an abundance of delicious aromas beckoned her to dine. The Seafood Shack finally lured her in, and she ordered clam strips to go. As she drove back out to the Cape, she popped a strip into her mouth, wondering how she'd ever survive again in Pittsburgh without The Seafood Shack's delicacies.

When she pulled up to the park's station, Ranger Mary Jane Mullins was on duty, and she apologized for requiring Bliss to show her identification before she allowed her to drive through the gates. Hiring private security to operate at a National Park was not customary, and by the time Nancy worked out the bureaucratic red tape to do so, the move would be completed.

Bliss was pleased that the Park Service had voluntarily increased their security, although she knew other than patrolling the shoreline, neither a private firm nor the government could completely secure Cape Destiny.

Her wheels crunched the gravel as she slowly drove into the parking lot. There were no other vehicles there. She turned off the engine, popped a breath mint, and checked herself in the mirror. She looked tired, the strain of the day reflected on her face. After applying some lip gloss, she stepped out of the Explorer, smoothed the wrinkles out of her khaki shorts and tucked in her shirt.

The light was nearly gone, and she hoped the twilight would soften the weariness on her face. Taking the box with the medallion out of her purse, she headed up the path. Crickets chirped in the brush and the air was cool under the trees. She hurried along, hoping not to meet any snakes or raccoons.

When Bliss cleared the copse of trees towering over the parking lot, she walked out across the broad lawn. Stars were beginning to appear. It was so beautiful here. How could this place be cursed?

Bliss looked over at The Keeper's House. It was dark. She walked up onto the porch, and called Parker's name into the screen door. No answer. Perhaps he'd gone out for dinner.

Disappointed, Bliss walked back down the porch steps and headed toward the Explorer. From the direction of the ocean, she heard a faint barking. Parker and Beau must be down on the beach.

She quickened her pace and headed down the path that led over the dune, toward the pounding surf.

Bliss trudged in her heavy boots through the sand, and as she stood atop the dune, she saw Parker and Beau swimming in the frothy sea. They were gray figures in an inky ocean, and she could barely make out Beau, his snout pointed in the air, as he paddled parallel to the shore.

The white cap of a large wave barreled in, and Parker standing in waist-high water joined his hands together and dove into the bottom of it, letting it wash over him. He rose, his back to her, as the wave crashed upon the beach. As Bliss was about to call his name, the words caught in her throat. The wave spent itself on the shore and rushed out quickly, leaving Parker in thigh-high surf. Naked.

Silhouetted against the darkening sky, she could make out the carved muscles of his back, the narrow waist, and his chiseled butt perched upon his strong legs. The same dark shade of the ocean, he looked like some water-God rising out of the waves. She stood there mesmerized by his unbridled masculinity, her mouth agape, admiring him. If he was cursed, every man should be so unfortunate.

Beau barked, snapping Bliss out of her reverie. The dog emerged from the surf, his coat dripping, and after shaking off a cyclone of water, he ran up the beach toward the dunes.

Not wanting to get caught ogling Parker, Bliss quickly turned and hurried back toward the house, her heavy boots kicking up sand behind her.

She trotted toward the car, deciding that she'd give Parker the medallion later. It was much darker on the path to the parking lot now making it difficult to find her way. The sound of small animals scurrying frightened her. Bliss stumbled over a tree root. An owl hooted above, and as she looked up, someone leaped out of the woods, slammed into her, throwing her to the ground.

She managed to let out a squeal before she landed hard on her side, knocking the air out of her.

Her first thought was that Beau hadn't been barking at her but someone lurking in the woods. Terrified and with her hair in her face, she squirmed beneath the weight of her attacker, beating at him with her fists. Her mind raced. *The threats weren't idle. If only I could get my breath back so I could scream. I wish Parker had seen me.*

As her attacker wrestled her onto her back, in her mind, she appealed to Beau. *Please, Beau. Help! Get Parker. I'm going to die.*

Chapter 18

"Parker, help!" Bliss shouted with all the air she could muster.

Her attacker stopped struggling. "Bliss?"

He knows my name. My attacker knows me. Her blood ran cold. *Most victims know their assailants.* Officer Bevans was right. This *was* personal. She had to get away. She squirmed against the heavy body lying on top of her.

Her assailant's powerful arms wrapped around her and drew her to his chest. "Oh, my God, Bliss. It's me. It's Parker."

He began to stroke her hair. Hysterical, she was much too frightened to believe him and punched against his bare chest.

He hugged her tightly, whispering in her ear, "Oh, I'm so sorry, Bliss. I thought you were the idiot who vandalized the trailer."

"Parker?" she whispered and then began to cry as she clung to him, the skin of his bare chest cool and damp against her cheek.

"I thought *you* were him," she said between sobs. "I thought I was going to die."

He kissed her forehead and then her cheek. "I didn't hurt you, did I?"

She sniffled. "I don't think so. Maybe just knocked the air out of me."

In the fading light, he held her away and looked into her eyes. Then he gently wiped away her tears and kissed her. Finally, she felt safe. She didn't care that she'd vowed not to get involved with him. She wanted Parker's arms around her, to be safe.

"Better now?" he asked, pulling some leaves from her hair.

"Yes."

"What are you doing out here so late?"

She took a deep breath. "I came to give you a gift." Bliss moved away. It was in my hand when you took me down." She felt around the ground.

"What does it look like?"

Bliss, sitting on a carpet of pine needles, turned and looked back at Parker, and she began to laugh. "You may want to look for something else first."

"What?"

She lowered her eyes and giggled. "Like your clothes."

"Oh good lord," Parker exclaimed as his hands flew to his cover himself. "I had a towel on when I jumped you." He scrambled around on the ground looking for it. "I'm sorry, Bliss. Cover your eyes, young lady."

Bliss covered her eyes. I'm not sorry, she thought finding his bashfulness charming. Although she knew exactly why Parker was naked, she though she'd have a little fun with him. "What goes on out here at night?"

"Ah, here it is," he said. And when he stood his back to her to wrap the towel around his waist, she sneaked a peek between her fingers and observed that up close he was even more exquisite. "I-I was swimming." He held a hand out to her and helped her up.

"Skinny-dipping?"

"There was nobody around, and I was hot and . . ."

"You don't have to explain."

"Just don't want you to think I'm some kind of red neck straight out of *Deliverance*, running through the woods at night naked."

"I was thinking more along the line of Tarzan." She kicked around in the dirt, looking for the velvet box. "I wish I had a flashlight."

"I have one back at the house. Stay here and I'll get it."

She grabbed Parker's arm. "And leave me here in the woods in the dark alone? Not on your life!"

"Let's go get my clothes then we can look," he said.

They headed down to the beach. "I hope I didn't interrupt anything coming out here," Bliss said as they strolled along in the dark.

"No, after I was done swimming, I planned to organize some of the research I've been doing on the lighthouse."

"You're researching its history?"

"Yes, for when the Oil House is turned into the museum."

"Must be quite an endeavor."

Once on the shore they became quiet. The beauty moved Bliss. Looking out over the water. The moon reflected a silver path that led straight to the horizon, the unknown.

After several minutes, Parker turned to her, his hair disheveled and wild wearing only a towel reminding her of an island king. "Know what's the most difficult thing about doing the research?"

"What?" she said softly.

"All my life I've heard stories about the lighthouse. What has happened out here. The hardest part is deciding what's true."

She looked up at him, his face outlined in moonlight. "What do you mean? The curse?"

"The curse. The myths. Everything. So much of what I know about this place can't be documented. I'm trying to separate legend from truth. Over time, the lines between them have seemed to have been erased."

Bliss sensed from his voice that he was troubled. She touched his arm. His flesh was warm as if it had trapped some of the sun's heat. "I think all of life is nothing but trying to separate the fact from fiction, Parker. When I married Jonathan, I thought I knew him . . ." Her voice softened. "Obviously, I had fallen in love with a sham."

"I just want to know what's real," Parker said. "But every time I think I've found it, it seems I'm left with nothing but a specter of what had passed for truth."

111

She leaned her head against his shoulder. "Did you ever think that maybe the purpose of life is not our finding the truth, but always retaining the desire for it. When you give up the search for what's real, I think that's when we get into danger."

He put his arm around her. "Maybe you're right. Maybe we can never know the truth."

Somehow, she sensed that he was relieved. Bliss reached up and touched his cheek. "But you'll never give up looking for it, will you?"

"No, Bliss, I won't," he promised before kissing her.

When he released her, Bliss had to step away to catch her breath.

*****

As they arrived back at the house, Beau emerged from the brush, covered with burrs, leaves, and mud. Parker shook his head. "Some great protector, huh? We're out being attacked in the woods, and he's chasing raccoons."

Inside, Parker turned on a light. She could see where his tan line ended and she found herself wanting to rip off the towel.

"There's a flashlight in the bureau in the dining room," Parker said. "I'll put these on and be back in a minute."

Bliss found the flashlight, but it wouldn't light. "I think the batteries are dead," she called.

"There are fresh ones in one of the drawers."

Bliss opened the first one and found some clam knives, a corkscrew, and a pack of matches from The Belle Island Fishing Pier. She opened the center one. It was jammed with papers. Rooting around, she found a pair of AAA cells. She moved some more papers until she found a pack of C's lying on top of a certificate of some kind. It was a marriage license. Must be some of his research, she thought. Curious, she read it. Then her mouth fell open. It was Parker's and a woman named Beth Hamilton.

He's married?

She searched the document for the date, but stopped when she heard the bathroom door rattling.

"Did you find them?" Parker called.

Quickly, she grabbed the batteries and shoved the drawer closed.

112

Parker walked into the dining room, wearing cutoffs, and carrying his shirt. Bliss fumbled with the package, dropping the batteries.

They both bent for them. Parker got to the batteries first. Bliss rose. "Sorry," she said.

He straightened up and handed them to her. "Bliss," he said, "are you OK? You're so pale, like you've seen a ghost."

Or a wife, she thought, as the hope for anything real with Parker died within her.

Chapter 19

Bliss sat at her desk and washed a Tylenol down with a glass of water. She ached all over from Parker's pouncing on her last night. Fortunately, she'd come away virtually unscathed with only a few brush burns and minor scrapes. His power and ferocity had impressed her. Had he not discovered her true identity any sooner, she knew she wouldn't have been so lucky as to come away relatively unharmed.

She recalled the image of him, naked in the moonlight, the muscles of his firm buttocks, the ripples of sinews down his back, and she knew, physically, she was no match for him.

Emotionally, she was in distress too. The thought that Parker was married disturbed her. And if she was honest, she was jealous. They'd only shared a few kisses, yet she felt betrayed. She'd promised herself she wouldn't get involved with Parker, but these yearnings to have his arms around her again, told her that her heart had other ideas.

They'd taken a flashlight out to the woods after she found the marriage license and scoured the grounds for the box containing the medallion but to no avail. She focused the beam of light on the pine-needle littered earth and stole glances of Parker as he moved aside leaves and rocks with the toe of his work boot, the faint moonlight turning his golden hair silver.

Leaning back in her chair, she raised her arms over her head, thinking that some stretches might loosen her ribs, but the muscles hurt like she'd overdone it at the gym.

Who *was* Parker Swain? And what secrets did he have? Was he a two-timing womanizer? Surely, someone would have told her that he was married. Obviously, he had been married at one time, but was he still? She tried to recall his hands. In her mind, she could see them tanned and nicked, workman's hands. She could feel them stroking her hair and touching her cheek. But Bliss couldn't recall a wedding band. Probably because it had never occurred to her to look for one before.

But what had happened to his wife? She swiveled her chair and faced the stack of papers on her desk. As much as she told herself she wouldn't get involved with him, she felt herself falling for his genteel charms. If he were still married, would it make a difference? She felt unable to resist him no matter his marital status.

Yes, it would make a difference, she told herself. She'd just gotten out of one disastrous relationship; becoming involved with a married man would only lead her back to heartache. She vowed if she found out that Parker was married, she'd force herself to forget about him.

She couldn't just ask him, but she needed to know. Then she had an idea.

Bliss walked over to Nancy's desk, booted the computer, and waited. She was glad she'd arrived earlier than Nancy. Bliss avoided the computer and therefore didn't know much about using it. Nancy would be suspicious if she found Bliss working on it.

Once, Nancy had shown her how to do a search on the Internet. She hoped she remembered how. Bliss hit the search button like she'd seen Nancy do a thousand times and pecked in Wellington County. After clicking on the county's official link, she read the site map, searching for a connection to the vital statistics department. As she finished entering Parker's name into the search window, there was a knock at the door.

116

Bliss quickly shut off the power to the computer.

When she opened the door, Parker was standing there in his customary jeans and T-shirt with Beau at his heels.

"Brought you something," he said, handing her a tube.

"Ben-Gay?" She laughed.

"I'm a bit sore this morning, and I wasn't taken by surprise. Figured you'd be a bit achy too."

"Come on in," she said, and he and the dog stepped through the doorway.

Bliss put her hand on her ribs just below her bra. "My side is the worst. Took a Tylenol."

"Why don't you let me put some on you."

"Oh, you don't have to."

"Come on. It'll loosen it up."

The thought of him having his hands on her frightened and excited her. "You don't need to."

He took the tube from her hands. "Look I'm responsible for banging you up. At least let me try to alleviate the pain."

What could it hurt? Bliss thought. It's not like we're going to make love in the office on top of the desks.

"Lift your shirt up."

Bliss pulled the tails of her pink oxford cloth shirt out of her khaki shorts, and lifted it, baring her midriff.

Parker moved behind her. He squeezed out a squiggle of Ben Gay on to his palms and reached under her shirt. When he touched Bliss with the ointment, she flinched and giggled. "That's cold."

"Sorry," he said. Then he massaged the balm into her side. She felt the cream working it's magic, soothing her aching muscles.

"How's that feel?"

"Fantastic."

Bliss closed her eyes and let his hands soothe her. Parker leaned in and whispered in her ear. "I love your perfume. I'm a sucker for menthol."

As Bliss giggled again and then moaned with delight, the door flew open. Bliss with Parker behind her, his hands under her shirt, turned and faced Nancy.

"Oh! Excuse me," Nancy said lowering her eyes and leaving.

"No, Nancy. Stop. It's not what it looks like."

Nancy halted, her hand on the knob.

"Parker's just taking care of me. Things got a little rough out in the woods last night."

Nancy turned and headed for the door. "I don't think I want to hear any of this."

"What Bliss means," Parker said, "is that when I jumped her, she got a little banged up."

"I don't need an explanation. I'll just leave until you're finished."

Bliss dashed over and grabbed Nancy by the arm. "No, let me explain. Last night I came out here to give him a gift, and when I didn't find him at home, I started back toward my car. That's when someone sprung from the woods and attacked me."

Bliss left out the part about Parker being naked.

"It was me," Parker said. "I thought Bliss was the person who vandalized the site."

"You see," Bliss said her dark eyes shining. "It was all a misunderstanding. Knowing that I'd be sore, Parker brought me some Ben Gay. I couldn't reach the tender spot." She said tucking in her shirt.

"How thoughtful," Nancy said and walked to her desk.

Nancy's closed-mindedness toward Parker infuriated Bliss. She raised her chin and tossed back her hair. "Yes, it was."

Parker smirked, apparently flattered that Bliss had come to his defense. "I also came to see if you want to resume our search," he said.

Bliss smiled. "Yes, I do, Parker," she said defiantly. "I looked around on the path this morning, but I'm not sure where it was that you sprang out of the woods *naked* and pounced on me."

Out of the corner of her eye, Bliss saw Nancy stop when she heard Bliss describe his lack of attire. Bliss smiled, pleased that she'd really given Nancy something to think about.

"I know those woods like the back of my hand," Parker said. "I'm pretty sure I dropped my towel near where the path curves."

Bliss moved toward the door and laughed. "You better hope there was no poison ivy or you're going to be needing more than Ben Gay. Come on."

"I didn't think of that," Parker said.

Bliss turned to the brooding Nancy, who was straightening papers on her desk, and said, "I'll be back in a few minutes."

Bliss closed the door and walked down the ramp. Then she looked at Parker and burst into laughter. "Oh, my God, Parker," she said, covering her mouth, "did you see the look on her face when she walked in?"

"I thought she was going to have a hissy fit."

"Well, I guess things did look a bit tawdry."

"And then you go and tell her that things got rough in the woods last night. Oh, that really helped."

They walked toward the path. "Well, how about you saying that you jumped me."

"Well, how about your telling her I was naked? You're a wicked woman," Bliss Sherman.

Bliss smiled devilishly. "Aren't I?"

"If she disliked me before, she'll surely hate me now."

"I love Nancy dearly," Bliss said, "but sometimes I think she needs to loosen up a bit."

They strolled companionably in the morning sun. Dew left dark water marks on the tips of her work boots.

"How's that?" Parker asked.

Bliss ducked under a branch and entered the path where misty shafts of sunlight filtered onto the forest floor. "She's so controlled and focused on work all the time. She makes me feel guilty. I just wish she'd enjoy life. It's all business with her."

Parker looked intently on the path. "Well, Bliss. I've learned that you can't change people."

Bliss sighed and tried to remember if any of the foliage looked familiar. "I know."

"What does she do for relaxation? A hobby? Or something?"

"She does exercise to keep fit. I know she brought along her dumbbells. She like to read too. Other than that, I don't really know."

Parker scanned the brush and then glanced at the sandy path beneath his feet. "I think this is the spot. See how it curves. And isn't that your boot print?" He moved over to the bushes. "You can see where I trampled some of the underbrush."

Bliss turned and faced the direction of the parking lot. "So if I was standing here, and you came at me from there," she pointed to the thicket, "then when you took me down, the box probably flew out of my hand and landed somewhere over there." She swept her arm across an expanse to her right.

They separated and began searching an area about ten yards long. After about ten minutes of moving aside branches, kicking over rocks, sweeping aside leaves and needles, Bliss spied the blue velvet case partially concealed by a compost of magnolia leaves. "Found it," she said with relief and picked it up. She weaved her way out of the thicket and met Parker on the path.

After brushing the dirt off the velvet, she handed it to him. "For you. For rescuing me."

Curious, Parker opened the case and stared at the medallion, a puzzled look creeping across his face.

"I know it's not very pretty, but I thought you'd appreciate it." She came and stood beside him and pointed at the smeared image on the coin. "If you look closely, you can see that it's a North Carolina State quarter." She gazed at Parker, and his expression reminded her of a little boy on Christmas morning. She wondered how she could ever speculate that he would be capable of cheating on his wife. Parker was not deceptive. Secretive and private, yes, but not deceptive.

He plucked it out of the box. She touched the coin. "It was put on the move beam and the lighthouse passed over it, pressing it."

He looked at her incredulously.

"It's a little bit of history. A souvenir. I had Desiree St. Jacques, the jeweler, make it into a medallion for you."

Speechless, he turned it over and saw the distorted image of the Wright Brothers.

"I don't know if you wear jewelry, but even if you don't, I figured you could save it."

He took her hand. "Bliss you went to all this trouble for me?"

She gulped under his penetrating gaze. "It was no trouble. Do you like it?"

"Like it? I'll treasure this always. Let me put it on."

He undid the clasp and reached behind his neck fumbling to fasten it.

"Here, let me help," Bliss said as she went on tiptoes, reached up, and covered his hands with hers and fastened the chain.

As she slid her hands down, Parker caught them in his own and held them. "Bliss, thank you. I've never had a more valuable treasure." Then he pulled her to his chest and as he kissed her passionately, Bliss wondered if he had at one time regarded his wedding ring as a valuable treasure too.

Chapter 20

Bliss pulled away. Like someone suspended over an abyss clinging only to a rope, she felt herself losing her grip, falling for Parker Swain. Sighing, she rested her head on his chest, listening to his heart beating, wondering how she'd managed to do exactly what she had vowed not to do—become involved in another doomed relationship.

With his fingertips, Parker raised her chin and peered into her eyes. "What is it, Bliss?"

She looked away and said softly, "That's it precisely, Parker. What is it? What's going on between us?"

He rubbed her arm. "What's been going on ever since God made a woman out of a rib and gave her to Adam."

Bliss frowned. "What I mean is where is this headed?"

Parker kissed her cheek. "I guess it will go wherever we allow it to."

She turned away from him. "That's just it. I feel like a wedge has been driven into my heart. One half tells me I'm deeply attracted to you and to enjoy your company, but the other half tells me I'm headed for heartbreak. I hardly know you, and what I do know is that you're tied to this place, and we have no future."

Parker came behind her and wrapped his arms around her. He kissed her neck and whispered, "Ah, Bliss, does anyone really have a future? All any of us ever really have is now. Can't we just be happy with being here together, for whatever little time we have?"

"But I'm afraid."

"Of what? Me?"

She gazed into his warm brown eyes. No matter Nancy's suspicions and his past, she knew she had nothing to fear from him. "No, not you. The pain when I lose you."

He hugged her. "You won't have to lose me. Just because you have to leave doesn't mean we still can't carry each other in our hearts. My granddaddy was swept away in a hurricane, but my granny never really lost him. She remained true to him until her dying breath." He took her face in his hands, "Oh, darlin', I know you want to feel safe. Want promises. But the only promise I can make is that I won't hurt you."

She placed a hand on his chest, feeling his heart pounding under her palm. "But what about you? Aren't you afraid *you* might get hurt?"

"Don't you worry about me now. I know how to deal with pain. And besides, Bliss, the way you've made me feel would be worth any hurt I may feel when you go." He traced a finger on her lip. "Can't we just enjoy the weeks that we have together. Can't we just live for now?"

She had to answer yes, for her heart had already committed her to him the first time she set eyes on him.

"I should get back to the office," she said after he had kissed her again to seal their arrangement. "Do you mind coming back with me? I want to prove to Nancy that I wasn't making this all up."

They walked back across the lawn, and as Parker told Bliss what he planned to work on, she watched him with false cheer. The pain was already there. The specter of never seeing him again beckoned like death.

When they walked into the office, Nancy ignored them.

"Well, luckily we found it." Bliss said brightly.

Nancy barely glanced their way. Bliss grabbed Parker's arm and pulled him over to Nancy's desk. "See what I had made for

Parker in appreciation for saving me when I collapsed with heat exhaustion."

Bliss pulled the medallion away from Parker's chest. Nancy, her nose turned up, slowly rose and looked over her bifocals to examine the jewelry, while Bliss explained how it was made. "I'm going to get one made for you, Nancy, as a souvenir. Something to take away from the move."

Nancy went back to her desk. "That's OK. Don't waste the money. Knowing that we did a good job will be souvenir enough for me."

Awkwardness hung in the air until Randy burst through the door. "Well, here she is—the most popular woman in all of Cape Destiny."

"What did Nancy do?" Bliss asked.

"Not Nancy," said Randy. "You."

Bliss raised her eyebrows warily. "I am? I'm afraid to ask why."

"I just told the crew that you've given them the Fourth of July off."

"Well, they've been working so hard. And my goodness, it seems cruel to bring them to such a lovely place and never give them a chance to enjoy it."

Parker looked at Bliss. "Are you taking the day off too?"

"Yes, I think we've all earned a break."

"If you're free, I'd like to show you how we celebrate the Fourth Outer Banks style."

Bliss's eyes lit up at the prospect. Then her shoulders sagged. "Sorry, Parker, Nancy and I planned to take in the gardens at the Historical Center."

"The gardens will always be there," Parker said with a wave of his hand. "But the Fourth on the beach only comes once a year." Parker looked at Randy and Nancy. "Why don't y'all come, too? We'll cook some seafood. I'll get some corn at the Farmer's Market."

"Remember, I don't like seafood," Nancy said.

"I love it," Randy said, "but I'm going to have to pass. Promised my wife I'd fly home."

Parker looked at Nancy. "I'll get you some burgers, Nancy. And Bliss here tells me you like to keep in shape. I have a pair of kayaks. I could borrow one for y'all, and we could go exploring out on the sound. Put your training to good use."

"I don't know."

"Oh, come on, Nancy," Bliss said. "It'll be fun."

"No, you go, Bliss. This tooth is still giving me trouble. Maybe I can fly home and get it fixed."

"I know a real fine dentist, over in Wingina," Parker said. "She could fix you up in no time. Save the expense of airfare."

"Mr. Swain, I'd feel much safer in the hands of my own dentist than someone from around here," Nancy said with a note of condescension

Bliss saw a flash of temper in Parker's eyes. "Suit yourself, Ms. Klempner," Parker said through clenched teeth, "but I assure you Dr. Owens is a great doc. And I'll have you know Southern isn't a synonym for stupid."

Nancy snorted and turned to face the computer.

Bliss was glad Nancy had declined Parker's invitation. If she couldn't be polite in passing conversation, they'd be at each other's throat if they spent any length of time together.

Bliss turned to Parker. "Well, if Nancy doesn't mind. I'd be delighted to spend the Fourth seeing how it's celebrated on the Outer Banks."

Parker's eyes softened as he looked at Bliss. "Great. I'll pick you up at the hotel around eight. We'll start off with a good country breakfast served at this little diner I know. Many fine chefs say when it comes to breakfast, the South has it all over the North."

Nancy seated at her desk, sniffed and muttered to herself. "Must have never heard of bagels and cream cheese."

Before the Civil War broke out again, Bliss put a hand on Parker's back. "I'll walk you out. I want to go check on one of the earthmovers. It keeps stalling."

They walked down the steps together. Parker looked at Bliss and pointed over his shoulder toward the trailer. "Sorry for getting peeved at her, but that woman has an agenda."

"And you're not on it," Bliss chuckled. "I guess she has a right to be put out. I did throw her over for you. I just wish she'd give you a chance."

"Well, to be neighborly, I did invite her too."

"Yes, you did."

When they rounded a bend, Bliss stopped in the shade of an ancient oak. She tucked a strand of hair that had blown across her cheek behind her ear. Gazing up at Parker, she sighed. "I honestly don't know how she resists you. She must have an estrogen deficiency."

Parker took her hand and looked over his shoulder toward the site, where workers were busily attending to the move. "Do you think she'd come out and whip me with her printer cable, if I kissed you here in broad daylight?"

Bliss looked playfully at him. "She might."

Parker looked back at the trailer then turned to Bliss. "Oh, hell. It'd be worth it," he said before sweeping an arm around Bliss's waist and pressing his lips passionately to hers.

Chapter 21

On the Fourth of July, Parker picked Bliss up early at the hotel. When she saw him standing in the lobby, she was taken aback by how stylish he looked. Dressed in khaki shorts, a green plaid sport shirt, and Topsiders, he looked more like a Palm Beach playboy than a teacher-turned-renovator.

Bliss wore a pair of white shorts and red boat neck T-shirt. She'd packed a tote with her bathing suit. Parker, as promised, took her to a small diner frequented by locals, where she had a massive plate of biscuits and sausage gravy.

"You are right," Bliss said. "You Southerners certainly have it all over us Yankees when it comes to breakfasts."

Next, they headed to Wingina, where King Street was decked out for Independence Day. Red, white, and blue buntings graced the facades of the stores and flags hung from every lamppost.

Parker had brought along two lawn chairs. He set them at the curb in front of the Outer Banks Booksellers, and Beau curled up under Parker's chair and slept as the Wingina High School Marching Band, Boys Scouts, and the Outer Banks Little League teams paraded past. Bliss felt it all charming, as if she were living inside a Norman Rockwell painting.

The parade ended near noon. The sun, high in the sky, beat down, and Bliss was glad to retreat into the shady park in the center of town. Parker bought them hot dogs and fresh-squeezed lemonade. They strolled through the craft fair, Beau nosing around, until they heard shrill laughter and someone calling, "Mr. Swain! Mr. Swain!" They turned and saw two teen-aged girls giggling and waving. "Come buy something from us."

Parker and Bliss went over to the table where a variety of cakes, pies, and cookies were displayed. "Hi, girls," Parker said. Bliss could tell by the way the girls beamed when he spoke to them that he must be the subject of many school-girl crushes at Wingina High.

Beau put his front paws on the table. "Back off, Beau," Parker said, pushing his dog away from the treats. "What's going on here, ladies?"

A pretty little girl with big blue eyes and long straight blond hair exclaimed, "It's for the National Honor Society."

"My mom made the brownies," a plumpish girl with rings on every finger said as she pointed at a plate on the table.

As she and Parker looked over the goodies, Bliss could feel the girls' eyes on her.

"What do you like, Bliss?"

Before she could reply, she heard someone say, "I got more napkins." Bliss looked up and saw Julie Marshall, the young school reporter, set a stack of white napkins on the table.

"You better put something on top of them this time," the blond said snottily, "or they'll all blow away again." Julie lowered her eyes.

"Julie?" Bliss said.

The girl looked up and when she saw Bliss, a smile spread across face. "Miss Sherman, I didn't see you there."

"How's the article coming?"

The plump girl looked surprised then blurted, "You're the lady moving the lighthouse!"

Parker looked at Bliss. "You know Miss Julie, then?" Parker asked.

"Yes," Bliss said. "She interviewed me the day of the press conference for your school newspaper."

"I submitted it to our editor today," Julie replied brightly. "It'll be in the back-to-school issue."

As Parker introduced Bliss to the rest of the girls, she heard someone laugh wickedly behind her and exclaim, "Honor Society! Huh, that's something you'd never find Bliss Sherman in."

She spun around and found Jonathan glaring at her. "What are you doing here?" she said, her pulse quickening.

"There's nothing around down by the Coast Guard Station, so I thought I'd drive up here for dinner. And what do I find? Jethro Bodine and The Whore of Cape Destiny."

Bliss gasped, while the girls stared in shock at her and Jonathan.

Parker stepped between them. "I thought I told you to leave her alone."

"And what are you going to do about it?"

Beau began to bark. Parker squared his shoulders and moved closer toward Jonathan. "Put your lights out permanently."

Jonathan laughed smugly. "Wouldn't the school board be pleased to hear about one of their teachers assaulting someone on the Fourth of July at the National Honor Society table?"

Bliss grabbed Parker's arm, before he could get off a punch. "Ignore him, Parker. He's not worth it."

She stepped up to her ex-husband. "Leave Jonathan. If you think you can intimidate me, you're wrong. And the next time you pull a stupid stunt like you did at the site, you'll be arrested for trespassing." She put her hands on her hips. "And wouldn't being arrested help you win The Coast Guard project?"

To her relief, she could see some of his bravado dissipate.

He smiled. "Well, dear Bliss. You're right. I wouldn't want to sully my reputation. But I guess you wouldn't know about that since yours has been shot to hell." He turned and walked away. Beau chased after him, barking until Parker called the dog back.

Bliss, trembling, felt tears stinging her eyes. Parker put an arm around her waist. "You OK?"

She nodded.

He gave her a little squeeze. "I think you need a brownie."

When they turned around, the girls behind the bake sale counter were staring at them wide-eyed with shock.

"Ladies," Parker said, "y'all know how I'm always pointing out 'teachable moments' to you. Well, you just witnessed one of life's most important lessons—never marry a jackass."

The girls laughed nervously.

"You're married to that creep?" the girl with the rings asked.

Bliss still shaking said, "Was married. We're divorced."

"No wonder. He's horrible," the petite blond said. "If he comes back here, I'm going to sell him Mrs. Oswald's bran muffins. They give you the runs."

Parker bought a plate of brownies and a sugar cookie , and then guided Bliss to a park bench under a shady oak where she could compose herself while listening to the small brass quartet in the gazebo play Sousa marches. "I'm sorry about that," Bliss said. "I hope he doesn't harm your reputation."

Parker broke off a piece of the cookie and fed it to Beau. "If I cared about my reputation, I'd have packed up and left a long time ago."

She stared at him, waiting for him to elaborate, but he dusted the crumbs off his hand then patted her knee. "Come on, let's go back to the house."

Chapter 22

Once Parker shut off the engine, Beau jumped out the back of the truck and bounded toward the house. "Well," Parker said as they walked up the path, "what'll it be now? Swimming or kayaking?"

Bliss opted for kayaking. They changed into bathing suits, Bliss sporting a navy one-piece Speedo and a pair of nylon shorts. Parker looked so much the outdoorsman as he emerged wearing an old pair of red trunks with the insignia OBX Lifeguard emblazoned on the leg. He was bare-chested, and she was touched to see that he was wearing the medallion she'd given him.

Parker led her down to the sound where he had already moored two yellow kayaks. Bliss watched him, his biceps bulging as he pulled the crafts to the bank. After they lathered up with sunscreen, he handed Bliss a life jacket, and she buckled it up snuggly.

"Have you ever done this before?" he asked as he assembled her paddle."

"No," she said with trepidation, recalling a disastrous attempt at canoeing on Lake Arthur when she was a Girl Scout.

"Oh, don't worry. You'll pick it up in no time." He handed her the paddle and took his. He instructed her on how to hold it properly and how to dip one end into the water then to rotate the shoulder to dip the other side.

She had trouble getting the rhythm of it. Parker came behind her and closed his arms around her helping her to get the correct motion. Her heart thudded in her chest at the nearness of him and the power she felt as he led with the paddle.

She got into the kayak, and he stepped into the water and pulled her into the sound. She sat and watched as he dragged his vessel into the water and climbed in. Beau stood on the shore, barking, giving them a canine send off.

The sun was intense and Bliss struggled with the kayak. She kept going where she didn't intend. Feelings of ineptitude, like when her dyslexia made it difficult to read, inspired panic, but Parker was patient and told her to relax and use a light touch, not to beat the water. Soon she found herself slicing through the still water, following him as he led her on a tour of the sound, pointing out inlets and the best spots for catching crabs.

Bliss was afraid she'd never be able to keep up with Parker, but after she relaxed, she was amazed to realize that they had been out on the water for two hours.

When they came ashore, Beau licked them like he hadn't seen them for ages. Then Parker took her down to where he had stationed his crab pots, and he was pleased to show her that he'd caught six large, angry looking ones for dinner.

Bliss took a shower in the outside shower, a wooden alcove attached to the side of the house. The cool breeze on her damp skin left her feeling invigorated. She changed back into her shorts and tank and came into the house.

"You've added new counter tops since I was last here," she said, running her hand over the smooth surface of the gray polished granite. "It looks great."

"Thanks. Louisa Barnhart from the state was really impressed with what I planned to do with the kitchen."

While Parker cleaned and steamed the crabs and ears of Silver Queen corn, Bliss fixed a salad with vegetables he'd purchased from a farmer's market.

"Now," Parker said, grabbing a mixing bowl, "it's time to give you a lesson in Southern cooking."

He dumped a packet of cornmeal mix into the bowl, added the rest of the ingredients, and then handed the bowl to Bliss. "Beat this for me, while I heat the oil."

"What's Nancy doing?" Parker asked as they fried the hushpuppies.

"She flew home to get her tooth fixed."

"Hope the dentist forgets to give her Novocain," he said.

Bliss playfully smacked him.

*****

After dinner, Parker poured them another glass of wine, and then they headed down to the beach. As they strolled along the shoreline, the waves washed around their feet.

They took turns throwing a weathered stick into the surf for Beau to retrieve. The summer sun began to set, sending up flares of pink and gold to the sky warning of the day's end.

"Let's watch the sunset and get ready for the fireworks," Parker suggested. Then he called Beau back to shore. The dog emerged from the ocean, ran up the beach, then shuddered, whipping Parker and Bliss with a shower of water.

They walked back to the house, where Parker refilled their glasses and grabbed a blanket and the rest of the wine.

"Do you think the mosquitoes will be bad?" Bliss asked.

"It seems to be clear tonight, and where we're going to watch the fireworks isn't usually bug infested."

Parker tucked the blanket under his arm and grabbed the wine. Then picking up Bliss's hand, he led her down the back steps. The light cast by the setting sun colored her skin a warm gold.

It had been so long since he'd been with a woman, he wondered as he walked barefoot through the cool grass, if this was a bad idea.

He'd talked things over with Wayne, told him how attracted he was to Bliss. "It's about time," Wayne had said as he slapped Parker on the back. When he told him that their romance had no future, Wayne had still encouraged him to pursue her. "Look, Parker, get with the program. You don't have to marry every girl you make love to. Have a good time, then cut your loses at the end of summer. After all you've been through, you deserve a little fun."

Will I remember how to make love? One look at Bliss as she walked beside him, refreshed his memory. He felt as anxious and

135

nervous as a schoolboy, and wondered how he, a country boy, would measure up against a sophisticated businessman like Jonathan when it came to love making.

Keep it cool, Parker chided himself. There's nothing riding on this. This is a casual summer fling. Like the catch and release program in fishing. Pursue Bliss for the summer, enjoy a good time, then at the end of the lighthouse project, release her. She was not a keeper.

The birds chirped their farewells to the day as Parker spread the blanket on the grass along the shoreline that afforded them an unobstructed view of the Wingina waterfront across the sound.

Parker and Bliss sat on the blanket, and Beau, who had tagged along, parked his hot, furry body in between the two of them.

"Who do you think you are, my chaperone? Move it, buster!" Parker said as he shooed Beau away. The dog settled at their feet and looked at them with sad brown eyes.

"You've hurt his feelings," Bliss said as she knelt and reached over to pet Beau. The dog yammered and lapped up the attention.

Suddenly there was a concussion. A streak of light shot into the air and burst into a chrysanthemum of sparkles in the sky.

"Here we go," Parker said.

Beau quickly rose and barked. "He's afraid of fireworks," Parker said. "Beau, go on back to the house." As another rocket lit the sky with purple and green sparks, Beau bolted for the Keeper's House.

Parker moved closer to Bliss and put an arm around her. "How's that for ditching my competition." Bliss turned and looked at him. He could see the reflection of skyrockets in her eyes. This is the perfect Fourth of July, he thought to himself.

Bliss lay back on the blanket and Parker joined her. Together they watched as a shower of colors exploded above them.

After a few minutes, a continuing series of launches and numerous explosions rocked the whole sound. Bliss turned to Parker. "This must be the finale."

"Seems so," Parker said, secretly knowing that as soon as the fireworks were over he planned to launch his finale for the evening.

When the last rocket extinguished its color in the night sky, Parker turned on his side and raised his head on his elbow.

"Did you enjoy that?"

Bliss sighed. "I've enjoyed everything——from the parade to the kayaking to dinner to this."

He reached over and stroked the inside of her wrist. "It's only about ten. There's still some time left to enjoy ourselves."

He bent and kissed Bliss, her lips warm and soft under his. He knew he must not have lost his touch, when Bliss softly moaned and wrapped her arms around him. He moved his mouth to her neck and anointed her with kisses and nibbles. Gently, he pushed aside the strap of her tank top and began to work his way down to her swelling breast.

Bliss seemed to freeze for a moment. Then she reached up and began undoing his shirt. She pulled it open and ran her hands over the fine hair of his bronzed chest. Then looking down into her wide dark eyes, he saw something that chilled him. What he saw was love.

He rolled off her and closed his eyes. "I'm sorry, Bliss," he said. "I can't do this."

Bliss was silent for a moment then touched his arm. "I understand. That's OK if you can't."

He looked at the star-twinkled sky and sighed loudly. "No, I mean I can. But I can't do this."

Bliss sat up and straightened her tank top. "I don't understand."

He covered his face with his hands and groaned. "I'm perfectly capable of making love, but I can't do it with you."

Bliss crossed her arm and gazed out across the sound at the lights of the small boats slicing through the water.

"Because you're married? I should have never let myself get into this position."

Parker suddenly opened his eyes and sat up. "I'm not married. Who told you I was married?"

Bliss looked at him. "No one. When I went to get the flashlight batteries, I found a marriage license in the drawer."

He took her hand. "Bliss, my wife died two years ago. I haven't even looked at another woman until you came along. You were going to let me make love to you even though you thought I was married?"

She hung her head. "You must think I'm some kind of tramp, but I rationalized that after all that I've been through, I deserved some happiness." She paused. "And I believed you when you said you wouldn't hurt me."

He put his arm on her back. "And I won't. That's why I can't make love to you." He put his head on her shoulder and whispered in her ear. "You see, when I first saw you, you stirred things in me I thought had died, and I knew I had to keep my distance because we have so many obstacles separating us. So I told myself the same thing—that after all I'd been through, I deserved some love, a fling, at least. I told myself to live for the moment." She turned and looked at him. He raised his head and gazed deeply into her eyes, "Be a 'now' kind of guy." He grasped her by the shoulders. "But, Bliss, I'm not a 'now' kind of fella, I'm a 'now and forever' kind of guy."

"I don't understand," Bliss said.

"What I mean is, Bliss. I love you. I'm not the type of man who can make love to a woman I care deeply for and then watch her walk out of my life."

Bliss blinked back tears, and placed a hand on his cheek. "Oh, Parker. This is terrible. This is the worst. It's just awful."

"I'm sorry. I didn't mean to get you all hot and bothered and then back away."

"I'm not upset about that," Bliss said wiping away a tear. "I'm upset because I've fallen in love with you too!"

Chapter 23

Parker swept her into his arms. "Oh, Bliss, this isn't terrible. Love is always a good thing." He kissed her enthusiastically, and then pulled away to look at her, as if checking to see if she were really there.

As he held her, she began to cry. "Not when it ends in heartache."

He wiped away her tears. "Who says it has to end in heartache?"

"You just said that's why you couldn't make love to me, because you couldn't bear the pain of walking away."

"That was before I knew you loved me too." He took her hand and held it to his heart. "When love is shared, that makes it indomitable."

"But what are we going to do, Parker? I've only a few more months here then I have to leave."

His thumb stroked her hand. "Perhaps I can lock you inside the lighthouse like my own Rapunzel."

"Or you could leave Cape Destiny to be with me," she said.

"Oh, Bliss, there's nothing more I'd like than to be with you, but if I left this place," he said, sweeping his hand toward the shimmering sound before them, "you'd only be getting half my heart because the rest of it would be left here."

She sighed and hugged her knees to her chest. "So then it is hopeless."

He put his arm around her. "For a woman whose motto is 'moving heaven and earth' and who's accustomed to doing the impossible like relocating lighthouses, you sure get discouraged easily."

"Well, how am I supposed to act?"

"Look, Bliss. All I know is that I love you, and that's something I'm not going to be sorry for. I realize we don't know where our love will lead us, so I propose that we take this slowly and be honest with each other about everything——our feeling and fears, hopes for the future—then I believe things will work out."

"I wish I could believe that."

He chuckled and kissed her hand, too joyous from being in love again to be gloomy. "O, ye, of little faith. Don't know if you have much of a religious background, Bliss, but round here every respectable boy is schooled in the Bible. And if I recall my scriptures right, there's a verse that goes something like 'if you have faith the size of a mustard seed . . .'"

Bliss chimed in, "I went to Catholic school for 12 years. 'You can move mountains.'"

Parker kissed the tip of her nose, "Or at least lighthouses."

*****

The next four days were very hectic, as Bliss was busy finalizing the bid for the Old Coast Guard Station. She was so absorbed she'd barely seen Parker and hadn't found the right time to ask a question that had been nagging at her ever since the Fourth of July. How had Parker's wife died?

With the bid on Nancy's desk for final revisions, Bliss sat at her own desk, poring over their budget. Things were tight. The troublesome earthmover had died, and they'd been forced to rent another. The lost time and added expense left Bliss with the uneasy knowledge that if another costly problem cropped up, they could be in serious financial difficulty. Then she might have to take Parker up on his offer to live in the lighthouse.

For a moment, she left her problems and allowed herself to imagine what it would be like to live with Parker in the Keeper's House. Then reality intruded on her fantasy. Certainly, Cape Destiny was beautiful, but she'd never lived in one place for longer than a few years. Her father had grown up in Pittsburgh, and after bouncing around as military brat, she decided to settle in his hometown. She just couldn't envision herself existing on this thin strip of land isolated by water. Parker's roots were here, but hers weren't.

And what would she do about her business? With the aid of technology, she could run it from here, but what about the others? Nancy's whole life was invested in Sherman Engineering. And the few employees back in Pittsburgh? She owed them more stability than to relocate the firm for the sake of her love life. What was she going to do? She sighed heavily. Maybe this was the curse of Cape Destiny—doomed love.

She tossed the report aside. "I know what I'll do. I'm going to win that other contract, and when things calm down, perhaps Parker's prediction will have come to fruition. Perhaps the impossible will become possible."

Bliss was glad that Nancy didn't have access to the financial reports. Over the Fourth of July holiday, Nancy's dentist had given her a temporary crown, but for some reason, she was still experiencing pain. Bliss didn't need to add to her surliness by burdening her with their financial woes.

Nancy had left forty-five minutes ago to pick up another case of soap for the move and another prescription for pain pills at the Beach Mart, leaving the office quiet. So when a knock came at the door, Bliss startled, then rose to answer it.

Ever since the vandalism, she'd been jumpy. Cautiously, she peered out the window and was surprised to see Parker. She quickly opened the door, and though he was tan, he was as pale as his white T-shirt. "Parker," she exclaimed. "What's wrong?"

"I hope I'm not interrupting, but I wanted you to look at this." He held out a letter, and he was so upset she could see it shaking in his hand.

"What is it?" she said as she took the paper from him.

"Read it."

The letterhead was very official looking and carried the state seal of North Carolina, Department of the Interior. It was dated July 6 and addressed to Parker J. Swain II.

As Bliss read, her jaw dropped.

Dear Mr. Swain:

It has come to our attention that you are in violation of our agreement with regard to the renovation of the Cape Destiny Lighthouse Keeper's Home. According to our good faith agreement, renovations to the former Keeper's Home and Oil House were to proceed in a timely manner in exchange for use of the property and first claim to it upon completion.

Unfortunately, it has come to my attention, that you have been negligent in your obligations. Therefore, the State of North Carolina has chosen to exercise its right and demand that the renovation of both properties be completed by September 30 or the State of North Carolina shall declare the agreement null and void.

Should you fail to meet that deadline, we ask that you remove all personal effects and desist from the property by no later than noon on October 1, 2005.

If you have any questions or wish to schedule an appeal, please call the office.

Sincerely,
Louisa Barnhart
Secretary

Bliss raised her eyes and looked at Parker, whose face now wore an expression of a gathering storm.

"Oh my, Parker. Can they do this?"

He paced. "I don't understand. I saw Louisa when she came down for your press conference. Gave her a tour of what I've been doing. She seemed pleased and mentioned how relieved her department would be when they could turn the property over to me. She mentioned nothing about any deadline."

"Was there anything about it in your agreement?" Bliss asked.

"Only that stupid clause that said they had the right to revoke it if I didn't make a concerted effort to renovate the place." He stopped and turned to Bliss, his face flaming red making his hair appear to be even blonder. "You've seen me busting my neck up on that roof. I've been working non-stop on the place ever since they turned it over to me. How can they say I'm in default? I don't understand."

But Bliss was beginning to, and she didn't want to face the reality that it may be her fault. "I could have my lawyer back in Pittsburgh look it over."

"This isn't your problem, Bliss."

"At least, let him see if he can sue for your time, labor, and expenses."

He grasped her arm firmly. "I don't care about that. All I care about is the Keeper's House. I can't lose it."

The sound of desperation in his voice alarmed her. She touched his hand. "I'll help you any way I can, Parker." Even though Bliss felt as if she was competing for his affection with the lighthouse, she knew how important it was to him. "I don't want you to lose it either."

Especially since it's all my fault.

He hugged her. "Thank you. It's comforting to have someone listen to my ravings. And I've come to ask a favor. I've already scheduled a hearing for next week. Could you look after Beau for me? I have to drive to Raleigh. He'd be no trouble. I'd ask you to stay in the house, but I'd hate to see you out here by yourself what with the things going on around here. I'll pen him up in the house, and if you could just feed him and see to it that he gets to run a little steam off now and then, I'd appreciate it."

She looked dubiously at Parker. "You and I both know Beau isn't the kind of dog to be locked up by himself. I'll stay with him."

"No, I'd worry about you."

"Look, if Jonathan wanted to hurt me, he would have already done so. He's only trying to intimidate me."

"Yes, but if anything happened to you . . . "

She laughed nervously. "Nothing's going to happen to me. Please let me take care of Beau. And besides I owe you."

"For what?"

She turned and looked away. "Because I'm responsible for placing the Keeper's House in jeopardy?"

"You are? How do you figure that?"

"Jonathan's behind this I'm sure. Remember after you punched him? He said you'd be sorry. Well, this letter is his way of making you pay."

Parker snickered with disbelief.

"I'm serious," Bliss said. "He has connections everywhere and has the resources to make people do what he wants."

"You really believe he'd do this?" Parker asked, shaking the letter.

"Yes, he can be cunning and cruel."

At that moment, Nancy walked in. When she saw Parker, she stiffened.

He folded the letter. "I better let you get back to work. I've taken up enough of your time."

Bliss stepped outside with him and shut the door behind her. She touched Parker's arm. "Please be careful. I know this is Jonathan's handiwork."

"Maybe I should pay him a little visit."

"No! Don't. It'll only make things worse, and besides I don't think he'd ever hurt a woman, but a man . . . I don't know."

"I'm quivering, just thinking about little ol' Jonathan."

"I'm serious, Parker. Promise me you won't go to see him."

"I promise. And when I get back from Raleigh," he lifted her chin and kissed her deeply, his lips lingering over hers as he whispered, "I'm going to really make him green with envy."

Chapter 24

"Looks like hurricane season is underway, folks," Hunter Rowan, the weatherman said cheerily as he opened the ten o'clock report.

Bliss replaced the phone and looked over at the television. Rowan, hair impeccable, was standing in front of a multi-colored map of the United States. His hand motioned to an image of several red-yellow masses of clouds as they came spinning angrily off the African coast as if the continent were a dragon spitting fireballs. Bliss moved closer to the screen.

"Tropical Storm Anita, our first of the season has been churning here two hundred miles off the coast of Cuba for the past week and seems to be losing steam. I expect Anita to be downgraded to a tropical depression later today." He moved his hand and highlighted another mass of clouds in the middle of the Atlantic. "Here we have our third storm of the season, Clotilde. It's too early to tell if Clotilde will intensify. But what the Hurricane Center is really focusing on is this baby." His hand moved to a vortex of clouds off the coast of South Carolina. "The Hurricane Center has just upgraded Blaise from a Tropical Storm to a Level 1 Hurricane."

Bliss didn't have a degree in meteorology, but she didn't need one to detect the well-formed eye. The storm spinning across the Atlantic looked like the blade of a circular saw, poised to wreak destruction on anything in its path. A sickening heaviness settled in the pit of her stomach.

"We'll be monitoring Blaise closely, and I fully expect The National Hurricane Center in Miami to post hurricane watches by tomorrow morning for the area extending from Northern Georgia up to the Chesapeake Bay." A blinking red line highlighted the part of the U.S. where the storm could make landfall. Cape Destiny lay in the center of the red zone. Bliss felt as if someone had painted a bull's-eye on her.

"You may want to keep an eye on Blaise. It could strengthen and move inland, or we hope it makes a big right turn and heads out to sea. These storms are unpredictable, folks, but as always, you should have emergency kits on hand and be prepared for the worst."

Bliss sat on the end of the bed and numbly watched as Hunter Rowan gave the tide schedule. What do I do? Bliss wondered. If Blaise were to make landfall, she'd need to start securing the work site, stabilizing the lighthouse, moving out sensitive equipment, and evacuating the crew.

She didn't want to go to all that trouble if it proved unnecessary. The expense and loss of time would be another burden, one that would break her.

She thought the wisest course would be to come up with a plan and estimate how long it would take to evacuate and secure the site. Tomorrow, when she moved into Parker's house, she'd get his opinion on what he thought this storm would do.

She reached for her microrecorder, but then remembered she had a more pressing and distasteful matter to attend to.

Taking a deep breath as a tonic to boost her confidence, she picked up the phone and punched in the numbers.

"What? You get tired of John Boy Walton?" Jonathan asked when he heard Bliss's voice.

She told herself not to lose it. She had called to make things better not exacerbate his wrath. Ignoring his remark, she said

146

sweetly, "I need to talk to you. I'm asking you to call off your dogs."

"Don't know what you're talking about, sweetheart."

How like him to play innocent. "You're—" her voiced sounded much too strident; she lowered the pitch and began again. "You're denying that you're out to get Parker Swain."

"Bliss, Bliss, Bliss," he said patronizingly. "Why do you always think ill of me?"

The image of him with Laura, her personal trainer, in their bed flashed in her mind. That's why, bastard, she thought.

"Look, I know what you're doing to him, and I'm asking you to please stop it."

He chuckled derisively. "And I know what *you're doing* to him."

Anger flared in her, and she struggled to maintain control. "All I'm asking is that you don't take your anger for me out on him. Don't punish Parker by taking away his house. Call whoever you've leaned on at the state and tell them to lay off."

Jonathan was silent for a moment. "What are you talking about?"

"Oh, don't play innocent with me. You and I both know damn well that you're responsible for the state threatening to take back the Keeper's House from Parker?"

"You think I'd do that?"

"Who else?" Bliss said sharply.

She could hear him breathing and almost the wheels turning in his devious mind. "OK," he said, "I'll see what I can do, but I want something in return."

Bliss gulped and braced herself.

"I want you to drop your bid for the Coast Guard Station project," he said.

"What? You're crazy!" With the precarious state of Sherman Engineering's finances there was no way she could withdraw her bid. She needed this contract.

"Am I? You and I both know you're too stupid to run a company. Why don't you come back and team up with me. It'd benefit both of us. I could be in the background. The silent partner. You could get the contracts being a minority, handicapped woman."

A bomb of rage exploded in her, unleashing a mushroom cloud of hate. "Handicapped? Stupid? Here's how stupid I am,

147

Jonathan. I'm so stupid I dumped you, won the biggest engineering contract of the decade, and I'm going to be awarded the Coast Guard Project. Oh, and by the way, you were right about something. I am Parker Swain's lover. In fact, I'm moving into his house tomorrow so we can make insane, sweaty, animal love whenever we please. And just for your information, Jonathan, let me tell you that until I met Parker Swain, I'd assumed that The Cape Destiny Lighthouse was the largest structure rising on the Atlantic Coast. Thank God I canned you, or I'd never have known what it feels like to be loved by a real man and not some puny, poor excuse like you." She slammed the phone back into its cradle.

*****

The next morning, after Bliss made sure that Nancy had mailed the bid for the Coast Guard Station, Randy brought a portable television inside the trailer and he, Bliss, and Nancy stood in front of it sipping their coffee, concern etched on all their faces.

While Hunter Rowan gave the forecast, a red banner scrolled across the bottom of the screen. It was a hurricane watch, alerting a stretch of the coast from South Carolina to Virginia to keep a weather eye, as the path of Hurricane Blaise was still not certain.

Randy pursed his lips and looked at Bliss. "What do you think we ought to do?"

Bliss sighed. "I wish they'd be more specific as to where and when it's going to make landfall. I hate to close up shop for nothing."

Nancy pointed at the screen. "The meteorologist said they'd probably know more by this afternoon, when they send up storm chasers. How long do you think it would take to move everything out?"

"A good thirty-six hours," Bliss said.

Randy looked at his wristwatch and made mental calculations. "We still have some leeway. Just a suggestion. Why doesn't Nancy investigate some storage places inland where we could move the heavy equipment in case we need to."

Bliss walked to the window and peered out. The sky was peacefully blue. She couldn't believe that a monster storm was churning a few hundred miles off the coast. What little she could see of the beach revealed that the sea was choppy.

She turned and looked at Randy. "Let's shut down and dismantle the sensitive equipment and stand by, ready to get it out of here if need be."

All day Bliss monitored the weather, and by the end of the workday, the storm system had made no progress; it had stalled 150 miles off shore.

Before everyone left for the day, Randy called all the crew together and had them leave phone numbers where they could be reached in case the storm began to move inland through the night.

Bliss took the paper and hesitated before she spoke. "I won't be at the hotel tonight if you try to reach me, Nancy. I'm staying at Parker's."

She saw Nancy stiffen and the corners of Randy's mouth quirk ever so slightly.

"It's not what you think. Parker has to go out of town over night. I offered to take care of Beau." She hadn't told Nancy about Parker's letter because it was none of her business.

"You're too busy to be bothered with taking care of a dog," Nancy said. "Why doesn't he just lock it in the house, and get someone to feed it?"

"That's what he suggested," Bliss explained. "But think of poor Beau, cooped up by himself. It's only one night, and besides, I'm getting a little sick of seeing the same four walls of my hotel room."

Randy held the phone number sheet. "So if I need you, how do I get hold of you?"

"I'll give you Parker's number and, of course, I'll leave my cell phone on."

"Well, let's hope this bugger dissipates," Randy said as he walked out the door, "and we can all get back to work."

After Randy left, Nancy frowned at Bliss. "I don't like you staying out here all by yourself. I'll stay with you."

No offense to Nancy, but Bliss was looking forward to sitting on Parker's back porch and unwinding with a glass of wine. Bliss touched Nancy's shoulder. "Don't be silly. You don't like dogs and besides, I'll be fine. People are concerned about the hurricane. No one is going to bother with me."

Nancy seemed unconvinced.

"I'll be fine," Bliss said as she ushered Nancy to the door. "Go home. Get a good night's sleep, because if this storm heads inland, we're going to be very busy tomorrow."

Chapter 25

Bliss locked the trailer and headed across the lawn toward Parker's. Midway there, Beau came bounding toward her. She knelt and petted him. "Looks like you and I are going to be roomies." Beau slurped her cheek. She walked up onto the porch and knocked on the screen door.

"Come on in," Parker called.

Bliss opened it and walked down the hall. "I'm in the living room," he said.

When she walked into the room, her heart leaped in her chest. She noticed it was doing that every time she came near him. He was dressed in navy shorts and printed golf shirt, and he smelled like soap and aftershave. He must have just taken a shower because the tips of his hair were still wet and clung in darker spikes. He was zipping a suitcase that was lying on the couch.

He glanced up at her. The muscles around his brown eyes were taut. "How's it going?" Bliss asked tentatively.

He straightened and set the case on the floor. "Wish I didn't have to inconvenience you."

"You're not. I'm happy to do it." She ruffled the coat of Beau, who stood next to her. "And besides, it's probably best that I'm close to the site what with Blaise offshore." She frowned. "You've lived here all your life. Do you think it'll make landfall, Parker?"

He put his hands on his hips. "We might get some heavy rain and such, maybe some wind. Chances are slim that it'll make a direct hit here. But if things should deteriorate, I want you and Beau to high-tail it out of here."

Bliss scowled. "I wish I knew what it was going to do."

"Well, I have a hurricane kit I keep on hand. I'll show you where it is. Has a flashlight, in case the power goes out. Has a radio too. You can monitor it to hear if an evacuation is called."

Parker took her to a pantry in the kitchen near the door to the back porch. He opened it, pulled on a chain, lighting an overhead bulb. The austere glow revealed several boxes stacked on shelves. Bliss's eye snagged on a rifle propped in the corner. He pulled one of the boxes off the shelf and opened the flap. Blankets were folded inside. "Wrong one." Opening another, he moved a few cans of tuna aside then pulled out the radio. "This is a weather one. Gives updates on a special channel. There's more batteries."

"What's the gun for?" Bliss asked. "To stop looters?"

"Hunting. Protection, I guess," Parker said. "It's the South, Bliss, everybody has a gun down here. Don't worry the shells are on that upper shelf."

"I know about guns. I know how to shoot. My father was military and taught me."

Parker got her acquainted with the house, where he kept Beau's dog food, the clean towels, and the keys to the place. Then he walked her into his room. A large bay window faced the sound. And Bliss imagined lying in bed and watching the lights of boats bobbing on the water.

Parker moved toward the bed. "I bought some new sheets for you."

Bliss was touched. "You didn't have to go to so much trouble."

"Mine were kind of threadbare and plaid. I just couldn't imagine you lying on them."

152

Bliss didn't know why she felt warm all of a sudden. Perhaps it was the realization that Parker had been thinking about her sleeping in his bed.

He lifted the edge of the quilt. "They're blue. I thought the color would be restful, and your dark hair would look lovely against the pillow case."

Bliss tried to contain her smile and walked toward the window. She watched a parasailor being flown like a kite. "This view will spoil me. I might not want to leave."

Parker came from behind and placed a hand on her shoulder. Her kissed her neck. "That would be fine with me."

She moved away. "Well, neither of us will be able to stay if you don't go. Do you have everything ready to present your case?"

"Yes, I got the pictures back this morning of all the work I've done, and I spent the whole afternoon getting things in order. You've been such a help."

"I wish I could be more of one, but I seem to keep making things worse for you."

"What do you mean?" Parker asked.

Bliss turned toward him. "I called Jonathan last night and asked him to lay off you."

Parker raised an eyebrow.

"He accused me of being incompetent and of having an affair with you." Her voice trailed off. "I lost my temper and said things I shouldn't have."

"Like what?"

Bliss lowered her head. "He had me so angry, I told him I was moving in with you." She hesitated then said quickly, "And I kind of exaggerated about you."

"What did you exaggerate?"

Bliss felt herself blushing as she stumbled for words. "Your manhood."

"My manhood?" Parker asked looking puzzled and amused at the same time. "What exactly did you say?"

She squeezed her eyes closed. "If you must know, I said I moved out here so we could make wild animal love and. . ." She looked at him sheepishly. "I said the lighthouse wasn't the largest structure rising on Cape Destiny."

Parker whistled and laughed.

"He became furious," Bliss said. "I'm sorry. Don't be angry that I made things even worse."

Before she knew it, Parker had scooped her up in a big hug and was laughing. "Oh, Bliss, how can I be angry after being complimented like that."

"I feel terrible, Parker. I'm the reason this happened. He's taking his anger for me out on you."

He hugged her tightly. "And that's the way I want to keep it. I saw what an idiot he was. I can handle him, but I don't want him coming anywhere near you."

"Oh, I'm not afraid of him," Bliss said, trying to act the independent, confident woman. "I feel terrible that you got caught up in our feud."

He kissed her on top of her head. "I don't. Not when my honor is being defended so spectacularly. Perhaps when I get back, I can make those boasts come true."

Bliss couldn't bear thinking what it would be like to make love to Parker, when she knew the brief moment of pleasure would lead to unimaginable heartache. She pulled away. "You better get going."

She walked out of his room, and he followed her down the stairs. Picking up his suitcase, Parker headed out the front door, with Beau close at his heels. The evening sun cast a warm, peachy glow on everything and fired Parker's hair with flecks of gold. The ends of his hair had dried in loose curls. His handsome face made her weak with desire. Looking away, she noticed the petunias wilting in the sun. "Do you need me to water your flowers?" she asked.

He started toward the truck. "Oh, you're so busy. Don't worry about them. I'll only be gone a day. I think they'll survive."

Bliss watched him unlock the door with the sense that maybe she'd not survive his absence.

He stowed the suitcase on the floor in front of the passenger's seat and shut the door.

"You be good for Bliss now, you hear," he said as he bent and held Beau's muzzle. When Parker hugged the dog, Bliss felt her heart melt. Parker was undeniably a virile, handsome man, but sometimes, glimpses of the boy in him rose and made her want to protect and mother him.

He stood and studied Bliss's face like he was trying to memorize her. She met his gaze as he touched her cheek. "Thanks again, Bliss."

154

"Good luck, Parker."

He tilted her head back and planted a brief but hot kiss on her lips. "I'll call you."

He got in the truck and pulled away. Bliss closed her eyes, feeling his kiss lingering on her lips, and silently prayed that things would work out for Parker. And for her.

Sighing, she strolled up the path, her cotton sundress skimming her legs, Beau by her side. Before leaving the woods, she picked up a stick, and when they came to the clearing, she threw it. Beau barked and headed after it.

Bliss walked over and took a seat on the porch step and for the next ten minutes she and Beau played fetch. The last time he retrieved it, he dropped it at her feet and then proceeded to lick her bare legs. Bliss giggled. She'd been cooped up so long in the hotel it felt wonderful to have so much room all to herself.

"Let's make dinner," she said, as she rose and opened the screen door, feeling like a teenager left home while the parents went out of town.

But instead of throwing a party, Bliss decided to cook. She opened Parker's cabinets and began to root around. Thoughtfully, he'd stocked the shelves. She found a box of penne pasta and decided some comfort food was in order. Filling a pot with water, she set it on the stove to boil. Beau followed her outside while she raided Parker's garden for a red pepper, some beans, a plump tomato, and a small zucchini. After cleaning and chopping the vegetables, she put them into a pan with some hot olive oil, sautéing them and then tossed them over the pasta.

Taking the bowl, she headed out to the back porch where she sat on the porch swing. She savored the fresh vegetables, tender pasta, and the way the sun blazed as it set over the watery horizon.

After cleaning up the kitchen, she planned to take a long, leisurely bath in that old claw-footed tub, this time without clothes.

As darkness fell, Bliss went into the kitchen. She placed her bowl in the sink with the dirty pots and pans. Beau, who had remained out on the porch, woofed, and Bliss heard him scratching the screen door.

"You need to go out, boy?" she said as she unlatched the door and held it open. He meandered over to the brush then disappeared into the blackness. "Now don't you get lost, Beau."

She went back inside and finished the dishes. Gathering up the garbage, she headed for the cans along side the house. "Beau!"

she called as she put the lid on the can. "Beau! Come on." She wanted to bring him in before she took her bath.

"Beau," she clapped her hands then heard rustling in the brush behind her. She turned around and gasped. *Jonathan!* He was standing there, the light from the kitchen shining on his black hair making it gleam like patent leather.

"Hello, Bliss," he said flatly, his tone setting her on edge.

Her heart hammering, Bliss said, "You better leave before Parker comes out and finds you."

A smile stretched across his face. He reached out to touch her, and she flinched. "Bliss, why so jumpy?" He moved closer. "You never used to be afraid of me."

She hadn't been afraid of him before, but she sensed something had changed in him, revealing a side she'd never known. Before she could move, he pressed her against the house and put his lips on hers. They were cool and slick and made her think of worms.

She pushed him away and ran for the porch. "Parker! Parker!" she yelled as she ran up the steps, hoping her bluff would scare him off. She scrambled to open the door and ran inside. As she was about to latch it behind her, his face appeared at the screen and she screamed.

He laughed wickedly. "You must be losing it, Bliss. Don't you remember? You told me Parker was going out of town."

Her fingers were shaking so badly she had difficulty getting the hook into the eye. Bliss, her mouth dry, ran across the porch. Hearing the sound of splintering wood behind her, she glanced over her shoulder and saw Jonathan pulling on the door and tearing the latch from the frame.

Jonathan ripped open the door, dislodging one of the hinges. She stumbled over the threshold leading into the kitchen and fell. Pain registered briefly, but was overridden by her survival instinct. *Get up! Get away!*

As she scrambled to her feet, Jonathan seized her from behind. Grabbing her by the waist, he spun her around and slammed her hard against the wall. Her brain felt as if it had been dislodged.

When her mind settled, she realized that Jonathan's cold hands were pawing her. He panted in her ear. "I'll make you remember what a real man is like," he growled. "And not some Southern-fried fairy."

"No, Jonathan," she commanded as she beat at his chest. He hit her. The sound of the slap of his palm meeting her cheek rang in her ears. Stunned, her legs sagged. He roughly stood her up against the wall and tore open her sundress.

Bliss's mind raced yet things seemed to be happening in slow motion, so much so that she felt as if she were observing herself. *This is Jonathan? The man I'd married? Had once loved? How could he do this?*

He smashed his lips against her, sticking his tongue into her mouth. She gagged on it. Then anger that he dare treat her this way boiled over in her and supercharged her with strength.

She sunk her teeth into his tongue and tasted his metallic blood. Taking her by the shoulders, once again, he slammed her against the wall so she would release his tongue. Dazed, she let go. When he grabbed his mouth, she suddenly realized she was free of him and bolted into the house.

Where could she hide? Seeing the pantry, she dashed inside. Bliss fumbled around, looking for a lock but there wasn't any. Feeling around for something to hit him with, her hands came upon the rifle.

Bliss trembled as she picked it up. Then desperately she searched for the shells. When she heard him outside the door, she froze.

Jonathan swung open the door, and his eyes widened as he stared down the barrel of the rifle.

Bliss slowly moved out of the closet, her eyes and the gun trained on him. She aimed the barrel at his chest, hoping he wouldn't test her with an unloaded gun. Blood trickled out the side of his mouth; that red was the only color in his face.

He slowly backed away. "Don't be ridiculous, Bliss. You know you'd never shoot me."

She continued to walk, forcing him across the porch. "That's what you think," she said her voice shaky.

"I'd like to confess something before you do away with me. If you're expecting a call from Parker, you can forget about it."

"Why?" Bliss asked, fearing what he would tell her.

He smirked. "Let's just say I took care of him."

Bliss's heart lurched at the thought that Parker could be dead and distracted her attention. In that instant, Jonathan grabbed the barrel of the gun and wrenched it away from her.

She screamed and dodged as he swung the butt at her. Then suddenly Jonathan lunged at her and fell to the floor as Beau leaped at his back and knocked him over. Beau, his teeth bared, began to maul Jonathan, who tried to rise and fend off the dog.

Bliss picked up the gun. With Beau tearing at Jonathan, he stumbled down the steps and out into the yard.

"For god's sake call him off, Bliss," Jonathan begged.

Bliss, the gun steady on him, cried, "Beau, come here." Jonathan, his clothes tattered and covered with blood, rose. Bliss glared at him. "Get out of here. And don't ever come back unless you want to die!"

Jonathan staggered away and disappeared into the darkness.

Bliss lowered the gun, and crying, went and took Beau by the collar and hustled him back into the house. After locking the door, she ran back into the pantry and loaded the rifle. Then after checking every window, she sank to the floor, shaking and began to sob.

As Beau licked her all over, she clung to him, the gun, and the hope that Jonathan was lying about Parker.

Chapter 26

Bliss watched the clock. It was too early for Parker to have arrived in Raleigh. Surely, Jonathan was only trying to frighten her. He's not capable of murder, she reassured herself. Then as she began to ache, she realized that she hadn't thought him capable of rape either.

She picked up the phone but it was dead. Jonathan must have cut the wires. She retrieved her cell phone and dialed the number of the Hampton Inn, but the desk clerk refused, for reasons of privacy, to reveal whether Parker had registered. She just wanted to hear his voice to know that he was safe.

Bliss contemplated calling Officer Bevans, but she hated to drag the police into such a personal matter. She didn't want to be the subject of the headlines in tomorrow's *Island Courier*. She was trying to establish Sherman Engineering as the premier civil engineering firm in the United States and win the Coast Guard Station bid. A scandal would undermine everything.

No, she wouldn't involve the law, but she made sure the rifle was never out of reach in case Jonathan decided to test whether she was capable of killing him.

Her injuries began to pain her. She shuffled up the stairs to the bathroom to raid Parker's medicine chest for any pain relievers. When she saw her face in the mirror, her hand flew to her mouth as she covered a small cry. Propping the gun in the corner, she came back to the medicine chest mirror and saw that a red welt, in the shape of a palm, had risen across her cheek. Blood stained her mouth and chin. She searched for cuts to her lip, but concluded that it must have been Jonathan's blood. She quickly splashed water on it; she wanted nothing of his defiling her.

Taking a washcloth, she ran it under cool water and put it on the welt, relieving some of the sting. Bliss felt some sense of victory that she'd been able to defend herself.

The back of her head ached. A tender lump where her skull had slammed into the wall had risen. New pains announced themselves as she pulled off the torn dress. Scratches marked her breast. She turned around and looked over her shoulder. Abrasions and red marks—what she knew would soon become bruises—were visible across her upper back.

Bliss opened Parker's medicine cabinet. She felt like she was invading his privacy but reasoned that she wasn't snooping. She truly did need to be in there. There was nothing interesting inside, no prescriptions that revealed a psychiatric disorder, or poor health. All she found were common first aid items—Band-Aids, antiseptic cream, eye drops. Taking out some ibuprofen, she swallowed the largest advisable dose with the hope of mitigating the pain.

Keeping Beau in the bathroom for protection, she stripped off the rest of her clothes and stood under the warm water of his shower and cried again.

Then after wrapping a towel around herself and retrieving the gun, she went to Parker's room. She didn't turn on the light. Instead, she crossed to the bay window and looked out warily into the darkness, afraid that she would see Jonathan. As she rested her head against the cool window pane, all she saw were the distant lights of a few boats bobbing on the water and those of Wingina docked on the opposite shore.

In Parker's dresser she found another of his T-shirts. She smelled it. A mixture of ocean air, and laundry detergent filled her nose, and when she pulled the shirt over her head, the soft cotton enveloped her battered flesh and made Parker seem close. *Oh, please let him be OK.*

Carrying the rifle, she made her way down to the kitchen with Beau following closer than a shadow. She leaned the gun against the wall, and as she was wrapping some ice up in a tea towel to apply to her face, her cell phone rang, startling her as if someone had splashed her with scalding water.

Trembling, she picked it up and said hello.

"Bliss." It was Parker. She was so relieved, she nearly started to cry.

"Bliss, are you there?"

"Yes, I'm here."

"Everything OK? I tried the phone to the house, but it's not working."

"Oh, everything is fine. Maybe with the approaching storm the service has gone out," she lied not to worry him. And now that she knew he was safe, she was sure that things would be fine.

"Good. Made it here in one piece. Got something to eat, and I was watching the weather and all the stations are predicting that Blaise is likely to come ashore within the next day or so. You've still got plenty of time, but I think it wise that tomorrow when you go to work, you start making plans to safeguard the site and your equipment."

"Where do they think it's going to make landfall?"

"They're not sure, but even if we get a glancing blow, the way things are shaping up, you'll still need to evacuate. I wouldn't be surprised if they don't put up a voluntary evacuation for tourists tomorrow."

"What about the house, Parker? You want me to do anything?"

"No, you concentrate on taking care of your stuff. My meeting is first thing in the morning. I'll leave right after it. I should get there late in the afternoon. That'll still give me plenty of time to board up and secure things. So how are things going there?"

"Fine," Bliss said, catching a glimpse of herself in the kitchen window. Even in that dim reflection she could see her face was red. "Beau is keeping me company, and I just finished taking a long, hot bath."

"How's it there?" she asked.

"Small and quiet. Not used to being cooped up in such a tiny room. And my view is exceptional. A parking lot and the interstate. Wish I were back home."

I wish you were too. Bliss smiled. "Well, right now I'm looking out at a slice of moon surrounded by silver tinged clouds, and it's all reflecting off the water."

"I'm jealous," Parker said playfully.

"It's such a calm and beautiful night, Parker, I find it hard to believe that there's a hurricane out there."

"Well," Parker sighed. "Isn't that the way it is with most everything in life. You're usually cruising along thinking things are just swell and then a storm comes and slaps you silly."

She thought of this evening, how she'd never expected to be attacked by Jonathan. Sadly she said, "Yes, I guess that's true."

"Well, best let you get some rest. You'll have a busy day tomorrow."

"Good luck with the meeting, Parker."

"Thanks. Sleep tight."

"You too, she said.

Sleep tight? Bliss mused as she hung up the phone. With these bruises, Jonathan lurking, my financial problems, and a hurricane making a beeline for Cape Destiny, Bliss wondered if she'd be able to sleep at all.

Chapter 27

Bliss woke and tried to shift her legs and found that she couldn't. Alarmed that perhaps Jonathan's attack had done more damage than she thought, she sat up and discovered that Beau had gone to sleep on top of her.

"Beau," Bliss called and jerked her legs. Then every part of her body spiked with pain.

He stirred, then walked up the bed, and began to slather her with kisses. "Oh, Beau," she cried, wincing and giggling at the same time. Even her face hurt when his tongue met her cheek.

Groaning, she rolled out from under him. He sat beside her and looked into her face. Putting her arm around him, she rested her head against his shoulder. He was warm, and his heart beat rhythmically. "How am I ever going to go to work like this, Beau?"

He yammered sympathetically.

"You're so understanding. Maybe I should forget about men and get a friend like you." She marshaled her strength and bit her lip as she stood. Hobbling into the bathroom, she took another dose of pain relievers. The welt had faded to a dull red, but it was still prominent and swollen. *How can I go to work looking like this?*

After letting Beau out, she went into the bathroom and stripped off the T-shirt. Her body didn't look much better than her face. But at least she could cover those bruises and cuts with clothing. She stepped into the shower, hoping the warm water would loosen her up.

After dressing in khaki pants and a long sleeved shirt to cover the bruises, she tried to conceal the mark on her cheek with makeup, but it didn't help much. Bliss made a bowl of cereal, fed Beau, and tidied up after herself. Every movement made her body scream with pain.

She petted Beau, who followed her to the door. "I'll be back later," she said and then locked the forlorn looking dog inside.

Slowly, she made her way down the porch steps. The sun was blazing. She rolled up the cuffs of the shirt and eyed the sky. It was still a peaceful shade of blue. How much time did she have before the hammer fell?

When she walked into the office, Nancy was already there. "You're here bright and early," Bliss said sounding more energetic than she felt. She tried to keep the bruised side of her face away from Nancy's line of sight.

"I figured with this storm looming, I better get here and start the ball rolling. I called Randy last night and told him to shift from moving to evacuation. I located a storage facility about fifty miles inland that can house the equipment."

"Great," Bliss said, "but before we move out the equipment, our first concern has to be securing the lighthouse. When Randy gets here, we'll see what he thinks is the best way to do that."

When he arrived a few minutes later, he and Bliss decided to remove as much of the sensitive equipment as possible and ship it out immediately to the storage facility. Then he would have the crew use the earthmovers to pile sand up around the base of the lighthouse. The only consolation was that the lighthouse was now located further inland, a much safer location, than it had been only a few weeks ago.

While the crew took care of the work site, she and Nancy decided to remove as much of the office equipment as possible. "I'll take the computer and put it in my car," Nancy said. Bliss opened the file cabinet and began to stack folders on top of it.

"Can you give me a hand here, Bliss," Nancy called with her upper body trapped between the computer and the wall.

164

Bliss strode over and hoped Nancy didn't want her to lift any of the components, as just the movement of unloading the file cabinet made her muscles screech with pain.

"See that gray cable attached to the printer," Nancy said. "Can you pull on it? This is a tangle of wires back here."

When Bliss turned to reach for the cable, she heard Nancy inhale sharply. "My God, Bliss, what's wrong with your face?"

Instinctively, Bliss turned away. "Nothing."

Nancy rose and came to take a closer look. "Nothing? Good Lord, your face is all swollen. What happened?"

"I said nothing."

Nancy put her hands on her hips and eyed her skeptically. Bliss felt like a child whose mother was demanding an explanation for something she'd done naughty on the playground. "What happened?"

Bliss sighed and lowered her eyes. "Don't be alarmed because I'm fine, but Jonathan came out to the house last night."

Nancy's eyes focused on the bruise and her body stiffened. "Jonathan did that to you?" Nancy touched Bliss's cheek and she winced. "Your neck is bruised too."

"Just what did he do to you?"

Bliss felt tears welling in her eyes. "I was in the yard letting Beau out when he sneaked up on me." Bliss told her how he had roughed her up and how she and Beau had fended him off. By the time she was done, she was sobbing and shaking.

Nancy, her face grim, went to the door and locked it. "Let me see if you have any other injuries." She made Bliss pull up her shirt.

"That black-hearted bastard," Nancy snapped. "I'm calling the police."

"No!" Bliss said. "I don't want this to be all over the papers. It'll jeopardize our reputation and our bid for the Coast Guard Station project."

"You need to see a doctor."

Bliss pulled down her shirt. "No, I'm fine."

"But he must be stopped," Nancy slapped the desk. "He can't get away with this."

"Let's worry about him later," Bliss said, touched that Nancy was so concerned, "we've got to prepare for this hurricane."

Nancy bit her lip. "Why do Laveres think they can always have it their way?"

165

"Well, we're going to make sure he doesn't have it his way," Bliss said. "We're going to move this lighthouse and win that contract."

*****

At nine, a mandatory evacuation order was issued. Officer Bevans rode out to let Bliss know about it.

"Have you heard from Parker?" he asked, curiously eyeing her face. "Did he leave any instructions for what to do with the house?"

"No, but I'm going to go over there as soon as I'm done here and try to prep the Keeper's House. His meeting is scheduled for ten. I suppose I'll hear from him afterward."

"Does he plan on coming back?"

"I think so."

"I hope he doesn't have any trouble. Right now they're predicting things will start to get hairy near dinner."

"We'll be out of here by then," Nancy said.

"Good," Wayne Bevans said. "I have to stay here, but I'm not looking forward to it." He stepped closer toward Bliss. "Hope you don't think I'm nosy, but what happened to your face?"

"Oh . . . um," she stammered, "tripped on my way to the Explorer while I was carrying some boxes. I'm OK."

"Well, be careful and keep safe," he said as he dipped his head and headed for the door.

*****

Near eleven Nancy answered the phone. "Yes, I'll get her." She pressed the hold button. "It's Parker."

Bliss took a seat at her desk. "Parker," she said, "how did it go?"

"They've postponed the meeting until two this afternoon. This hurricane has everyone here at the capital in a tizzy."

"I suppose you've heard they've ordered a mandatory evacuation?" Bliss asked.

"Yes, and I want you to get off the cape as soon as possible."

"Is there anything you want me to do for your house?"

"No, as soon as I get out of this meeting, I'm coming back to batten the hatches."

"Parker, if it gets nasty out there, stay put. I'm going to have some of my crew, board up your windows and make sure things are secured. I'll take Beau and head inland. Nancy has already booked us some rooms in Elizabeth City."

"Thanks, Bliss," Parker said, "and promise me you'll get out of there quickly.

"I will. Call me after the meeting."

"If the phone lines are still working."

"Good luck, Parker."

Bliss turned on the portable TV and watched the projected trajectory of Blaise. It appeared as though it was heading straight for Cape Destiny. She doubled her pace of cleaning out the office even though she ached all over.

After working through lunch, she headed up to Parker's house with Stu and two other crewmembers. With a nail gun, they boarded up the windows of the Keeper's House in little over an hour.

As she was about to go inside and attend to Beau, she saw Nancy jogging across the lawn, a piece of paper in hand. The wind was whipping her hair and clothing.

Alarmed, Bliss came walking down the steps to meet her.

"Oh, this is an outrage," Nancy said.

"What? What is it?"

"Right before I disconnected the machine, this came in over the fax. They've awarded the Coast Guard contract to Jonathan."

Bliss's heart sank to the pit of her stomach. "Already? They've only closed the bidding. They couldn't have even evaluated our proposal. What a farce! He probably called in a favor." She took the letter from Nancy's hand.

Sitting on the porch steps, she read the faxed press release. "No wonder he was so cocky," she said. "He knew all along that he had it in the bag."

"Our proposal had to be much better than his. He probably pulled some strings."

Probably with the same person he used to try to get the Keeper's House from Parker, thought Bliss.

Nancy looked out to sea where the sky was growing increasingly cloudy. As the wind blew her hair, she glared. "Laveres are born manipulators."

Chapter 28

Bliss stood. "Well, no sense fretting about it now. If we don't get this area secured, we won't have to worry about bidding on anything."

"I only have a few more boxes to move to the car, and then that's about all we can do," Nancy said.

"How's Randy coming along?"

"They're winding up too. They've buried the base of the lighthouse, and he sent the heavy equipment out of here about an hour ago."

As they walked back to the trailer, Bliss noticed that the sky had darkened, and the wind had picked up. A soft drizzle began to fall. She eyed the dark ominous clouds that were rolling in. "Must be the outer bands. Can you imagine what it must have been like down here before weather forecasts, Nancy? Why, you'd be thinking it was another rainstorm and then bam! a hurricane. You'd never know what hit you." Bliss wished life had an early warning system too that could prepare you for its storms.

When they returned to the trailer, Randy was piling sandbags around its base. "I sent the rest of the guys home. There's nothing more we can do around here," he said as he stood and wiped the sweat from his brow. "It's in Mother Nature's hands now. I'm just a little concerned about this trailer. After the wind gets cranking, this thing could take off like a glider."

Bliss looked at Nancy. "Well, we've cleaned anything of value out of it. So if we lose it, we lose it," Bliss said. "Trailers can be replaced. What really worries me is the lighthouse."

Randy gazed up at the towering structure and the clouds seemed to be thickening around it. "Well, it's half way to its new site, and I feel better about it weathering a hurricane where it's sitting now than where it was when we started."

"I hope you're right," Bliss said, raising her voice to be heard above the whipping winds.

Randy put a powerful hand on her shoulder to reassure her, but the pressure pained her battered back. "That baby weighs a ton. Don't worry about it"

A gust of wind buffeted them and sand stung their legs. "Guess we should get out of here," Bliss said, pushing the hair out of her face.

Nancy sprinted up the walk and locked the trailer. They each picked up a box and hustled to the parking lot.

"Need me to haul any of this stuff?" Randy asked as he opened his truck.

"No, I've got room on the back seat," Nancy said.

"Drive safely, you two," Bliss said. "See you at the hotel."

"I'll wait for you, Bliss."

"No, you go, Nancy. I have to get Beau and his things. I'll be right behind you."

"Are you sure?" she said, using her car door as a shield against the gusting wind.

"Go. I'll meet you at the hotel."

Nancy looked at her skeptically.

"I'll be fine."

"You said that last night too."

"I'll be fine," Bliss said emphatically. "I'm just going to get Beau, his food, and lock up. Go."

Rain pelted them and pebbled the lenses of Nancy's glasses with droplets. She took them off and wiped them on the hem of her shirt. "OK, but please be careful."

Nancy closed the door and started her Buick. Bliss, her shirt and pants flapping against her skin, ran to the house.

When she got to the front door, she heard Beau barking wildly. She let herself in and was surprised to see him so wired. Bliss knelt and petted him and spoke into his ear. "It's OK, fella. It's just a bad storm."

Bliss didn't want to tell Nancy, but she was expecting Parker to arrive at any moment. While she waited for him, she went to the closet in the kitchen and took out the weather radio. An evacuation warning repeatedly advised everyone near Crystal Shoals to leave immediately. If Parker didn't soon arrive, she'd have to go. She decided to call his hotel room, but she when she picked up her cell phone, the battery was dead. *Damn, where was the recharger?* In her desk drawer. It was probably in one of the boxes in her car. If the rain let up, she'd go to her car and try to locate it. She hoped Nancy hadn't put it in her car and driven off with it.

As the wind rattled the plywood over the windows, Bliss hoped Parker had stayed at the hotel and nixed the idea of returning to the Cape.

Beau whimpered and encircled her legs. "Better let you out before it gets any worse out there." She opened the door and Beau, looking like a gold streak against the leaden sky and sheeting rain, took off. Wearing only her windbreaker, she fought her way to the car, but failed to find the charger.

Bliss glanced at her watch. They were projecting landfall in another three hours. She wished Parker would get there.

To occupy herself, she hurried back to the house and began to move anything of value to the second floor. When she lifted his toolbox, her muscles cried with pain. It was growing darker, and she turned on the lights. When she saw Beau's dog dish, she realized that she'd forgotten about him.

Concerned, she went to the porch and called, "Beau! Beau!" The wind had become so fierce her words were lost in its howling. Her thin windbreaker offered no protection in this weather. She went back inside and found Parker's slicker hanging on the rack. After pulling it on, she ran down the steps. Fighting the gale, Bliss headed in the direction where Beau had gone. The limbs overhead creaked as the wind ripped through the branches; the trees bowed deeply in deference to the storm's might.

Bliss caught a glimpse of Beau running and followed him down a path she'd never been on before, holding her arm up to shield herself from the biting rain.

Suddenly, the path opened to a small well-tended clearing dotted with tombstones. *The family plot.* She'd seen a cemetery on the survey of the land, but had never been there. How charming she thought to be buried on the property where you'd spent your days. Some of the stones were so old they were nearly crumbling.

"Beau, Beau," she called and in reply, heard a howl coming from the left. She threaded her way through the headstones and found Beau lying on the soggy earth in front of a shiny, new granite slab.

"Beau, come on."

He bayed mournfully, like he was cursing the storm. "Let's go, Beau." When she bent to grab his collar, something caught her eye on the stone—the name engraved on it: PARKER J. SWAIN III, 2001 – 2003.

Her heart ceased beating and the raging storm receded from her senses. She rose and staggered backward in shock.

Oh my God! Parker had a son?

Chapter 29

Bliss touched the wet granite, and began to cry. The wind gusted and blew the hood off her head. Rain lashed her, yet she was numb to it. *Why didn't Parker tell me he had a son? A son who was dead?*

A bolt of lightning split the gray sky with a flash, jerking Bliss back to reality. She pushed her wet, matted hair out of her eyes and looked around for Beau, but he was no where to be seen. "Beau! Come on!" she called, her voice edged with fear as she wiped the rain and tears from her face.

Nancy was right. She was a fool to have become involved with Parker. How could she have trusted him with her heart when he couldn't even trust her with something so important as the fact that he'd been a father?

"Beau!" she cupped her hands around her mouth and yelled louder. *Where did he go? Why wasn't he coming?* She just wanted to get him into the car and leave before Parker arrived.

A mixture of sadness and betrayal enveloped her. She felt pity for Parker that he'd lost his son, yet how could he keep this from her? Especially, when he'd pledged that he'd never hurt her? Didn't he know that secrets hurt too?

"Beau," she called again into the wind. As the shock diminished, a sense of anger rose in her as furious as the storm. *What else is he keeping from me?*

A squall buffeted her and the rain slashed sideways. "It's no use." She began to fight her way back to the house.

When she arrived there, she'd hoped to see Beau waiting for her, but he was not. As she walked into the house, the lights went out. "Oh, great," she groaned, and with her hands out in front of her, she felt her way down the hall. She remembered that Parker kept the flashlight in the buffet.

Bliss carefully made her way into the dining room and opened the drawer. The lights flickered once, twice, and then stayed on. Taking the flashlight, she once again saw Parker's marriage license. Her curiosity getting the best of her, she pulled it out and read it carefully. He'd gotten married seven years ago.

One of the sheets of plywood that she and the crew had nailed over the windows ripped away and flew through the air. Rain beat at the window like BB's. It was time to go.

As she went to return the license, a clipping lying in the drawer captured her attention. Bliss moved away the spare batteries and lifted it out. The edges had begun to yellow. Bliss read the headline: LOCAL MAN HELD FOR MURDER. Beneath the bold black banner was a picture of Parker in handcuffs being lead into a police car. Bliss felt her legs turn to liquid, but she forced herself to read the caption.

Parker Swain, 30, a Cape Destiny native and history teacher at Wingina High School, was arrested today in connection with the death of his wife, Beth Swain.

Bliss's vision dimmed, and she felt as if she were going to faint. Dropping the clipping, she braced herself against the buffet. She was having trouble breathing. As she bent to pick it up, the lights went out again.

Panic filled her. She had to get away. She wanted to get as far away from Cape Destiny as possible. The puzzle pieces all fit now. Parker had been hostile when she came. There was the vandalism. He'd had access to the trailer to spray paint those slurs. He'd shown a propensity for violence when he'd attacked Jonathan. And he'd murdered his wife. Had he also killed his son?

Nancy had warned her. She'd been suspicious of Parker all along. Why hadn't she seen through his charm? Why hadn't she seen through Jonathan's?

Because you are a stupid fool, Bliss.

"Bliss?"

She gasped as every muscle in her body hardened. It was Parker. In the darkness, she fumbled for the drawer, stuffed the clipping inside, and quickly closed it. When a wet, strong hand touched her back, she flinched. As she turned around, her heart pounded against her breastbone. Bliss then realized she was alone in the dark with a murderer.

"I was just looking for a flashlight," she said her voice high and tight.

"What are you still doing here? I'd have thought you'd have left hours ago."

Act normally Bliss, and you can get away from him. "Beau ran off in the storm and won't come back."

Bliss turned the flashlight on him. She wanted to keep him within sight. His hair hung in wet locks, and his windbreaker was dripping. "How long ago?"

"A while ago. I went looking for him, but he takes off whenever I approach. I came back inside to get a flashlight. I've never seen him act this way."

"It's the hurricane. Storms spook him."

"Well," Bliss said, backing away, "I should be leaving. Nancy is waiting at the hotel for me."

"Wait, it's really starting to whip up out there."

"No, I can't. I promised Nancy." She fumbled her way to the front door. She heard Parker coming after her. Bliss ran down the steps. As she started across the lawn, the wind battered her and the rain beat at her, slowing her. "Wait, Bliss," Parker said, as he caught up with her and took her by the arm.

"I can't," she yelled her voice high in the roaring wind, as she wrenched herself free from his grasp.

"Bliss, what's wrong with you? You can't go off by yourself in the storm. There are power lines down everywhere, and when I was coming in, waves were washing over the road."

"I've got to go," she said, tears forming in her eyes and sounding as if she were pleading. She took off running toward her car, her body still aching from the beating she suffered at Jonathan's hands.

Half way down the path, Parker caught up to her and grabbed her from behind. The odor of broken, wet pine branches smelled sickening like a disinfectant. "You're not leaving."

Bliss, trembling, realized that her only hope was to catch him off guard and strike first. She raised the flashlight and swung it at him. He intercepted the blow and wrapped her in a bear hug. As the rains and wind assaulted them, she stared defiantly at him, looking into his dark brown eyes. "I know about you, Parker Swain. And I'm not afraid of you. I'm not going out without a fight."

"What are you talking about?"

"I know you're a murderer."

In the darkness, she felt his arms tighten around her. "Who told you?"

"I found the clip when I got the flashlight," she said calmly masking her terror.

Bliss felt his arms loosen. She backed away wondering if he was toying with her. In any case, she wasn't going to wait to see. She took a step and heard a crack above them like the heavens were splitting in two. They both looked up as a tree limb broke off from the trunk.

He lunged for Bliss, knocking her away before the limb could strike her. Bliss landed on her back, Parker on top of her.

She began to cry. "Please don't kill me."

"Kill you? Why would I kill you?"

"Because of the lighthouse." She scooted away in the mud.

"Would I save you from that limb if I were going to kill you?"

She wanted to believe him. But she'd seen it written in black and white in the paper—he was a murderer.

"Please let me go," she begged.

The trees were creaking. Pine needles shot through the air like darts.

"As much as I want to prove that I won't hurt you, I can't, Bliss," he shouted over the howling wind. "I love you. You'll have to trust me, because there's no way we can leave now. It's too dangerous."

She was trapped in a hurricane with a killer.

"Look back at the road," he yelled. "Trees are down everywhere. You can't get out. We can't get out."

176

She scrambled to her feet and ran, her will to survive blocking the pain. She didn't know where she was going. She just knew she had to get away from him. Looking over her shoulder, she ran toward the beach, into the hurricane. The door peeled off the trailer and sailed like a Frisbee toward her. She fell as she leaped out of its way.

Parker was at her side, panting. "Come on, Bliss. It's too late. Blaise is coming ashore. We have to go into the lighthouse."

"No!"

He scooped her up, and as she struggled to break away, he fought the whipping wind and carried her off. "It's the safest place."

As he trudged up the mound of wet sand that had been pushed around the lighthouse's base to stabilize it, she wondered how he could consider a lighthouse in a hurricane with a killer to be a refuge?

Chapter 30

"Bliss," Parker said, his voice echoing up the dark tower, "climb up to the second landing, we'll ride the hurricane out there. It should be well above the storm surge."

Bliss was shivering now as her wet, muddy clothes stuck to her skin. The lighthouse's thick walls muffled the wind raging outside.

"Go on, Bliss," Parker commanded, handing her the flashlight with which she'd tried to hit him.

She started up the spiral metal stairs, her footsteps ringing hollowly. The air, damp and stale, smelled like a tomb. She looked behind and saw him watching her from the doorway.

"I'm going to get some supplies," he said. "Stay here."

Bliss was a hostage. Where could she go? She'd escape if she could, but there was no way now. She had no choice but to remain.

When she reached the landing, she shined the light around and wondered how they would be able to survive in such a small place. It was nothing more than a crescent of metal grating, only a few square feet of space.

She sat on the cold, hard metal step below the landing. And waited. For what? To be attacked by a killer? For the lighthouse to be engulfed by the sea? Either way she'd be dead by morning. Shivers wracked her, not just from the wet clothing, but the thought of what'd she'd discovered about Parker.

The beam of light slicing through the blackness alerted her that Parker had returned. He closed the door to the lighthouse and began the ascent up the stairs, so weighted down with supplies he looked like a Sherpa readying to scale Mt. Everest. There was no sign of Beau.

Parker was soaked through and his hair was lashed across his face. When he neared her, he stopped, hung the lantern on the railing, set his load on the step below her, and handed a sleeping bag up to her. "Here, spread that out on the floor, Bliss. It'll be warmer and more comfortable than the metal grating."

Perhaps he'd brought something from the house she could use to defend herself, Bliss wondered, as she unrolled the sleeping bag that was wet on the outside and smelled as if it had been stored in an attic.

Parker opened a box and pulled out the weather radio. "Don't know if we'll get reception in here." He switched it on, and it crackled indecipherably. He shut it off. "Guess there's no point anyway. We know it's coming ashore."

Standing two steps below the landing, he looked up at Bliss and his gaze softened. He reached to take her hand, but she kept hers stiffly at her side. "Bliss, I'm not going to hurt you. As soon as we get out of these wet clothes, I'll explain. I didn't kill my wife."

Bliss cowered and watched him warily as if he were an animal waiting to attack. He removed more items from the emergency box. "Here's a blanket," he said as he held out a cotton woven one to her. "Take off your clothes and wrap yourself in it."

"I'm fine."

"You're going to get cold. Take them off and hang them over the railing to dry. I'll turn my back."

Bliss watched him turn and face the wall. She was shivering. She took off the slicker, her boots, and socks then struggled to peel off her shirt and pants. As she was about to remove her panties and bra, she glanced over her shoulder to make sure Parker was not watching and saw him wiggling out of his wet boxers. The light from the lantern fell softly over the hard, sculpted muscles of his back, buttocks, and thighs.

Bliss quickly turned around, stripped off the wet panties and bra, and wrapped the blanket around her. It felt good to be out of the soggy clothes. Holding the blanket tightly around herself, she walked up a few steps and spread her clothing across the metal stairs.

She came back down to the landing, and sat, knees drawn to her chest, huddled in the blanket, resting against the wall. Parker, wrapped in his blanket, came up to the landing and sat next to her. She flinched. "Are you hungry or anything?" he asked? She shook her head no.

Sighing heavily, he crossed his legs, the blanket falling off his shoulders in a puddle in his lap, the medallion around his neck glinting in the lantern light. He touched her gently. "Forget settling in. I can tell that you won't relax until I set everything straight."

He pushed the wet hair off his face, closed his eyes, and with another sigh, rested his head against the wall. "As you already know, Bliss, I was married before. I fell in love with Beth in college, and we were married a year after we graduated. I took a job teaching at Wingina, and she worked as a nurse. When she got pregnant a few years later, that's when I began to dream about restoring the Keeper's House. I wanted it for my child." He turned and looked at Bliss, the soft light of the lantern sparkled in the puddles of tears in his eyes.

"We had a boy, P.J." His voice caught. "I loved the little fella so much and couldn't have been happier. In the summers, when I was out of school, we spent all our free time here playing on the beach. One day in July when he was about two, I brought P.J. to Cape Destiny while Beth was working."

He stared absently as if he were being transported to the past. "He was such a great little guy."

The pang of longing echoing in his voice touched Bliss.

Making fists, he beat them together like he was trying to pound some strength into himself to get through his explanation. "We were sitting under an umbrella, because Beth was fanatical about him not getting any sun. It was a windy day, and he was digging in the sand at my feet near the shoreline, when a gust, uprooted the umbrella and sent it rolling down the beach. I chased it about twenty yards. Beau was just a pup then. He barked and followed after me thinking it was a game. When I turned around and looked back, P.J. was gone." He stopped beating his fists and his voice became somber. "I scanned the beach. Then, I looked toward the water." He was silent for a few seconds then said, "The surf was tossing him like a rag doll."

His voice lowered an octave. "I ran toward him and dove in, but a huge wave came, sucked him out, and then drove him headfirst into the sand." He lowered his head. "Snapped his little neck. He died instantly. Right here on the beach."

Bliss' heart swelled with sympathy for him, and she wanted to reach out and hug him, but that only explained his son's death. What about his wife's? She reminded herself that he was a murderer. "I'm sorry," was the only expression of sympathy she allowed herself.

Cold now, she wrapped the blanket around herself more tightly and watched as Parker sat for several minutes with his eyes closed. Then he wiped his tears away and, once again, spoke, his voice sounding as if calling from a wilderness of pain.

"Beth never forgave me. Oh, she said she knew it was an accident, but that was her head talking. Her heart convicted me with her coldness. We stopped making love. She had an affair with one of my students—Jesse Taylor—a big, handsome linebacker on our team."

Bliss was shocked by his honesty.

"Wingina is too small a place to carry on in such a way, and I guess Jesse got to bragging about how he was getting it regularly from Mrs. Swain. That kind of news spreads faster than poison ivy.

"One afternoon, Jesse cut school to have a little fun with my wife. Seems he was in the middle of scoring big with her when his mother, who'd grown a little suspicious when the principal called and reported that Jesse hadn't showed up for school, went home expecting to find him in bed sleeping. When she opened the door to his room, she saw that he was in bed, but he wasn't sleeping.

"Mrs. Taylor immediately called me and told me about my wife's "indiscretions" as she put it, and warned me she'd have my job if I didn't keep my shameful wife away from her son.

"At first, I was hurt, humiliated, and then furious, but as I drove home from school to confront her, I realized that this was just another way for her to punish me for killing P.J.

"By the time I reached the house, I'd concluded that she was only acting out of her pain, and in some perverse way, it felt good being cheated on. Like my agony was paying some debt I owed for allowing P.J. to die.

"When I walked into the house, I found Beth with my rifle stuck under her chin. I rushed to her and grabbed it, but she got off a shot that sent her into a coma for five days before dying."

He was silent; the storm raged violently and wind sang through the small cracks in the mortar.

"Because of the circumstances surrounding her death and because my fingerprints were on the gun, they charged me.

"At my trial, Jesse, to his credit, fessed up and stated that Beth often talked of ending her life, she was so distraught over P.J.'s death. And the coroner testified that her wounds were consistent with a suicide. Thankfully, I was acquitted."

He looked at Bliss. "You've got to believe me. I may have been responsible for P.J.'s death, but I didn't kill Beth."

She touched his hand. "I do believe you, Parker. But I don't understand why you would keep a clipping of a murder in which you were unjustly accused and the rifle that killed your wife? Most people wouldn't want any part of those things unless they were like those serial killers who collect souvenirs of their victims."

He squeezed her hand. "That rifle? I let Wayne destroy it. The one in the house is my granddaddy's. It's more or less an heirloom. And the reason I kept the clipping? To remind myself to never fall in love with another woman."

Bliss could barely speak, "Did it work?"

"No, Bliss. You know I love you."

She leaned over and rested her head on his shoulder.

"I'm sorry, Bliss, that I never told you all of this, but I didn't plan on falling in love with you. It wasn't my intention to drag you into my little universe of misery."

She turned to him and moved her hand to his cheek. "Being in your little universe has made me very, very happy. I'm sorry I ever doubted you."

Without regard for her blanket slipping off her shoulder, she reached out and drew him to her. His hair was damp and smelled of rain. "Please forgive me and more importantly, Parker, please forgive yourself."

"Oh, Bliss, I forgive you."

"And yourself?"

He shook his head that he couldn't and buried his face in his hands sobbing. Bliss held him until he could cry no more.

When he had quieted, she kissed his brow.

He raised his head. "Sorry, Bliss, for burdening you with this, but I've never had anyone I could tell about this. How empty my life has been. Why I'm so obsessed with Cape Destiny. You know my boy's buried here?"

"I know," she said stroking his wet hair. "I found his grave when I was looking for Beau."

"These last few years, the only things that have kept me alive is this land—the Keeper's House and that tombstone." He raised his head and looked at her. "Until you."

She held his face. The stubble of his beard was damp with tears. Looking deeply into his dark, sad eyes, she said, "You are a good, kind, gentle man, Parker. P. J. was lucky to have had you for a father. He wouldn't want you to live like this. I love you. Please stop blaming yourself." She kissed him softly.

He tentatively accepted her kiss. Then as if the howling storm had breached the walls of his hardened heart, and begun to wash away some of the misery, she felt his lips responding, reclaiming his right to happiness and to love again.

Parker swept Bliss into his arms, laying her across his lap. Pulling her tightly to his chest, she felt her breasts pressing against his warm, rock hard muscles.

He kissed her passionately then moved his lips to her throat. With her hands sunk deep in his golden hair, she arched her back offering her breasts to him. Before he honored them with kisses, he held her away and sighed, "Ah, Bliss, you're beautiful." Then she saw a frown wrinkle his brow. "You're all scratched and bruised." Tenderly, he touched the marks. "Did you get hurt in the storm?"

She raised her head and looked at him. "No," she whispered. "I wasn't going to tell you, but since we're being honest with each other . . ." She sat and faced him. "Last night, Jonathan came out to the house. He attacked me."

"Attacked you? How? What did he do to you?"

She shivered and Parker pulled a blanket over them. Bliss told him how cruel Jonathan had been. When she got to the part where Beau saved her, she began to cry.

184

"Oh, Bliss," Parker said, gently comforting her with a protective embrace, "it's so dark in here I can't tell. Are you badly injured?"

Her hot tears fell on his shoulder. "I'll be fine. She turned and held on to him tightly. "I'm just so afraid of being hurt. Promise me you'll never hurt me."

"Oh, darlin'," he said as he patted her. "All I want to do is be good to you." He kissed her, his lips reissuing an invitation for intimacy. She replied with passion, her mouth open to welcome him and his love.

Parker gently settled Bliss on the sleeping bag, and then he caressed and kissed every bruise and scratch, until she no longer felt aches and pains, but tingles and pure pleasure. He lay beside her and then pulled her on top of him, taking care to watch her battered back.

Then Bliss took him into her and made him her own, part of her flesh, her heart, her soul.

And as the wind howled and the surf pounded, Bliss felt herself and Parker, two broken people, becoming whole while melded as one flesh.

Chapter 31

Bliss was cuddled in Parker's arms while he slept. Behind that boyish face, lay the tragedy and pain of several lifetimes. How could someone who had suffered so much be so kind and considerate and unselfish a lover?

The wind had diminished through the night, and she could only guess what time it was. Parker stirred and slowly opened his eyes. When he saw Bliss watching him, he gave her a lazy smile. "I must have been swept away by the storm surge and died," he said, "because I've awoken in heaven."

She snuggled in tighter and played with the medallion around his neck. "Now I know why they called you Bliss."

She pressed her hips against him. "Feel like another trip to paradise?"

"What's the fare?"

"Depends if it's one way or round trip."

"Oh, Bliss. It's one way. I'm never comin' back from loving you."

She lifted her head a little. "Do you think the hurricane's passed? It seems quieter."

"Want me to find out?"

"How are you going to do that?"

"I'll go down stairs and peek outside. And besides, I'd like to stretch out a bit. Not exactly roomy up here."

He rose, naked, and stretched, appearing relaxed, at peace, and sublimely male. Adam must have looked like that on the first day of Creation, Bliss thought.

Parker headed down the steps. Bliss rose and stretched too, only she didn't feel refreshed but sorer than the day before. She wrapped a blanket around herself and went down two steps to where Parker had unloaded the emergency kit. She wondered if he had any pain medication. Inside the box, she found some aspirin and a bottle of water. Hungry now, she located a box of Pop-Tarts and some Slim Jims.

Bliss carried them up to their lair, and giggled as Parker came bounding up the steps.

"What's so funny?"

"You. You look so silly. I'm used to being in here with men in hard hats and jeans and work boots. To see you come strutting up the stairs without a stitch," she shook her head laughing, "it's just priceless."

He got under the blanket with her and snuggled closer.

"It's cold down there."

"Has it passed?"

"I think so, but I couldn't get the door open to see for sure. There's about two feet of water in the base. We'll have to wait until it recedes before we can try it again."

"I'm worried. Do you think Beau is OK? I owe that loveable old dog. If it weren't for him, I don't know what would have happened to me."

"Don't worry about him, Bliss. Animals know what to do when storms hit. He'll be fine."

"I'm hungry," she said, breaking into the Pop-Tart's silver sleeve and pulling one out. "Are you?"

"Yes."

He took one from her and bit it. "I don't know what it is about love, but even these things taste good today. Lord, I don't think I ever want to leave this place."

"Same here," Bliss said, "but I guess we have to face reality."

Parker looked serious as they sat shoulder to shoulder, wrapped in the blanket munching on junk food. "About last night. I'm sorry, Bliss, but I never thought of using any protection. I shouldn't have been so careless. But you have nothing to worry about. I wouldn't care if you became pregnant. I'd love to have another child. Sometimes my bones ache missing P.J. But what I mean to say is you don't have to worry about any diseases because I haven't been with anyone since Beth."

Bliss closed her eyes. "I'll be fine, Parker." She didn't know whether she should risk telling him her secret, but if she truly loved him, she knew she should be honest. It would be better that he knew upfront. "I wish I could get pregnant," she said sadly. "For two years, I tried with Jonathan. I intended to make an appointment with a specialist. That was until I found him with my trainer."

"Maybe it was a blessing," he said.

Maybe to him it was a blessing, Bliss thought, but she didn't think infertility in any way could ever be a blessing.

"And you needn't worry," she said as she handed him a Slim Jim. "I had myself tested after I found them together. Luckily, I didn't catch anything from him."

She curled against him, absorbing his warmth, feeling the soft hair on his legs brush against her. "You never called. How did the meeting go?"

He exhaled heavily causing the blanket to slip a little off her shoulder. He pulled it around her. "When they issued the mandatory hurricane evacuation, all hell broke loose. They hustled me into this meeting, and I tried to make my case, but they were distracted. What it boils down to is they've given me until the end of the year to complete the renovations."

"That's only a little more than five months! There's no way anyone, not even a whole crew of workers, could complete it in that time. And who knows what's happened to it since the hurricane."

"It's like they're dead set against me."

"Oh, they're being unreasonable."

"I can't get upset about it now."

They sat quietly for a while, staring into the darkness.

"Can you pass that bottle of water?" Bliss asked. "I found some aspirin in the emergency kit."

"Are you in much pain?"

She popped the pill into her mouth and followed it with a gulp of water. "Some. And I don't think sleeping on a metal mattress helped.

"When we get out of here," Parker said, "we're going to see Wayne Bevans. Jonathan can't get away with this."

"No, please, Parker. I don't want this to end up in the paper. It'll be bad for my business."

"If you're dead, Bliss, there is no business. Vandalism and threats are one thing, but assault and attempted rape is another. What are you waiting for? Him to kill you?" Parker shook his head. "No, there's a progression here. He must be stopped. Tell me, what did you ever see in that guy?"

"I've been thinking a lot about that," Bliss said. "He was handsome, powerful and from a well-known family, and I guess when he took an interest me, I was flattered. I think I felt so bad about myself for being biracial and dyslexic, that when he showed me the least bit of attention, I fell for him." She shook her head. "He wasn't always cruel, but when he came out here the other night, I saw something in him I'd never seen before—a darkness, a capacity for brutality."

He held her face in his hands. "Listen to me, Bliss, I couldn't save P.J. and I couldn't save Beth, but I'll be damned if I'll stand by and let something happen to you. If you won't let me call Wayne, then I'll go see that coward myself and knock some sense into him with my fists."

"No, Parker. Jonathan's not rational. Promise me you won't go to see him."

"The only promise I'll make you, Bliss, is that I'm never going to let another person that I love be harmed."

Chapter 32

After a lunch of canned chicken noodle soup cooked over a candle and a pack of cheese crackers, Bliss and Parker retrieved their clothing. Her pants were still damp and the fabric felt cold against her skin.

Parker, fully dressed now in the clothes he'd worn home from Raleigh, sat on the landing. His tan pants and navy sport shirt were rumpled and wrinkled. "Nothing like wet socks to start the day," he remarked, struggling to pull the soggy socks on his feet. He slipped his feet into his wet leather loafers.

On the step above him, Bliss was trying to do rake her hair out of her face. After being caught in the hurricane, making love, and then sleeping on it, she knew it must look like a tangle of seaweed.

Parker smiled at her adoringly, and she felt a warmth grow in her chest. He moved up onto the same step as her, smoothed her hair back, and kissed her gently.

"I know we were caught in a terrible hurricane, Bliss, but I'll treasure last night as one of the most wonderful nights of my life."

Of all the places where she and Jonathan had made love—Paris, Rome, their penthouse in Pittsburgh, none of them compared to the night she'd just spent wrapped in Parker's arms lying on a sleeping bag, on the metal grating in the dark, cold lighthouse. "Parker, I've never felt so . . ." she struggled to find the right word. What she felt was more than love. He'd opened a new world to her. One where she felt complete. "I've never felt so valued."

He hugged her. "Oh, Bliss. You are a remarkable, intelligent, beautiful woman and any one who doesn't recognize that is a fool."

Tears swam in her eyes as she closed them to accept his kiss. Even if I'm infertile? she wanted to ask, but stopped because she didn't want to know his answer.

He took her hand and squeezed it. "Now, I guess we've got to see what Blaise has done. Parker headed down the metal stairs with Bliss trailing behind. At the bottom of the tower, water, ankle-deep high, had pooled. Parker and she waded through the fishy, briny water, and he shoved the door.

Sand had drifted against it making it immovable. Parker shoved a shoulder into it and pushed. It budged a few inches. He then dug out the door, pushed it open a little more and continued digging and pushing until he could slip out. Inside still, Bliss heard him exclaim, "Good Lord."

When she stepped outside, she felt like Dorothy opening the door to Munchkin Land. Only Bliss saw no colorful, flower-filled fantasyland, but a vista of utter devastation. Limbs and debris littered the site and a heavy scent of pine from all the trees that had been snapped off like toothpicks lingered in the now calm air. Sand and puddles pockmarked the lawn. She gazed up at the lighthouse. It appeared to have weathered the hurricane unscathed, but a complete inspection of the structure would be needed.

Parker took her hand, and she was glad of it because the destruction made it seem as if they'd landed on another planet. The feel of his strong hand closed around hers tethered her to reality.

He looked at her, disbelief in his eyes. "If this wasn't a direct hit, I'd hate to see one."

It was a beautiful, sun-drenched day, and it seemed as though Mother Nature was asserting her capricious nature. Parker turned and shaded his eyes with his hand and looked up at the lighthouse. "Seems like it's OK." He looked at Bliss with a frown. "Wonder how the rest of the place fared?"

"And I wonder how Beau is?" she said. "I feel so responsible."

"Bliss, he's gotten away on me too. That dog has a mind of his own. Come on, let's take a look around."

They walked with difficulty up the move corridor. The smooth path her company had cleared for the lighthouse to move along was now drifted over with sand. Bliss calculated that clearing this alone would set the project back several days, days she couldn't afford to lose if she wanted Sherman Engineering to remain solvent.

The trailer was knocked off its foundation and lay on its side. It was a rental, so Bliss hadn't lost anything there, but it became apparent that it would be days before operations would be up and running again.

"I'm almost afraid to see what the house looks like," Parker said solemnly.

They picked their way around the downed limbs, their feet squishing as they trod on the waterlogged ground. When the house came into view, they both stopped, dumbstruck. The porch roof was curled back like the lid of a tin can and slats of clapboard had been blown completely away.

A towering oak leaned against the house; it had collapsed a portion of one gable.

"Oh, Parker," she said as she put a hand on his shoulder.

He shrugged and snickered sarcastically. "I was never going to be able to meet their deadline anyway." His voice strained with emotion. "This really puts the nail in the coffin." He lowered his head, stuffed his hands in his pockets, and walked toward the brush.

She gave him a few minutes then followed. When she found him, he was at P.J.'s grave angrily tossing branches, leaves, and odd bits of debris off his son's burial plot. When he bent to wipe away the sand and dirt from the granite head stone, Bliss touched his back. "Parker, I'm so sorry. I know how hard you've worked and how much the house means to you."

He rose and faced Bliss, his eyes filled with tears. "Everything I've ever loved has been taken away from me. My wife. My boy. My house. And I've probably lost my dog too. I have nothing."

She hugged him, laying her head against his chest, and she could almost hear his heart breaking. "You still have me, Parker."

He held her at arm's length and stared at her, the depth of all his losses reflecting in his eyes. "But for how long, Bliss? How long will it be before I lose you too?"

She wanted to tell him that he'd never lose her, but she didn't want to make promises that she couldn't keep.

Chapter 33

The storm surge had pushed a mountain of sand across the narrow road leading out of Cape Destiny, cutting them off from the mainland. Parker estimated that it would be at least several days before help would come.

Bliss and Parker spent the rest of the day trying to clear the debris away and make the house habitable. Fortunately, the interior only seemed to have suffered water damage from the driving rain and the tree crashing into the attic.

As Bliss was helping Parker to pry off what remained of the plywood sheets she and her crew had nailed over the windows, she heard a weak woof coming from the direction of the Oil House.

"Parker, did you hear that? It sounded like a bark. From over there."

Parker turned around, crowbar in hand, his eyes keen as he angled his head toward the Oil House and listened.

They both heard it again. Parker took off running. The Oil House barely resembled a structure now. It had collapsed into a pile of weathered lumber. Parker began pulling away the rubble. Bliss came to his side and began flinging aside debris. She heard the woof again. The barking was coming from beneath wreckage. Parker began working faster. Through the boards Bliss could see Beau's golden coat.

Parker and Bliss tugged on a window frame, which was wedged under the pile of boards. It wouldn't move. He grabbed the crowbar, braced a foot against the foundation and pulled with all his might. It refused to move. "Bliss, how about you grab the frame on this side and shimmy it, while I use the crowbar." The frame shifted, they lost their footing and fell backwards onto the soggy ground. Before they could get their bearings, Beau, wet and smelling like seaweed, was on top of them kissing and licking them.

Bliss sat up and watched with delight as Parker wrapped his arms around the dog's neck and hugged him tightly. "Oh, boy, you're safe." Parker relaxed his hold on Beau. "Are you hurt, buddy?" He ran his hand over the dog, picking out leaves and splintered wood from his fur.

Parker smiled at Bliss. "He seems like he's OK."

"Bet he's hungry," Bliss said.

As if he could understand, Beau barked at Bliss.

Parker stood, gave Bliss a hand, and said, "Come on, Beau. Let's get you something to eat."

After Parker fed Beau, he examined the dog more closely. He seemed to have suffered nothing more than scrapes and bruises.

Although the electricity was out, the house still had running water, and he and Bliss gave Beau a bath.

It was near dusk when Parker lit a fire in the fireplace and cooked hot dogs that had thawed in his freezer. The physical labor combined with the stiffness from the beating Jonathan had inflicted on her, left Bliss feeling as if the Oil House had collapsed on her.

When she rose from the table to clear away the dishes, Parker noticed how stiffly she was moving. He stood and took her dirty plate. "Bliss, you've done enough. What we both need is a long hot bath."

"Go take yours first," she said. "I promised Beau I'd brush him."

Parker went upstairs and opened the spigots. At least he had hot water. It was dark now, and he rounded up what candles he could find and clustered them around the tub. When it was full, he called for Bliss.

"Wow, that was quick," she said as she entered the bathroom. She stopped short. "You haven't taken one yet."

He grasped her hand and led her into the room. "You go first. I'll leave you to relax."

"You mean you're not going to bathe me again?"

A glint of mischief flickered in his eye. "If you'd like, I'd be happy to."

She slid a hand up his chest and touched his neck. "I'd like it very much."

Parker cleared his throat. "Well, I wouldn't want to scrimp on Southern hospitality." He pulled Bliss's hand away and kissed her knuckles, in the glowing light he could see that they were scraped. He looked piercingly at her, his gaze owning her. "I guess we should get out of our clothes then."

He lovingly undressed her, taking care with her injuries, kissing them like a devoted mother soothing a child's pain. Cold, and feeling more vulnerable now that they were outside the safety of the lighthouse, Bliss slipped into the warm water. Reflexively, she closed her eyes and moaned as the heat penetrated her battered, chilled flesh. Then she opened them and watched as Parker removed his shirt. When he dropped his pants, Bliss chuckled.

He stopped and stared at her.

"What?" she said in response to his glare.

"A giggle isn't exactly what a man who's just bared his essentials wants to hear."

"It's not your essentials I find amusing. It's your tan. Your bum looks like the Coppertone baby's."

He glanced over his shoulder and looked at his white backside. "What do you want me to do? I can very well go buck naked around here while I work on the house?" He stuck a foot into the tub. "Move up, Bliss," he said as he crawled in behind her.

She moved forward in the old tub and felt him slide in behind her, his brown, muscular legs folding around her.

Bliss leaned back against his chest and closed her eyes as his arms encircled her. "If I ruled the world, I'd let you go naked."

He kissed the top of her head and whispered. "What else would you do if you ruled the world?"

She sighed and began to speak, although something inside her kept warning her not to reveal her heart's wishes because doing so would make her vulnerable. But perhaps it was the primordial womb-like waters that made her feel safe enough to bare her soul to him. "Oh, Parker," she whispered, "if I ruled the world, I'd take away all the pain your past has caused you. I'd restore the lighthouse for you——"

"Know what I'd do?" he said.

She turned and looked back at him, and the longing in his deep brown eyes reached into her heart and made it ache.

He took her hand. "I'd find a way to love you enough so that you'd never leave me."

*****

Bliss lay on her side in the dark, watching the way the moon peeking into the bedroom window outlined Parker's body in silver. His chest rose and fell heartily, the slumber of a man who'd spent a long day laboring and a long evening loving her.

Her body still hummed from the love he'd made to her. He'd been so passionate, she knew it was more than an expression of his feelings for her, but an unspoken attempt to seduce her into staying. It was a silent promise that if she'd remained on Cape Destiny, she'd enjoy this passion for the rest of her life.

Her gaze traveled down his flat stomach to where he'd pulled a corner of the sheet over him. The ridge under the cover was resting too now against his thigh, and she wondered how something so hard could reach the softest parts of her heart.

She rolled over on her back and stared at the ceiling. Maybe it's because it's been too long since you've had a real man make love to you. The last year of her marriage had been such a strain. Jonathan had been pressuring her for a baby, an heir to the Lavere fortune, but she hadn't conceived.

Sex had become another item on her to-do list then. The romance and mystery of love and conception was stripped away by readings from ovulation predictors and the charms of vaginal mucous.

Bliss could still hear the derision in Jonathan's voice when she suggested they adopt. "I don't want somebody else's baby. The parents would find out we're wealthy and be constantly looking for a handout."

Bliss told him they could adopt from outside the country.

"I don't want some foreigner," he said, meaning someone like her.

When she found Jonathan cheating, she gave up the thought of ever having a family again. She'd left him, left the company, and thrown herself into her career. Now, she had her career, and Parker was asking her to stay.

When he spoke about his late son, she saw in his eyes the longing for another child. She'd reconsider her devotion to her career if she thought they had a chance. Parker loved her now, but when she couldn't provide him with children, she knew his love for her would fade. She preferred to leave while still in love, rather than to stay and see their love sour.

Hot tears welled up and spilled out the corners of her eyes when she thought about living without him. She wiped them away and rolled over on her side.

Parker signed in his sleep and turned toward her. He draped a heavy arm around her and pressed closer.

Biting her lip to stifle a sob, she thought, *I'm in love with a man I can never make happy*.

Chapter 34

Bliss and Parker spent the next several days repairing the hurricane damage by day and making love by night. To Bliss, her time there felt as if she were living in a dream world, a paradise where only she and Parker mattered. She didn't have to think about the business, the move, Jonathan, or the future. Bliss would have been content to spend the rest of her life cut off from the rest of the world.

Three days after they emerged from the lighthouse, an earthmover rumbled up the road pushing the sand that had choked it out of the way. Not long after that, while Bliss and Parker were hauling limbs into a pile on the edge of the wood, they heard a voice calling them. Emerging from the forest in the direction of the parking lot, came Wayne Bevans. "Parker, Parker!"

Bevans hustled over and shook Parker's hand, planting a firm slap on his back. "Oh, man. Am I glad to see y'all are OK."

He turned to Bliss and hugged her. "We were hoping that you were safe out here. And not with Lavere."

"Why would I be with him?" she asked.

"Your secretary called alarmed when you didn't show up at the hotel. Your secretary said he'd been to the Keeper's House while Parker was away and had been abusive. And since he's disappeared, we thought that perhaps he had something to do with your not arriving at the hotel." He bent and petted Beau who was snaking in and out of their little circle.

"Disappeared?" Bliss said. "What do you mean?"

"Vanished. No one has seen him. He had a reservation in Elizabeth City at some hotel where he could ride out the hurricane, but he never arrived. His office reported him missing. No one has heard from him. As far as we know, Bliss, you were the last one to see him. Did he mention anything to you?"

A mixture of emotion coursed through her. A small part of her, a part that Jonathan had not managed to kill, was concerned for his safety, but an even greater part of her felt guilty for feeling relief that perhaps he'd been lost in the storm. "No," she said.

"And you didn't have any contact with him after that night?"

Parker squared his shoulders and stepped toward Officer Bevans. "What are you implying, Wayne? That Bliss had something to do with Lavere's disappearance?"

"Take it easy, Parker. I'm not implying anything. I'm just asking Bliss a few questions. I'm trying to get to the bottom of his disappearance."

"Well, I don't like you casting suspicion on her. I know what it's like to be accused."

Bliss stepped between them. "Jonathan Lavere came out here and nearly raped me. If it hadn't been for Beau fighting him off, I don't know what would have happened. Believe me, Officer Bevans, after what he nearly did to me, Jonathan Lavere is the last person I would want to see."

"Nearly raped you?" Bevans looked at her. "I thought he'd just been threatening. Why didn't you file a report?"

She put her hands on her hips. "A little thing like the hurricane got in the way."

"There was ample time to file one before the storm hit."

Irritated, that she was being treated like a criminal instead of Jonathan, Bliss sighed. "I didn't report it because I didn't want to be the subject of a scandal. My reputation would be damaged. I'm trying to win the bid for another job. Who would want to hire a woman tied up in a criminal case?"

"Well, I just wish you would have informed the authorities."

"And why is that?" Parker asked belligerently.

Wayne Bevans lips became tight, making his pudgy cheeks plumper. "Because then it wouldn't look so reasonable to conclude that Bliss may have meted out her own justice."

Parker grabbed him by the shoulders. "You get the hell out of here. Bliss did nothing to Lavere. You're not railroading her into something the way they railroaded me when Beth died."

Bevans pushed him away and straightened his uniform shirt. "Now, take it easy, Parker. I don't want to have to run a friend in for assaulting an officer." At the word friend, Parker seemed to turn down his temper to simmer. "I'm just doing my job, trying to find out what happened to him. Most likely, he was lost in the storm surge. But until we find him, you might want to watch yourself, Bliss."

"You think I did something to Jonathan?" she said in disbelief.

"No, but if he's as violent as you say, and he hasn't drowned, why isn't he checking in with his office? Maybe he's laying low so he can finish what he started with you."

Suddenly, Bliss felt chilled. Was Jonathan capable of such treachery? A few weeks ago she wouldn't have believed so, but that was before he'd assaulted her.

"Well," Parker said, putting his arm around Bliss. "If you'd do your job instead of casting doubt on innocent people and find this lunatic, then we wouldn't have to worry now, would we?"

Wayne Bevans grinned and slapped Parker on the back. "You got it bad, don't you, boy?"

"What are you talking about?"

"You're like a mamma bear protecting her cub. I've never seen you like this." He turned his gaze to Bliss. "I congratulate you, Bliss. It's a pleasure to see Parker Swain in love again."

Parker took Bliss's hand. "Don't you concern yourself with my personal life. Y'all concentrate on finding Lavere and protecting Bliss."

To change the subject, Parker asked how the area had fared.

"Blaise was a bad one," Wayne said as he ran a hand over his face. Bliss could see that he was fatigued. "Though the experts say it could have been worse had it come in at high tide. There's trees down everywhere. Power and phones lines are out from Virginia to Georgia, and you won't believe Beachfront Road. Not a place on this island that didn't suffer some kind of damage."

"You mentioned that Nancy was worried about me?" Bliss said. "I assume she's OK?"

"Yes, she's fine. She said to tell you that she was heading back to that cottage on Wellington Island." He closed his eyes and shook his head. "That woman is another force to be reckoned with. She's been calling me, driving me crazy, wondering when she can get back over here and start moving your equipment back in."

Bliss smiled. Nancy was as determined as a hurricane when she had a goal to meet. Then Bliss's smiled faded. How would she explain that they were on the verge of bankruptcy? If they could have just won the Coast Guard Station contract, it would have given them some cushion against the cost of the lighthouse delay. *Damn that Jonathan.*

Then she caught herself. Jonathan was missing. She shouldn't be condemning him. He could be hurt or worse. Worse? Worse would be dead. *Jonathan dead.* A feeling of relief swept over her as she allowed herself the guilty pleasure of thinking him dead. Her life would be so much easier if he had been lost in the hurricane. The Coast Guard contract, in all likelihood, would reopen for bids, and she'd never have to fear him harming her again. What a stroke of luck!

Shame filled her. How cruel to wish him dead. His cruelty was what she hated about him—the cutting remarks, the degrading behavior, the way he was able to home in on her vulnerability and made her feel bad about herself. While Parker pointed out to Bevans how the Oil House had collapsed on Beau, she sighed and looked off toward the beach lost in thought. *How terrible I am for wishing him dead.* She hugged herself. *And how terrible are you Jonathan Lavere for not only being able to make me feel ashamed in life, but in death as well?*

Chapter 35

The move of the lighthouse wasn't the only engineering marvel at work on the Outer Banks. Bliss was amazed at the speed and efficiency of the utility crews, relief workers, and charitable organizations who poured into the area after the hurricane to rehabilitate the place, save the remaining tourist season, and help those residents who had been displaced.

Once the roads were cleared, it was only a day before Randy was able to round up the crew, and they began putting in long hours getting the site back into working order.

The following week the trailer was righted and inspected for damage, and to Bliss's relief, it passed as functional. Nancy and Bliss spent another week setting up the office and waiting for phone service to be restored.

It was August by the time they had service again, and with the phones, came the heat. Unfortunately, when the trailer had flipped over, the air conditioner had been demolished. The windows and door of the trailer were left wide open, hoping to catch a breeze.

Nancy, who was trying to place weights on the papers lying on her desk so that the fan they'd recently purchased didn't blow everything away, chased a wayward paper and said, "Bliss, do you think it unseemly for me to call and see if they've reopened the bidding for the Coast Guard Station?" Jonathan still had not appeared and most everyone had concluded that he was lost during the hurricane.

Accompanying the arrival of the heat were insects. Bliss, with swatter in hand, slapped at a sand fly and missed. "If you do it tactfully, I don't see why not. It's not as if Jonathan was one of their employees."

Bliss stalked a green horse fly while Nancy picked up the phone and dialed. From her replies, Bliss could read nothing. "I understand," Nancy said, her voice falling. "Thank you."

Bliss stared expectantly at Nancy as she hung up the phone. "They haven't reopened it yet, have they?"

"No, they haven't. And they're not going to."

Bliss, beads of sweat forming between her breasts, rose. "What? Why?"

Nancy massaged her temple. "The Coast Guard Station was so heavily damaged they don't believe it's worth the investment to move it."

"Oh, wonderful," Bliss said, slapping the swatter against the file cabinet. The heat seemed to engulf her. She needed air. Dropping the swatter, she walked to the window longing for a breeze. They were sunk. Randy was projecting that the move would be delayed at least a month. The penalties for missing the deadline would put them under.

If that weren't enough to depress her, Bliss knew that it was time to move out of the Keeper's House. The Destiny Cove had reopened that morning and as much as she dreaded it, she felt it was time to tell Parker she was leaving. It was understandable that she had remained there while the hotel was closed, but now to avoid a scandal, she felt she had to move out.

*****

After a long, hot day spent working in the trailer, Bliss headed for the Keeper's House. The smell of the charcoal grill told her that Parker was out back cooking dinner. She found him, holding a bottle of beer and tongs. He took a swig of the beer, flipped the chicken breast. "Yow!" he said, quickly snatching his hand away as a tongue of fire licked at his arm. He lay the tongs on the shelf and set the beer down.

Bliss came to him. "Are you OK?"

He looked at and rubbed his forearm. "Singed my arm."

She touched the soft golden hair near his wrist feeling a rough spot, where the flames had touched him.

"You're blistering." Bliss said. There was a darkness to his eyes, something she'd not seen since the night spent in the lighthouse. "Want me to get you something for the burn?"

With his finger he tucked a loose strand of hair behind her ear. "What I want, Bliss, is for you to stay." He paused. "I saw your things in the car. I know you're planning to leave tonight, and I want you to stay, Bliss."

She withdrew her hand from his arm and turned to face the sound. The silhouettes of gulls peppered the pink clouds scudding across the sky. All around them the world was about its business, but Bliss felt as though she and Parker were held in suspended animation. They were going nowhere while life moved on.

"Parker, we knew this was coming."

He came and took her by the shoulders, facing her. "But it doesn't have to end this way. Stay here. I love you, Bliss."

She leaned against his chest. "I love you too, Parker, but I can't. It wouldn't work. I have my business."

"You're the boss. Move it here."

"I can't ask that of my employees. When I came to them with my proposal and persuaded them to join me, they risked everything to invest in my dream. I can't expect them to relocate because I've fallen in love."

"You wouldn't have to. They could remain in Pittsburgh and you could have an office here. I'll build you an office. You can have one of the bedrooms. "

"Here? You may not even have this place for much longer if the state has its way."

"We'll work something out. Love will find a way."

"That's rather naïve, don't you think?"

Angered flashed in his eyes. "What about your motto? Moving Heaven and Earth? I happen to believe love *can* move heaven and earth."

She began to tremble as tears streaked her cheeks. "I'd like to believe that, Parker. But I'm a realist. There are just too many things stacked against us. Things you don't even realize."

"I'm a realist too, Bliss. Nothing is more real than having love and then seeing it stripped from your hands. I know that nothing is more important than love."

She didn't want to tell him that her infertility was the reason she couldn't stay because he'd only protest that it didn't matter. And he would be honest. Right now, it didn't matter to him, but with time, his feelings would change. He'd known the joy of being a father, and he'd want to experience it again. Her infertility would matter, and it would kill whatever love they shared. Only someone who had seen a marriage wither under its curse could know this. Let him believe the real reason was that her career was more important. "Then leave the lighthouse, Parker," she said, knowing he'd never agree. "Come with me. You could move to Pittsburgh. Get a teaching job."

"I thought by now you'd understand that I can never leave this place. I am the lighthouse. The water I drink comes from the rain that falls here. The food I eat comes from this soil. The North Carolina sun has baked itself into my bones. My past is here," he said as he nodded toward the cemetery, "and so is my future."

"Then this place really is cursed." Bliss began to weep. "It takes prisoners, trapping them with love then destroying them."

"It doesn't have to be cursed. We can make it work."

Her heart pleaded with her to give in to his pleas and stay, but she knew their relationship was doomed as hers had been with Jonathan. She'd rather leave him now than later. It would be less painful.

She clutched her hands to her chest. "Even though my heart is breaking, Parker, I'm not sorry I fell in love with you. You're the closest I've ever come to real love." She quickly kissed him and hurried toward the parking lot.

He charged after her. "Stay, Bliss. Don't go!" he cried.

As she broke into a run, she heard him call, "When you discover that it's love that moves heaven and earth and not some hydraulic lift, come back to me, Bliss. I'll be here. Waiting for you. Loving you."

Chapter 36

Bliss stared out the trailer's window, watching as the sun-bleached sea oats on the dunes slowly ruffled in the breeze. Their hypnotic dance lulled her and made her sleepy.

Everyone had gone for the day, and it was quiet. She'd been so tired, she hadn't accomplished anything. Way behind in her paperwork, she thought it best that she remained and tried to catch up.

She knew the source of her fatigue. It was grief. When her father had died, she had expected to feel emotionally wrung out, but she'd been surprised when her sorrow had physically exhausted her as well.

Bliss was now mourning the loss of Parker. It had been more than a week since she'd left him, and she was so tired she couldn't concentrate.

After a few days had passed without Parker stopping in, Nancy had asked if he had moved back to his house in Wingina since they never saw him anymore and because the Keeper's House had been damaged. When Bliss told her that they'd had a falling out, Nancy had tried to conceal her happiness, but Bliss could see the hint of a smile on her lips.

Bliss had only seen glimpses of him coming and going. She'd gone out of her way to avoid him.

Her eyes now drifted toward the lighthouse. It was three-quarters of the way to its new location. Only the top of it was visible above the tree line. Bliss believed Cape Destiny was cursed. Parker's ancestor had been swept out to sea, his wife and son had met with tragic deaths, and now their love was doomed.

Yet the lighthouse didn't seem cursed at all to her. When they were holed up in it during the hurricane making love, it had become a magical place. That dark, dank tower had opened to her a world of light and love. Even though more than a month had passed since that night, the way Parker, gently yet passionately, had overwhelmed her with pleasure was still vivid in her mind.

It would be something she carried with her always. She yawned and leaned against the window.

Then suddenly she raised her head. A burst of energy surged through her. She turned and quickly began locking up. Work could wait until tomorrow, she thought as she shut the door behind her. She had something more important to do.

*****

The bell on the door of the Beach Mart and Pharmacy jangled, unnerving Bliss. She felt like ripping its clapper out. Looking over at the counter, she was relieved to see that no one was there. The store was empty too; the tourists had been slow to return after Blaise. June was probably back in the stock room. Cartons were scattered throughout, and Bliss assumed they were still in the process of restocking after the storm.

She hurried down an aisle. Perhaps she could make her selection, pay Boyd at the pharmacy counter, and slip out before June could pry into her business.

After glancing up at the overhead marquees, she located the right aisle and section. The array of products confused her. Selecting one, she began to read the instructions.

"How late are you, honey?"

Startled, Bliss rapidly took in a breath that sounded like a squeak and whirled around, red-faced, to see June behind her grinning.

"How far along do you reckon' you are?"

Bliss clutched the pregnancy test kit to her chest and sputtered nonsensically.

June slapped her arm. "Don't be embarrassed. We were so relieved when no one could find you after the hurricane to learn that you were safe with Parker. It's only natural when you're trapped together to get a little cozy. This won't be the first baby conceived during a hurricane. I should know. My mama named me after Hurricane June. Besides being made during hurricanes, babies like to be born during them too."

Stunned, Bliss said, "I didn't think I could get pregnant. I tried when I was married, and nothing ever happened."

"Wasn't your fault, darlin'. What you needed was a strapping Southern boy to plant his seed in your field. Parker must be so happy."

"Please don't say anything to him. I haven't even taken the test yet. I don't know for sure."

June ignored Bliss's admonishment. "Oh, he'll be just tickled when he finds out. Losing his baby sucked the life right out of him. He's been beside himself ever since. Poor boy's never been the same."

"June, please don't leap to conclusions. I haven't taken the test yet."

"Well, how are you feeling? Your breasts tender? Hungry?"

Bliss nodded to all her questions. "And I'm nauseous and tired all the time."

"I lay you dollars to doughnuts, Bliss," June said sweeping her up into a big hug "that you're expecting."

Bliss began to cry.

"Oh, honey, what's the matter?"

"Everything," Bliss said.

"Here, here. Come back into the stockroom and collect yourself."

June took Bliss by the hand and led her to the back. She directed her to sit in the desk chair. The old woman grabbed a box of tissues and handed it to her. While she dabbed at her eyes, June pulled over a large carton and sat. Looking quizzically at Bliss, she said. "Now, what's bothering you?"

"I don't know what I'm going to do. Parker and I have broken up and now I'm pregnant." She covered her face with her hands and sobbed.

"Do you love Parker?"

"Yes."

"And I know he loves you. So I don't see any problem. Since you moved out of the Keeper's House, he's been in here moping around. Got a million ailments. Looking for things to help him sleep. Antacids to calm his stomach. I told him what he needs is a cure for a broken heart. But I don't stock that. Wish I did." She chuckled. "I'd be richer than King Solomon."

Bliss, for the first time, felt the least bit hopeful. "But I told him I couldn't get pregnant."

"Well, that's the risk every man takes when he puts his dipper into a woman's well. And besides I can't think of anything that would make him happier than his being a daddy again."

"He did mention how he missed his son. But what'll we do? He won't leave the lighthouse, and I can't stay here."

June patted Bliss's knee. "I'm sure you'll work something out. When there's a baby involved, you'd be surprised how people change their attitudes."

"I hope you're right."

June kissed the top of her head. "Now take that test on home and use it."

Bliss opened her purse and pulled out her wallet.

June held up her hand. "My treat."

"No, I can't."

"I insist. All I ask is that you call me soon as you know."

Bliss stood and hugged June. "Thanks for being such a good shoulder to cry on."

She patted Bliss's cheek. "I hate to brag, but I make a swell godmother too."

*****

Bliss looked at the urine stick. There was no mistaking the result. She was pregnant. She threw the stick in the garbage can and stumbled out of the bathroom. Lightheaded now, she had to lie down.

I am pregnant.

She was delighted and frightened all at once. Stretching out on the bed, she marveled that another human being was growing inside her. I didn't seem real. Bliss slid her hand to just below her navel and held it there, loving the baby blooming inside her. Her baby. Parker's baby.

What would he say when she told him? She had no doubt that he loved her. She hoped he would love their child.

The phone rang. Before she raised the receiver to her ear, she knew who was on the other end.

"Well? Have you taken it?" June asked excitedly.

"Yes," Bliss said, trying to prolong the suspense, but her joy was spilling over into her voice.

"And? And?"

"It's positive!"

Bliss had to hold the phone away from her ear as June squealed like a pig.

"Sweet Jesus!" June said, "That's the best news we've had round here in ages. I'm so excited. I got to get me some yarn and start knitting. Why, I knit Parker his first blanket. I can't wait to congratulate him."

"Please don't say anything to him, June. I'm going to call him after I hang up."

"Oh, OK, but I feel like I'm going to bust a gusset."

Bliss laughed.

"Now you be sure to rest and eat right. Oh, get yourself some milk. And vitamins. You're going to need vitamins. And a doctor. You should see a doctor. I know a real good one. Lady doctor over in Wingina. Knows all about hormones and such. Prescribed me some after I went through the change, cause I was drying up down there. Made things difficult for me and Skeeter. Well, never mind about that. You just take care now."

"I'll be sure to."

Bliss lay back down. She was giddy with excitement and nervousness. How and when should she tell Parker? She didn't want to tell him over the phone. It had to be in person so she could gauge his reaction. And if he wasn't happy, she told herself, at least she'd have something to remind her of his love.

Bliss rolled over onto her side. She didn't want a souvenir of his love. She wanted a family. She was not one of those women who would be content to walk away with just Parker's baby when she could have him too. What was preventing her from having them both? The business? She chuckled. What business? We're probably bankrupt. Perhaps it's time to cut my losses and start again. *I'm good at starting over. All my life I've been moving things and starting over.* Something will work out.

She reached over and picked up the phone. Scooting upright, she rested against the headboard. While she punched in Parker's phone number, Bliss massaged her stomach and whispered to the baby, "We're calling your daddy."

Bliss heard the joy come into his voice when she said hello.

"It's good to talk to you again," Parker said rather dreamily.

She wanted to blurt out the news, but restrained herself.

"Parker, I've been thinking a lot about us . . . well, and I think we should talk."

"I'm free tonight."

Bliss saw her reflection in the mirror above the desk. She looked pale and tired. She needed to get some saltines. She needed time to pull herself together.

"I'm tied up tonight. I was thinking that perhaps we could meet for dinner tomorrow night. I don't know if any of the nicer restaurants have reopened."

"Why don't you come here? It'll be more private, and I'll cook you something special."

"You sure you don't mind?"

"Why it'd be a pleasure. Come at seven."

"OK, I'll see you then."

"Goodnight, Bliss."

Yes, it is a good night, she thought, as she hung up the phone and rubbed her tummy. "And it's going to be an even better day tomorrow."

Chapter 37

Bliss wiped her mouth with the back of her hand and flushed the toilet. In a cold sweat, she sat on the tile floor, hoping her stomach would stop pitching. How could something so small cause so much physical distress?

She closed her eyes and rested her head on the side of the tub. Why hadn't she left the hotel last night and picked up a box of saltines? June had called her three more times before she turned off the phone's ringer, put out the DO NOT DISTURB sign, and stumbled into bed.

Perhaps room service could send up some saltines. If she could just muster the will to rise, she'd give them a call. When the door rattled, Bliss raised her head. Hadn't housekeeping seen the sign hanging on the door? She couldn't recall putting on the chain. "Come back later," she called.

When the door opened, her heart began to pound. Who would ignore her warning?

Jonathan!

Struggling to her feet, she quickly scanned the bathroom for a weapon.

"Bliss, are you here? Are you OK?"

Her chest rose and fell in a huge sigh of relief. Nancy. Thank goodness it was she. "I'm in the bathroom."

Before Bliss could pull on her robe, Nancy appeared in the doorway, her brows knit into a sharp vee of worry. "Are you OK? I've been calling you all morning and nobody answered. I thought something terrible had happened. Like Jonathan had returned."

"I'm sorry," Bliss said. "I was so tired last night I shut off the ringer and went to sleep." She put her hand to her mouth to stifle a gag. "Excuse me."

"Are you sick?"

As if to answer her question, Bliss's stomach churned, and she bent over the toilet and dry heaved. She straightened up, clutched the counter to steady herself, then shuffled past Nancy and flopped onto the bed. She didn't want to tell her that she was pregnant before she told Parker. If he accepted the pregnancy, it would be much easier to have him by her side when she broke the news.

"I think I got some bad seafood last night," Bliss said looking up at Nancy.

"Would a cold compress help?"

"I guess it couldn't hurt."

Bliss heard Nancy running water. Then there was a long period of silence. Closing her eyes, Bliss concentrated, trying to will her stomach to settle.

When she felt a presence beside her, Bliss opened her eyes and saw Nancy, her eyes sharp, her mouth a tight slash across her face. "Bad seafood? What do you call this?" She thrust the pregnancy test kit box Bliss had left on the bathroom counter out. "Are you pregnant, Bliss?"

She didn't have the stamina for this now. And she didn't have to answer to her. And she also didn't have to deny something she was happy about. "All signs indicate that I am."

216

Nancy crumpled the box and threw it aside. "I knew Parker Swain was trouble the moment I saw him. That bastard. I could kill him for doing this to you."

Bliss sat up, walked past Nancy, and sat at the small table. "He didn't do this to me. I was a willing participant."

"Well, I'm sure we can find a doctor to take care of this. With the business in jeopardy, the last thing we need is a pregnancy."

How dare she make plans to abort my baby! Bliss's anger vanquished her queasiness. "You know I've always wanted a baby. I wouldn't dream of aborting it. Not that it's any of your affair."

"But what about the business? How will you run Sherman Engineering like this, puking your guts out?"

"That's what I was thinking. Maybe this baby is a sign that I should just let the business fail and begin again. With something less high profile. Start a new business here, like renovating hurricane-damaged structures."

"You're willing to let everything I've— We've worked for go down the drain? I can't allow that. Has Parker been filling your head with this nonsense?"

"Don't blame Parker. He doesn't even know about the baby yet. I'm going to tell him tonight at dinner." Bliss's voice became tight with anger. *How dare she disparage the man I love.* "And don't worry. If I have to work until the day I die, you'll get your investment back."

Nancy's eyes bored into her. "You think this is all about money?" She pounded the wall with her fist. "This is my life. My dream. To some day bury Lavere. I thought it was your dream too."

"Well, dreams change, Nancy."

"I wish you'd told me that before I went out on a limb and arranged a meeting this evening with the Coast Guard Project people."

"They agreed to reopen the contract?"

"They're thinking about it. That's why I was trying to get hold of you. We need to get things in order and leave after lunch."

"Can't we postpone? I'm too sick."

"Look, I'll call room service and get you something to eat. Then you take a shower and get yourself together while I go out to the trailer and prepare the documents."

"How will I get through a meeting without getting sick?"

217

"I'll stop by the pharmacy and get you something to settle your stomach."

"But I'm supposed to meet with Parker."

Nancy's jaw tightened at the mention of his name. "Call him and put it off. We can't let this opportunity to salvage the company go by."

Bliss knew that she couldn't let it pass either. Perhaps they could win this contract, and then if she decided to leave the company, she'd leave it solvent for the others and begin again with a clear conscience.

"Oh, fine. I'll call him."

Bliss thought Nancy would go, but she stood watching as she dialed Parker. After letting it ring numerous times, she hung up. "He's not answering. Now what do I do?" No doubt he was out buying things in preparation for their dinner.

"Write a note. I'll post it on his door when I'm out at the trailer getting the paperwork."

"I don't want to leave a note. Can't you wait for me to get hold of him?"

"No, we don't have time. A note will be fine."

Bliss was too weak to argue with her. She took a piece of the room's stationery and began to write. "Here," she said as she handed Nancy the note.

*****

Parker, his arms laden with groceries, walked up the steps. A piece of paper taped to the frame of the screen door caught his eye. After setting the bags on the porch floor, he plucked it off.

Parker—

I'm sorry. I don't know what I was thinking when I decided to meet with you tonight. On reflection, I think it would be a grave mistake. We have no future, and it would be pointless to see each other again. Please don't call me or come to see me. It's best for all that we forget that we ever met.

Bliss

Parker threw the paper aside and kicked the bag of groceries. Limes destined for the filling of a key lime pie rolled across the porch.

Parker stomped down the front steps. "You can't jerk me around, Bliss Sherman. Don't call or come see me, hmph. You're not getting off that easily."

*****

Parker turned the knob and pushed open the door to the trailer so hard it swung back, hit the wall, and nearly slammed back into his face as he stormed inside.

"Have you ever heard of knocking?" Nancy said as she rose from behind her desk.

"Where is she?" Parker said, his eyes scanning the office.

"Where is who?"

"You know damn well who. Bliss!"

"She doesn't want to see you."

"Well, I want to see her."

"I always thought you were a little thick," Nancy said. "Let me explain something to you. I'll try to go slowly so you'll understand. You were nothing more than an amusement to Bliss. A diversion. A way to relieve stress. To put it in your vernacular, you were nothing but a good roll in the hay."

"You're crazy. That's not the Bliss I know." He charged toward Bliss's desk and picked up her phone. "Is she at the hotel?"

As he punched in the number to Bliss's room, Nancy walked over and hit the disconnect button. "You may want to look at this first," she said smugly. "Save yourself some embarrassment."

"What is it?"

"Read it," Nancy said and walked away.

The letter was on the official Sherman Engineering stationery and was addressed to Louisa Barnhart.

As President of Sherman Engineering and lead for the move of the Cape Destiny Lighthouse, it regrettably has come to my attention that the Cape Destiny Lighthouse Keeper's House is in severe disrepair. It is my understanding that the State of North Carolina previously entered into an agreement with Mr. Parker Swain by which he must make a good faith effort to restore the property in exchange for the use of the premises, and when completely restored, be able to claim the house.

After visiting the premises and meeting Mr. Swain, I feel it is my duty to report that he is negligent in abiding with his responsibilities of the agreement. In short, the Keeper's House is a shambles. The quality of what little work Mr. Swain has accomplished is sub-standard, and I feel the Keeper's House is a blight on the site and will serve as an embarrassment to the State of North Carolina. When the CDL move is complete, I feel the lighthouse deserves to have a Keeper's House that is worthy of this grand structure. Therefore, I urge you find

Mr. Swain in default of the agreement and make other arrangements to have it quickly renovated.

Due to the sensitive nature of this letter and my desire to maintain a good relationship with the local citizens, I ask that you keep this letter confidential. Any questions may be directed to my assistant, Nancy Klempner.

Sincerely,

Bliss Sherman, President

Red rage clouded his vision and nearly prevented him from reading Bliss's signature.

He looked up at Nancy, who stood watching him, her arms crossed. He wanted to slam her against the wall. "I don't believe this. Bliss wouldn't write this."

Nancy turned her back and sauntered toward her desk. "Believe it, Mr. Swain. She was so outraged when she saw that poor excuse of a house that you're so attached to that she even composed and typed the letter herself."

He thought of how Bliss told him she felt responsible for his losing the Keeper's House. Perhaps she had written it. No, she couldn't be that deceitful.

"I don't believe she wrote this," he said, "but even if she had, it was probably before she fell in love with me."

Nancy turned around. "If that makes you feel better, Mr. Swain, believe whatever you want. All I know is that you fell in love with an illusion. Bliss Sherman cares nothing for you. Or your silly house. Now I suggest you leave before I call the authorities."

Chapter 38

After showering and drying her hair, Bliss pulled on her black suit and noticed that the skirt's waistband was loose. It should be getting tighter. *As soon as this meeting is over, I've got to see a doctor to get this nausea under control.*

Bliss took a seat at the table in her room and pulled out the file on the Coast Guard project to refresh her memory before Nancy returned. She found it difficult to concentrate on anything but the baby. By next spring, she would be a mother. She wished everyone could feel the joy bursting inside her.

Spying the microrecorder in her briefcase, Bliss took it out and clicked it on. With her hand on her lower abdomen, she spoke into the recorder. "Hello, little one. This is your mommy. I found out today that you exist, and I wanted to tell you how much I love you. Your daddy doesn't know about you yet, and I feel like I'm going to explode with excitement I want to tell him so much. Parker, your father, is such a wonderful, gentle man, and I know he'll love you too."

The phone rang. Bliss shut off the recorder, stuffed it into her skirt pocket, and answered it.

"Ms. Sherman, this is Julie Marshall."

"How are you?"

"Fine, thank you. I heard that you rode out Hurricane Blaise in the lighthouse. I was wondering if I could interview you about what that was like?"

"Sure. When would you like to meet?"

"Today, if that's OK with you?"

"Oh, I'm leaving this afternoon for an appointment."

"My advisor for the school newspaper would like me to get it to him as soon as possible. They want me to add this information to my upcoming article. I could be there in a few minutes if you have the time. It won't take long."

Bliss looked at her watch. Perhaps doing the interview would take her mind off her nausea. "Sure, if you can come now, I can fit you in before I leave. I'm at the Destiny Cove Hotel. Room 421."

"Oh, thank you, Miss Sherman. I'll be there in half an hour."

*****

Parker staggered away from the site. How could he have been so stupid? How could he have allowed himself to be duped by Bliss? He sat on the porch step and stared at the letter. As he reread it, his anger diminished but something worse replaced it. Betrayal. After years, of keeping up his guard, he'd allowed himself to become vulnerable. Now he had not only lost his heart, but he was going to lose his house as well. He stared up at the porch roof. The paint was peeling and the gutters were bent back. *It's hopeless. Be a man, Parker. Cut your losses. Forget Bliss. Forget the house. You may as well just pack it in and move back to the little cottage on Wingina.*

He stood. That's what he'd do. At least out there, he wouldn't have to see Bliss everyday. "Come Beau," he said. "Let's get the hell out of here."

*****

The door rattled. Bliss went to the peephole and saw Nancy scowling impatiently. She opened the door and Nancy swept in. "Good you're ready."

"Did you leave my note for Parker?"

"Actually, he was there. I gave it to him."

222

"Did he say anything?"

"He didn't seem pleased."

"Oh, I hope he's not angry. Maybe I should call him."

"Sorry, but we don't have time. " Nancy stepped between her and the phone. "How are you feeling?"

"Still sick to my stomach," Bliss said slumping into the chair and resting her head against its arm.

Nancy went to the sink. "Well, I stopped by the pharmacy on my way here. Got you something to settle your stomach." Bliss heard her unwrap one of the hotel glasses and the water running.

"Here, drink this," she said, handing the concoction to Bliss.

"What is it? Are you sure this is safe for pregnant women?"

"It's bicarbonate of soda. That pharmacist, what's his name? Boyd recommended it. Said it's perfectly safe. "

Bliss raised her head. She was feeling so sick and the thought of riding in the car added to her queasiness. Taking the glass, she held it under her nose. It smelled lemony and fizzy bubbles tickled her nose. "Are you sure?"

"It's an over-the counter. How harmful could it be?"

"I don't know," Bliss said. "Maybe I'd better not."

"Do you want me to call him?"

Bliss felt her stomach pitch. "Oh, OK." She gulped the drink.

"Were you able to keep down any of the food I had room service bring you?"

"Only the noodle soup. Nothing else appealed to me."

Nancy frowned. "Now, why don't you go lie down and rest while I take your things down to the car."

Bliss didn't even try to fight Nancy's mothering. As she curled up on the bed, a strange weightiness began to creep up on her. She was so tired. Not her usual pregnancy fatigue, but a paralyzing ennui as if her limbs were turning to cement.

Bliss wasn't sure how much time had passed, but Nancy was suddenly beside her touching her shoulder. "All set. Let's go."

In the gray fuzziness clouding her brain, Bliss remembered something. "We can't leave yet. I'm waiting for someone."

"What?" Nancy snapped. "Who are you waiting for?"

"Julie Marshall, the reporter from Wingina High School," she said, her tongue feeling thick. "She called while you were out at the trailer. She wants to interview me about how it felt to weather the hurricane in the lighthouse. She should be here in a moment. It'll only take five minutes."

"We don't have five minutes," Nancy said sharply. "Get up."

Nancy's tone startled Bliss, yet she was so tired, she felt powerless to argue with her or to rise. She came and took Bliss by the arm and dragged her up. "I said let's go."

Bliss's head swam, and she felt disconnected from her legs. "I can't."

Nancy's arms swept around her, hauling her to her feet. Her strength surprised Bliss. It was as if she'd leached all of Bliss's and taken it for herself. "We've got to get out of here. Now. I'm not going to let some little gook ruin everything."

Gook? Had she heard Nancy correctly? This wasn't the Nancy she knew. Bliss could barely walk let alone reprimand her for her slur. What is wrong with me? Bliss wondered. As Nancy roughly dragged her out of the room, the bottle of bicarbonate caught her eye. "You've drugged me," she slurred.

"Shut up," Nancy commanded.

In the dark well of Bliss's mind, alarms were going off. She needed help, but her blood had seemed to have turned to molasses, trapping her in a body that was refusing to respond. Then a thought entered her head. She felt it forming and watched as it burst into her consciousness. Fumbling for the microrecorder in her pocket, she depressed the record button and struggled to form the words, "Where are you taking me? Why did you drug me?"

"You don't need to know. You just be quiet, and I'll take care of everything. As I always do."

Helpless, Bliss slumped against her as they waited for the elevator. When the bell dinged, Nancy pulled her toward it, but stopped abruptly as the doors parted and Julie Marshall stepped forward.

"Ms. Sherman," Julie said, "Are you—are you OK?"

Bliss tried to say something, but her lips felt as immovable as icebergs.

"No, she's not OK," Nancy said with annoyance. "I'm taking her to the hospital now. I think it's her appendix."

Julie held the elevator button while Nancy helped Bliss inside. The girl looked at Bliss, concern wrinkling her smooth brow.

Bliss pleaded to her with her eyes because she could no longer speak. She was just so tired.

"Let me help you," Julie said to Nancy and moved closer as the doors closed.

"No, I can manage myself," Nancy snapped.

The elevator arrived at the lobby. "I could get the manager," Julie said. "We could call an ambulance."

"No," Nancy barked. "I can have her at the hospital before it even gets here."

Nancy, her arm wrapped around Bliss, dragged her out of the elevator.

"I hope you're OK, Miss Sherman," Julie said as she followed.

It took every ounce of Bliss's mettle, but she slowly sneaked her free hand into her pocket and grasped the microrecorder. Bliss turned toward Julie and moaning, held out her hand.

When Julie reached to give Bliss's outstretched hand a reassuring squeeze, Bliss slipped the recorder into the girl's palm. Julie stood still, a look of puzzlement crossing her face.

"Let's go," Nancy said curtly, dragging Bliss down the hall toward the back entrance. Bliss kept her eyes fixed on Julie, and then lost sight of the girl as Nancy pushed her out the door, took her to her car, and shoved her into the back seat.

*****

Parker walked into The Beach Mart and Pharmacy. June's head jerked toward the door when the bell jangled. She closed the latest edition of *Cosmopolitan*. "Well, I didn't expect to see you here."

"I didn't expect to be here," Parker said sourly as he walked over to the counter.

"Guess you weren't expecting a lot of things?" June said with a giggle. "But I told Bliss not to worry. Just cause it wasn't planned, and you're not married doesn't mean you won't love it any less."

Parker felt as if he turned too many pages in a novel and skipped some vital information. "What are you talking about?"

June covered her mouth. "Oops. Forget I said anything. I thought Bliss had told you already."

"Told me what?"

June turned her back on him and began straightening the cigarette packs behind the counter. "Please don't ask me, Parker honey. I promised her I wouldn't say anything until she told you first."

Parker walked around the counter and put a hand on his aunt's shoulder. "Look, you have to tell me what's going on here. First, Bliss calls me last night and asks me to have dinner with her tonight. Then when I went home today, there's a note on my door telling me she never wants to see me again."

"What? That doesn't make any sense. Why, I know she was a little frightened. That's understandable, but she was excited." She took Parker's hand. "And happy. She was so happy too."

"Happy about what, Aunt June?"

"The baby, Parker. Bliss is pregnant! With your baby."

"She's pregnant?" Blood rushed to his head making him dizzy. *Bliss is pregnant. With my baby.* "Oh, I don't understand. "

June tittered and blushed. "Well, I think it's a little too late for me to explain it to you now. The horse is out of the barn so to speak."

None of this made any sense. "I've got to talk to Bliss," he said. "May I use your phone?"

"Use the one in the back room. You'll have more privacy." She led him down the aisle and showed him the phone on her desk. He didn't know the number to the hotel. His hands shaking, he dialed information and searched for paper and a pen. He found a pen and then remembered the letter Nancy had given him. He'd stashed it in his pocket. He jotted the number on it and then dialed Bliss's room. While he waited for her to answer, his mind raced. Bliss was pregnant with his child. She wanted nothing to do with him. She wrote the letter to the state. The phone rang and rang.

Then his thoughts, swirling in his mind like snowflakes in a snow globe, slowly settled, and he suddenly realized what was bothering him about the letter. Quickly, he hung up the phone and ran out of the pharmacy without even pausing to say goodbye to Aunt June.

Chapter 39

Parker raced down Beachfront Road. Rage surged through him. How dare Nancy meddle in their lives! She was clever, but she'd overlooked one thing. She'd underestimated how close he and Bliss had become. Nancy assumed that Bliss would be too ashamed to admit that she was dyslexic. There was no way Bliss could have written that letter, when she had confided that she couldn't type and didn't know how to use a computer.

Obviously, Nancy disliked him, but he didn't think she was capable of such low-down, dirty tricks. "It's going to take more than a phony letter and an old maid paper pusher to keep me from Bliss. And my baby," he ranted to Beau.

My baby.

The thought of being a father again thrilled and terrified him. He pictured the baby growing inside Bliss and was grateful for the second chance at fatherhood. He gripped the wheel tightly, "I promise you, little one, I'll never let anything happen to you."

Parker pulled into the Destiny Cove lot, shut off the truck, and stepped out. The sky was gray and the air clammy. It felt like rain. Beau leaped out and Parker slammed the door.

227

Practically stomping, Parker made his way to the front entrance.

"Mr. Swain! Mr. Swain!"

He stopped before entering, and looking over his shoulder, he spied Julie Marshall hurrying toward him. Parker set his teeth in a grimace. As much as he liked her, he didn't have time to give a quote on how he thought Wingina's football team would do in the fall. He had to see Bliss.

"Mr. Swain," Julie said between rapid breaths. "I'm so glad you're here." The look on her face alarmed him. Her eyes were darting nervously.

"Are you OK?" he asked, touching her shoulder.

"I didn't know what to do. Who to call."

"What is it?"

"Something's wrong with Bliss, er ah, Ms. Sherman. I came here to interview her, and when I arrived, that woman who works for her, Miss Klempner. . . She was dragging Bliss out of here. She looked so sick."

Parker's grip tightened on Julie's shoulder. "Who looked sick? Bliss?"

"Yes."

He immediately thought of the baby. He hoped she wasn't miscarrying. "Did they say what was wrong?"

"Bliss couldn't talk, and it was strange but Ms. Klempner was acting weird. She was being kind of rough with Bliss."

"Rough? How do you mean?"

"She was yelling at her and jerking her around."

"Where did they go?"

"I don't know. She said she was taking Bliss to the hospital, but when she pulled out of the lot, she headed toward Wellington Island, not the hospital."

Parker felt that helpless, spiraling out of control feeling like when he'd found P.J. being tossed about in the surf. No, this was not P.J., and he was not going to let anything happen to Bliss.

"I've got to find them." Parker turned to leave.

"Wait, Mr. Swain. She sneaked this to me." She gave Parker the microrecorder. "I was about to listen to it when you pulled in."

"Thanks," Parker said and ran to the truck. He opened the door, Beau leaped inside, and he fired up the pickup. His wheels squealed as he zoomed out of the lot. Driving with one hand on the wheel, he turned on the recorder. As he headed toward Wellington Island, he heard Bliss's voice, warm and full of love, as she talked to the baby. *Their baby.* So powerful and moving was the pledge of love she'd made to their child that Parker nearly had to pull over to rein in his emotions. Then after a gap in the recording, a different Bliss came on. Her voice sounded slow and stodgy yet filled with fright. Bliss was accusing Nancy of drugging her. He stepped on the gas as he listened to Nancy barking orders like a mad woman.

As his speedometer passed sixty, he hoped that Wayne would see him speeding and pull him over so he could enlist his help. If they were headed toward Wellington Island, then Nancy must be taking her to the bungalow. He couldn't think of anywhere else on the island where they could go. God help them all if he was wrong.

*****

Bliss slowly came to, her eyelids feeling as heavy as lead curtains. Slowly raising them, she was blinded by an intense overhead light. *Where am I?* She tried to sit up but only her head was able to move freely. Raising it off the mattress, she saw that she was lying in a twin, four-poster bed. Her legs and arms were lashed to the bedposts with clothesline. She was so cold and clammy. A cotton sheet was all that covered her naked body. *What is happening to me?*

Then some of the fuzziness cleared, and she remembered. Nancy had drugged and kidnapped her from the hotel. But why? Why would she do something like this? They'd often joked that Nancy probably had a kinky private life. Perhaps she was going to take nude photos and sell them to blackmail her into keeping the business. Bliss began to panic.

What if she'd restrained her so that she could be raped for a porn video? As she struggled against the ropes, the sheet slid off, revealing her naked breast. *Think Bliss.* If you ever want to see Parker again and live to deliver your child, you must keep your wits about you. You cannot give into the drug. Whatever Nancy had in mind, Bliss knew remaining conscious would be her only chance of survival.

*****

Parker crossed over the long bridge that tethered Wellington Island to the Outer Banks, keeping his eyes peeled for Nancy's silver Buick. The island was a sad place. A dilapidated gas station whose windows were broken sat as the sentinel on the other side of the span. The road ran through a pine forest, past ramshackle trailers, and abandoned boatyards.

Three miles onto the island, the road came to a fork, and Parker took the left branch, as he knew the right ended at a boat launch. Not far past the fork, a small white cottage that could use a coat of paint sitting nestled among tall pines came into view. His heart leaped when he spied Nancy's car pulled closely to the house.

Slowing the truck, he eased into the sandy patch scratched out of the stubby grass and cut the engine, parking the truck next to a rusted oil tank. A fine rain, like spit, began to fall.

The blinds were pulled. Parker left the truck and warily looked the place over. If it weren't for Nancy's car, anyone coming upon the scene would have assumed no one lived there anymore. Uncharacteristically, Beau began to whine nervously. "Shush, boy," Parker said as he noticed how the carpet of pine needles looked as if something had been dragged over them toward the back door.

*****

Someone was coming. Bliss closed her eyes and pretended to be unconscious. She hoped she hadn't flinched when a clanking sound like silverware falling onto a metal tray startled her.

Bliss peeked and saw Nancy wiping down what looked like a metal skewer and several knives of various lengths. Terror telegraphed throughout her body.

"Oh my, what a naughty patient." Nancy's tone sounded sweetly maniacal. "Your drape has slipped."

Bliss felt the cool sheet skim her breasts as Nancy pulled it up to her neck. "If you had kept yourself covered, missy, we wouldn't be in this predicament, now would we? But don't you worry, Bliss," Nancy said, patting her shoulder. "This will all be over in a flash. Then we can put this unfortunate episode behind us, forget about babies, forget about old Parker Swain, and concentrate on building Sherman Engineering into the company I've always envisioned."

She must have taken me to some back alley abortionist. Bliss's heart pounded and hammered in her ears. She said a silent prayer. *Please, Julie, call Parker. Give him the recorder. He's my only hope.*

"Well," Nancy said, "every thing is in order." Bliss waited to hear a doctor enter the room. She jerked when Nancy pulled up the bottom of the sheet, and began to swab her thighs with a cold solution.

230

"You're awake?" Nancy said, the sweetness fading from her voice. "Well, we can fix that." She pulled the sheet down and looked menacingly at Bliss.

"Nancy," Bliss said, her voice sounding thick and her speech slurred, "what are you doing?"

"Never you mind. Let me get you another Vicodin, and when you wake up, it'll all be over."

Bliss summoned her energy and railed futilely against the lashings. Panting, she watched as Nancy broke up a pill in a glass of water and walked toward her with the drug.

*****

Parker crept up the back steps to the porch while Beau sniffed around in the yard. He peered into the window next to the door but could see nothing. Pounding on the back door, he called, "Bliss are you in there?"

Nancy froze and looked over her shoulder. "You drink this, and then I'll take care of Parker Swain." Roughly, she raised Bliss's head and put the glass to her lips. Bliss kept them sealed. "Drink this, damn you." She slapped Bliss. As Bliss cried out in reaction to the blow, Nancy poured the drug into her mouth. Bliss coughed and spat the liquid back at her, and with a scream that seemed to emanate from her toes, she cried, "Parker, I'm in here!"

Parker heard Bliss and rammed his shoulder into the back door. It didn't budge. Desperate, he kicked in the window next to the door. Shards slashed his jeans and cut his leg. Reaching inside, he unlocked the door and burst into the house. "Bliss, where are you?"

As she opened her mouth to call for him, Nancy jammed a wad of gauze into it. Bliss gagged and tried to dislodge it with her tongue, but to no avail. Nancy picked up a gun and flashed it in front of Bliss. "If you know what's good for you," she whispered in Bliss's ear, "you'll keep quiet."

Nancy, gun in hand, crept toward the doorway, stationing herself beside the frame.

Parker stormed into the room and was shocked to find Bliss half-naked and shackled. "My God, Bliss are you OK?"

Bliss finally spat out the gauze. "Parker, she has a gun!"

Parker whirled around, and saw Nancy, dressed in scrubs, holding a pistol on him. Her eyes were like two black bottomless pits as they trained on him.

"You just couldn't take a hint, could you, Mr. Swain? I tried to discourage your little romance with the vandalism, and the letter, but you just couldn't stay away from her. Now I have to take care of you and the baby."

"What do you mean?" Parker asked, watching Nancy's index finger as it curled around the trigger.

"If you hadn't followed us out here, I would have taken care of the baby and everything would have been tidy. But no. Typical man. It's always what *you* want. Imposing your will. When will you learn? Perhaps you need to be taught a lesson. Perhaps if you watch while I abort your baby, you'll learn."

She's mad, Parker thought. He could almost see the cracks in her sanity and the mania bubbling up. *Think fast, Parker. Keep her talking until you can figure a way out of this.* "You're going to abort the baby? You'll kill, Bliss. If you care about her, take her to a hospital."

"Please take me to a hospital, Nancy," Bliss pleaded.

"Kill you? I assure you, Nancy, the doctor knows what he's doing."

Parker was confused. Why was she calling Bliss Nancy?

"Oh, but Charles, I want this baby. Your baby," Nancy said, her voice sounding young and frightened.

"Be reasonable, Nancy," she boomed, her voice taking on a masculine baritone. "I'm a married man."

Parker watched Nancy's grasp on reality slip away before him, waiting for an opportunity to wrestle the gun away.

Bliss gasped as she realized Nancy was having a psychotic conversation with Jonathan's father, Charles Lavere.

"I'm a respected business man with children," she continued in a manly voice. "The scandal would ruin me. If you love me, Nancy, you'll do this for me."

"I do love you, Charles," she whispered.

Parker saw tears roll down Nancy's cheeks as she plunged further into her past.

"Please don't take away my baby," Nancy was pleading now.

"Do it for me, darling," her voice deepened once again. "It'll be painless, and I promise you'll be rewarded for your loyalty. When I die, I'll make you a principal owner of Lavere. Do it for me, Nancy. For us. For yourself."

Her eyes narrowed as she glared at Parker. "But you didn't make it up to me, Charles, did you? You died and left it all to your poor excuse for a son. I could have given you my son. A good son. One worthy of the Lavere name. But now I don't have my baby. I don't have you. And I don't have the company." Her voice became shrill. "You lied to me, Charles. You lied about everything." She raised the gun, aiming it at Parker's heart and growled, "And now it's time for you to pay."

Chapter 40

Nancy, her finger curled around the trigger, walked closer. Parker knew he was moments from death. Perhaps that would be more merciful than having to watch Bliss and his baby die.

"No, Nancy! No!" Bliss was crying. "I pursued Parker. I seduced him. It's not his fault."

Nancy's eyes darted to Bliss, seeming perplexed by her outburst.

I'll die before I let another woman and child die, Parker thought. The only way to save them was to launch himself at her and hope that she was a lousy shot. As he tightened every muscle in anticipation of springing on her, he heard a bark.

"Beau, help!" Bliss screamed.

Nancy took her eyes off Bliss for a moment, and in that instant, Parker lunged for her as Beau leaped on Nancy. They hit the floor. A shot rang out. Bliss screamed. The squeal from Beau told Parker that his beloved dog had taken the bullet.

"Parker! Parker!" Bliss was sobbing hysterically.

Nancy and he wrestled for the gun. Parker was surprised by her strength, but it still was no match for his. He knocked her aside and grabbed the weapon.

"Parker, are you hurt?" Bliss cried.

"I'm OK," he said. "But Beau's been hit."

He scrambled to his feet, training the gun on Nancy. "Get up, and sit in that chair," he shouted.

Nancy, her hair disheveled and her scrubs twisted, slowly rose, straightened her clothing, smoothed her hair, and settled in the chair.

"Don't move," he commanded. Holding the gun on her, he went to Beau. The dog was lying on the floor bleeding, but he could feel a heartbeat. "You're going to be OK, boy," he said, patting him. Anger overwhelmed Parker. He wanted to empty the gun into Nancy. "Where's the phone?" he screamed at her. She was unresponsive. "Where's the damn phone?"

As Parker's eyes darted around the room, Nancy leaped to her feet, grabbed a knife from the tray of makeshift surgical instruments, and plunged it into her abdomen. Her face twisted in pain as she collapsed.

Time stood still. Stunned, Parker couldn't process what he'd just seen. Then the blood appeared as a spreading red blotch on her scrub top, jolting to his brain, telling him that what his eyes had just witnessed was true.

"Good, God!" Parker cried, dropping the gun and coming to Nancy's side.

"What's happened?" Bliss asked.

"She's stabbed herself." The image of Beth lying in a puddle of blood flooded his mind. Frantic, he grabbed some of the gauze Nancy had laid out in preparation for the abortion. Should he try to remove the knife? "Oh, God! Oh, God, help me!" he exclaimed, panic and nausea seizing him. As the blood pooled on the floor beneath her, Parker, sank to his knees, cradling Nancy in his arms, trying to apply pressure to the wound.

"No!" she screamed, writhing in his arms. "I want to die. Leave me alone."

"Let Parker help you, Nancy," Bliss cried from the bed. "You're sick that's all. We'll get you help."

"No," Nancy said her voice growing faint. "Nothing can help me."

Bliss closed her eyes and tears ran out the sides as the life ebbed from her tortured, trusted assistant.

As Parker struggled to save her, and she grew paler in his grasp, a liberating realization—the death to his guilt—came to

Parker. He could never have prevented Beth's suicide. Death is too seductive to a sick soul. Life is for those who wish to embrace it. Nancy went limp in his arms. He felt for a pulse. She was dead. Gently, he laid her aside and stumbled over to Bliss, covered with blood.

"Are you OK?" he asked.

"Is she . . . ?

He looked into Bliss's tear-filled, terrorized eyes and nodded. "She's gone."

Bliss gasped and began to sob. Parker untied her arms and legs and then wrapped her in a hug, smothering her with kisses.

"Did she hurt you?"

Bliss sniffled, "I'm fine. Tend to Beau."

Beau! In the chaos, he'd forgotten about him.

Suddenly, there was a commotion on the porch, and then Wayne Bevans's frame filled the doorway. "Good Lord!" His face blanched as he took in the scene. "What the hell?"

"Call an ambulance." Parker commanded. "And tell them to bring a vet too."

Chapter 41

Parker walked into the room. Bliss lay sleeping, her black hair a striking contrast to the white hospital linens. The peaceful look on her face gave no indication of the terror she'd suffered at Nancy's hands.

Silently, he walked over and took a seat next to her bed. He stared at her in amazement. This woman who'd come to his town to move a lighthouse had done something far more incredible. She'd moved his heart.

He gently took her hand. Her wrist was raw from the clothesline that had tied her to the bed. Parker shuddered when he thought about what could have happened to Bliss had he not gotten to her in time. He blinked, putting that thought out of his mind. He was determined to no longer dwell on the past. From now on, Parker resolved to enjoy what he had and look forward to the future.

Bliss stirred and slowly opened her eyes. Then a look of panic crossed her face, and she pulled her hand away struggling against phantom lashings. Parker stood and grasped her shoulders, "Bliss, you're OK. You're in the hospital."

She ceased struggling, sighed, and relaxed. "For a moment, I thought I was back there. With Nancy."

She slid her hands to her belly.

"The baby is fine," he said. "*Our baby* is fine."

Tears pooled in her eyes. "Are you sure? What about the drugs?"

Parker raised the head of her bed. "The doctors have assured me that you'll . . . We'll have a healthy baby. They give a larger dose of pain killers to mother's in labor."

Her forehead wrinkled. "And Beau?"

"He's going to be fine too. They operated on his right haunch." He shook his head in disbelief. "That crazy dog took a bullet for me."

Parker sat down again beside her. She looked up expectantly at him. "Are you upset about the baby?"

"Oh, Bliss," he kissed her hand. "I can't tell you how happy I am."

She beamed. "I didn't mean for you to find out that way. I wanted to tell you myself, but Nancy said we had to go to meet about the Coast Guard Station project. They were reopening the contract since Jonathan has gone missing."

"He's no longer missing, Bliss."

"So I guess the contract reopening was just a ruse on Nancy's part."

Parker hesitated a moment. "Well, yes and no."

Bliss stared at him, puzzled.

"I'm afraid I have some bad news." He paused. "They found Jonathan. Dead."

She bit her lip, and felt tears stinging her eyes. The sorrow filling her heart surprised her. When she had composed herself, she said softly, "After all this time, I had assumed that he'd been washed away in the hurricane. But the confirmation still comes as a shock."

Parker was silent for a moment, then patted her hand. "It wasn't the hurricane. Wayne believes Nancy killed him."

Bliss gasped. "Nancy killed him?"

"They're gathering evidence. His body washed up in the sound not far from her cottage early yesterday morning. Some kayakers found him. Wayne and his men were nearby dragging his car out of the water when they heard Nancy fire the gun. That's how Wayne came to be in the area."

Bliss shook her head. "She killed Jonathan? I can't believe it."

"Wayne says there are people at the Destiny Cove who can place those two together the day of the evacuation. And they've found a voice mail message on Jonathan's cell phone from Nancy telling him that you've agreed to collaborate with him on the Coast Guard Project and instructing him to meet you at the hotel. They think she lured him to your hotel, drugged him, and then drove his car into the sound with him inside."

"Where did she get the drugs?" Bliss asked. Then as soon as she had posed the question, she knew the answer. "The pain killers her dentist prescribed when her tooth was bothering her. That's where she'd gotten them. That's what she used on me."

"They're going to do an autopsy," Parker said. "They'll know more when the results come back."

Bliss massaged her tummy. "How ironic. Charles Lavere took away Nancy's baby, and now she has taken away his only son."

As much as Bliss wanted to hate Nancy, in a feral part of her, Bliss knew that she loved her baby so fiercely that if anyone ever harmed it, she thought she would lose her mind too.

"Did you know that she'd had an affair with Jonathan's father, Bliss?"

"No. But that explains so much about her life. Her dislike for Jonathan. Why she encouraged me to leave the company after Charles died. And why she was so upset when she found out I was pregnant. Evidently, she'd been promised a share of the business when Charles died. I guess when I told her that my business was nearly bankrupt and that maybe I should just liquidate and stay here with the baby, it sent her over the edge. She was losing her share of the business again."

Parker didn't want to tell her, but he knew he must. He couldn't trap her on Cape Destiny. "You may not have to give up the business, Bliss. When I called Randy to tell him what had happened, he said that the people behind the Coast Guard Station project have been in touch and are interested in Sherman Engineering doing the work."

"Wonderful!" Bliss's face brightened. "Did Randy say how the move was proceeding?"

"He said things were going smoothly and for you not to worry. He thinks you may come in only a week over schedule."

241

Bliss mentally ran figures in her head. "I think we'll be fine. I won't have to liquidate."

Parker felt sick. "So I guess you won't be staying on the cape then?"

"I'd like to, but I don't know if I can."

He stared blankly at her, surprised by her answer.

"See," she said, "with all the hurricane damage down here I figured there's a great need for reconstruction services. I was thinking of expanding into renovations and making Cape Destiny my Southern office and the base for that part of the business. Randy can head the Pittsburgh office and oversee the moving end."

"Why don't you know if you can?"

"Well," Bliss said, "because I have a certain place in mind for my office, but I don't know if the current resident will agree with allowing me to move in there."

"What place is that?"

"It's a little presumptuous of me, but I'd like to move into the Keeper's House. I was think of finishing its renovation so the present resident can keep it and then using one of the vacant rooms as my office."

Parker, his heart beating wildly, stood. "Well, what's stopping you?"

Bliss shrugged. "The person who lives there hasn't asked me to stay yet."

Parker wrapped his arms around her and kissed her. "Stay, Bliss! Stay. Marry me. Have my baby. I can't believe you'd move here to be with me."

She touched his cheek and laughed. "Oh, Parker, don't you know. I'd move heaven and earth to be with you."

*****

Read an excerpt from Janice Lane Palko's next novel,

Most Highly Favored Daugber

Chapter 1 – Sunday, January 25

The mallet paused above Cara's head then swiftly crashed onto the wedge, driving the pointed vee into her skull. *Why am I not dead?* Death would be relief. The mallet arced again, readying for another blow. Cara thrashed against the restraints. It delivered another cranium-crushing blow, and Cara's eyes flew open. *Where am I?* The phone rang again, inducing another skull-splitting shock of pain. Her heart racing, she disentangled herself from the twisted bed linens and reached for the phone to silence its painful trill. As she brought the receiver to her ear she glanced down at herself and froze. *Why am I naked?*

"Hello," she said, trying to recover her wits, but her mind was spinning in an endless loop of questions and offering no answers.

"Where the hell have you been, Cara?"

She finally placed the voice. It was Wesley. *Where the hell have I been?* Every light in the suite was blazing, and her clothes were strewn all over. *What happened? Why do I feel so strange? What did I do?*

"Right here," she said, buying time to clear her mind of the fog obscuring her memory.

"I've been calling you all morning, and you never answered. I left messages on your cell phone. It's nearly noon. I was about to call the front desk to have them check on you. Why weren't you answering?"

She didn't know. She tried to think back, but her mind felt as if someone had poured thick oatmeal into it. Her hair had worked itself loose and hung in disheveled strands about her face. Bobby pins litter the white cotton sheets like black ants. Panicked, she looked over her body. She appeared to be unharmed yet why did she feel as if she'd been beaten?

Cara spied her blue silk gown lying in a heap on the gray plush carpeting near the small table. *I wore it to the awards banquet. I was honored last night. With the Mother Teresa medallion. The medal? Where was it?* Her eyes searched the room for the medal until she caught a glimpse of herself in the mirror above the dresser and realized that the ribbon was still around her neck. The gold medal, however, was dangling between her shoulder blades. She righted the medal and then pulled a blanket around herself. She was cold but not because she was naked, but because thinking about the possibilities of what had happened in this room chilled her to the core.

Why would I be so careless with such an expensive dress? What did I do last night after the banquet?

"Cara! Are you listening to me? What the hell is with you?"

I got sick. At least that was something, a bread crumb she hoped that would lead her down the road to fully remembering how she had gotten in this state.

"I'm sorry, Wesley," Cara said, feeling calmer now that she had at least some excuse to offer her husband. "I must have gotten food poisoning or some super virus. I got sick last night, and I must have passed out."

"Passed out? Who blacks out from the flu?"

"I don't know. All I remember is feeling terribly ill and coming back to the room."

"How much did you have to drink?"

She pulled the blankets more tightly around her and checked her hand to make sure that her engagement and wedding rings were still there. Thankfully, they were as were her grandmother's aquamarine and diamond drop earring, which were still dangling from her lobes. *At least, I wasn't robbed.*

"Cara, you still there? How much did you drink last night?"

"I don't know. I'm not your child, Wesley. I didn't think I had to keep a tally and report in."

"I've been calling for hours. I thought something terrible happened to you."

"Nothing's happened to me. I'm fine." *Am I? Why can't I remember anything past getting sick? Why am I naked?* Had she been hot? Had she had a fever? She touched her cheek with the back of her hand. It felt cool. Had she done something bad like that other time? She closed her eyes, near tears. *Why can't I remember?*

"Are you sure you don't have someone with you?"

Her eyes flew open. "What? Are you accusing me of hooking up with someone?"

"Come on, Cara. I'm not stupid. You're there all by yourself, and when I called you last night, you were in a bar."

That's right. I was in a bar. Another crumb.

"Then I tried calling all morning and no one answers. It doesn't take a genius to connect the dots."

She stood, pulling the blankets off the bed. "How can you say such a thing? I booked this room for us. So we could be together. You were the one who stood me up. Maybe you're feeling guilty." Her head began to spin and she sank back onto the bed, clutching her temple.

"Guilty? For what?" his voice came booming out of the phone. "Working? Trying to make a nice life together? You forget, I don't have the connections and name recognition you do. Some of us have to work hard."

She stifled a scream. She worked hard too and being so well-known was no picnic, but she felt too feeble to argue. Cara sighed. "Look, Wesley, I'm sorry. I love you. I'd never cheat on you. You know that. I got sick last night—the sickest I've ever been. I came back to the room and fell asleep. That's all. Seriously, you don't think I'd ever want someone else, do you?"

He didn't answer.

"Do you?"

"I'm sorry, Cara. It's just that sometimes I get so crazy when I think of all the other guys you could have married."

Exasperated, she closed her eyes. "Wesley, don't."

"It's true. You could have married any number of other men. How did your grandmother phrase it? 'Someone more suitable.'"

"But I didn't want them," Cara said softly. "I wanted you."

The silence hung there. They'd been over this so many times, it was maddening.

"I was calling to tell you that my plane will be boarding soon," he said. "I'll be home before dinner."

"Good."

"Right," he said and then hung up.

She put the receiver in its cradle, and her stomach rumbled with hunger. *I don't think I threw up last night. My stomach doesn't have that kicked-in-the-gut feeling. Perhaps I was drunk.* She tallied the drinks she'd had during the evening, but concluded that too much alcohol wasn't it. She'd certainly had more to drink on other occasions without feeling this hung over.

Maybe I'm pregnant. She held her head in her hands. You'd have to have had sex for that, she thought. With Wesley so involved in this case, she couldn't remember the last time they'd made love. That was why she had booked the suite in the first place.

Sighing, Cara picked up the phone again and dialed room service. She ordered dry toast and tea, and after straightening the bed linens, she crawled back under them, rolling onto her side, clutching a pillow. As she closed her eyes, she heard her grandmother's voice in her lilting Irish brogue coming through clearly in her cloudy head, "A wee bit of tea and toast is just the thing to cure what ails you."

Cara smiled wryly, thinking she'd need more than a cup of tea and slice of toast to fix this mess. As she tried, once again, to reconstruct the previous evening in her memory, a thought reached out and clutched her, sending a ripple of panic through her. *What if this is like the last time?*

One other time while she was still a child she'd had a memory lapse, and many times over the years, she had trod down that well-worn path in her memory hoping to discover what her mind kept from her, but each time her foray into the past had lead her into forests of confusion and dead ends of frustration. No matter how she tried, she couldn't remember. Her pulse quickened and her heart beat into her ears as fear seized her. *I couldn't remember then and if I can't remember now, will the same thing happen?* The metallic taste of terror was on her tongue as she pondered the question that provoked the most turmoil in her heart: *Will I be abandoned again?*

Sign up for Janice Lane Palko's newsletter at www.thewritinglane.blogspot.com so that you will be the first to know when **Most Highly Favored Daughter is available.**

Made in the USA
Charleston, SC
19 November 2015